Sometimes everything you want is right before your eyes. Have patience it all will be made clear.

–Blue Saffire

Prodigal Son

Gio

"It's done," Jace whispers in my ear as I sit in this irrelevant meeting.

I grunt and give a slight nod as he fades back into the background. Then I focus on the room around me.

I'm discounted, forgotten, unconsidered, but I'm okay with that. These men have no idea what's coming for them. Old age has made them all complacent and out of touch.

The world has changed, and they haven't. Leadership has failed and they've become sloppy in their antiquated ways. This generation has no care or respect for the past or the rules. As a result, these men are becoming obsolete.

My grandfather, on the other hand, has remained sharp. He asks questions. For everything he teaches, he asks for a lesson in return. I admire him for this.

He will be the saving grace for a few. The others will get what they deserve. Their greed will consume them. Their lack of foresight will end their world as they know it.

My gaze lands on Dario. My twin brothers are unique and the complete opposite of each other. While Dante responds with brutal force and builds from the hand he's dealt. Dario is a quiet storm.

He's the thinker, he always has a million questions. He's going to say what he thinks, and he'll come at you once he figures out the problem he needs to solve, but Dante is the one who's going to silence you and ask questions later. Not Dario—unless provoked into a blinding rage—which takes a lot or involves Carleen.

This is why he was chosen for this part. Yet here he sits with a stern scowl on his face. I know this isn't what he wants.

He still doesn't fully understand what he's needed for. His mind is elsewhere. What he wants belongs here in America. Dario found his forever years ago, but there are others who have tried to map out his future and take that away from him. Or at least they think they have.

Dario won't be the one to make the sacrifices in this family. That will always be me. I'm the tsunami they don't see coming.

Ever wonder why magicians say abracadabra? It's to get your attention off their next move. The word calls to your ears and distracts the eyes. It's like brain confusion. Like biting down on a virgin's ear as you break their barrier.

Well, I, Gio Di Lorenzo am the biggest fucking abracadabra there is. I'm the wand, the hands, and the curtain the wizard is hidden behind, the smoke and the damn mirrors.

They fucked up writing my ass off—but wait, I'm getting ahead of myself again. This isn't about me. This is about my little brother and how I'm going to make sure he gets to have the life he should. He was never meant to be the Don of our family—yet another illusion. He's not the one with the dark soul. Not as dark as it would need to be for what's coming.

No, they started this, and I will finish it. There are layers to everything I do. They fucked up thinking they could replace me. Like I'm not a fucking Di Lorenzo by blood.

We'll see. I promise you this, if you're going to come for me, make sure your ass is smart enough or at least smarter than me. I wish these motherfuckers luck, I have never been anyone's fool.

Just because I don't turn my head every time a snake rattles doesn't mean I don't hear the rattling. My axe is always at hand, ready to chop heads. I am Gio Michelangelo Di Lorenzo, put respect on my fucking name.

CHAPTER ONE

Musings of a Child

Dario

I look down into my palms as I sit on this park bench. This is the same park where Carleen became my best friend. My mother would bring me and Dante here to play. It was like an escape from that big house.

While Car and I were friends for years before we could run this place, some of my fondest childhood memories happened right here on this playground. It was a time so much simpler than now. My mother would tell me to enjoy being a child.

I get it now. When I have the weight of the world on my shoulders it all makes sense. I rub my thumb into my palm, longing to talk to my mother.

I feel like she would tell me the right thing to do. I'm not like Dante or Gio. They have accepted who we're supposed to be. I accepted it on the one hand, but I still have a life of my own I want to pursue.

I have dreams beyond becoming the Di Lorenzo Don. I've wanted more for my life than being one of *Nonno's* Capos. If not for my Italian pride, I probably would say fuck it all and run off with the one constant in my life—Carleen.

I stare off at the slide and remember one day in particular on this playground. Dante had been on the swings, and I sat at the top of the slide watching my mother.

I tilted my head to the side and observed all the men and women standing around her. There were always people with us. None of the other kids had an entourage with them. Not like this. Then there was Gwen. She was always there to whisper in my mother's ear.

I focused on my mother and watched her movements. Something about Mama made her different from the other mothers. Even at eight I knew this. My curiosity got the best of me. It always did.

I slid down the slide and walked over to my mother. She gave me a bright smile when she saw me walking over. The moment I stopped in front of her, she ran a hand through the front of my hair.

"Are you having fun, my handsome boy?" She took my face in her hands to kiss both of my cheeks.

"Yes, Mama, but I have a question."

"Oh really?" She smiled.

"Yes, why do we always have so many people with us? None of the other kids do. What makes us different?"

She reached to cup my chin in her hand. "My dear, Dario. Always the watchful one. You have plenty of time to learn about life as a Di Lorenzo. Don't be in a rush to grow up, my sweet boy."

"But what makes us different?"

She puckered her lips. I didn't think I was going to get an answer. However, her eyes lit up and she tugged me onto her lap.

"Do you remember your books about the dragon families?"

I nod.

"Well, remember how some dragon families were more dangerous than others?"

"Yes. The hero had to protect his friends and family from the other families. Bad people wanted to hurt them."

"Yes, that's exactly what it's like. You will always have to protect your friends from our life and people will always be after our family's power. This is why we always have people around to protect us."

"Oh."

"But this is not the time for you to worry about such things. Be a child and enjoy every moment you can. When the time comes for this life to pull you in, you will wish you had. Look, there's your friend. Why don't you go play with her?"

I look up to find Carleen looking at Dante with her brows pinched. I know that look. She knows my twin isn't me. Not like everyone else. She turns her head my way and her face lights up. She's so pretty.

Her brown face and those long puffy braids always draw my attention. She's taller than most of the girls on the playground, but she's also really skinny, but it's her smile that stands out. Her lips are so soft and puffy looking.

"But Mama, does that mean I'll have to protect Carleen from our family? She's my best friend. I don't want anything to happen to her."

"Essere un bambino. Be a child, Dario. I will always keep you and your friend safe. You be a child and allow me to do the rest."

"But Mama, the hero in my book couldn't trust all of his family. It was his own family that took his happiness."

Her face hardened instantly. Her lips pinched. I knew I said something wrong.

"Marone. I forgot about that. I guess I picked the perfect example. Forget everything I've said. Go play."

She kissed my cheeks again and sent me on my way. I shrugged and followed her instructions. Running as fast as I could, I joined Carleen on the slide. I only looked back once to see Carleen's mother sit next to mine. They always sat together.

All of my questions forgotten, soon, I ran the playground chasing after my friend. Suddenly, she tripped over what seemed like nothing and fell to the hard ground. I rushed to her side. She turned over with tears in her eyes.

"Are you okay?"

"No," she cried looking down at her skinned knees.

"Don't cry." I moved to blow on her cuts like Mama did for me and Dante when we fell. I frowned as I realized there were other steps before the blow. *"Wait here. I'll get Mama."*

"Dario." She sniffled and held out her hand. *"Don't leave me."*

I remember holding her hand as I waved for our mother's help. Mama came with a first aid kit and Carleen's mother fixed up her knees. From that day, I vowed to protect Carleen from the other dragon families.

It's the reason I've fallen in love with my best friend and refuse to tell her. We can never be together. I now know my role in the Di Lorenzo family. Carleen would never be safe with me.

My thoughts turn to my mother, she didn't stick around to keep us safe. However, I don't think she was safe. Dante thinks she left us.

I've never believed that. My mother loved us too much. Something else happened. Back then I was too small to find out what.

I didn't have the money, power, or respect to gain answers. Now, all of those things are at my fingertips, so I won't run, and I'll give up all hopes of ever having Carleen as more than a friend. Even that has its dangers, but I don't think I could breathe if she weren't in my life at all.

However, I'm going to find out what happened to my mother. That last night before she disappeared, I overheard something, and I think I know where to start looking for answers. If that means going through with this trip to the other side to get them, so be it.

I pull my phone from my pocket as it buzzes. Seeing it's Grandpa Esposito, I groan. He's been calling nonstop.

Gio already told me to avoid his calls. I don't know what that's all about, but Gio always has a reason for everything he does. I don't dislike my grandfather.

Of us three brothers he's always been the kindest to me. He's the one who has spent most of my life talking about me running the Di Lorenzo family someday. Now that I'm older, I've wondered why we've never taken the Esposito name. To be honest, I don't think my mother ever took it either.

"More bullshit and secrets," I mutter.

I know why Dante hates him, but I don't know the deal with him and Gio or what happened between him and Nonno. Frustrated with it all, I dial the one person I need to talk to in order to clear my head. All of this shit is ready to crush me.

Carleen

"Ugh, what do you mean? I thought we had all the permits."

"We did, then you asked for a few changes, and I had to pull new ones."

"Okay, fine but I can't live like this. What happened to moving in sections so I wouldn't have to move out during the renovation? You've torn my entire place apart," I seethe at my contractor.

"The guys messed up. Joey got confused and told the guys to demo everything."

"Got confused? He got confused. Do you guys not communicate? What am I supposed to do? I don't have time for this."

I'm fuming. It's bad enough Dario will be leaving the country and for the first time, I'll be running the restaurant by myself. I'm so nervous, I could shit my pants every time I think about it.

Now this. I knew I should have waited to do this.

It's not that I don't think I can run the restaurant on my own. Dario insisted we open a restaurant together. I had no idea he planned for us to open it under his family's empire. I mean, it does make sense, but the Di Lorenzo name comes with so much pressure.

Pressure I tried to avoid by dropping out of my residency and becoming a chef. My father still looks at me with so much disappointment. As a third-generation surgeon and the chief of staff at his hospital he had such high hopes for me as a surgeon.

I loved having a scalpel in my hands, but the politics and pressure were threatening to snap me. I would leave the hospital no matter what time of the day or night and go to hang with Dario in whatever kitchen he worked in. I found myself happiest with an apron on.

I'm a fast learner, some call me a sponge. I have always been determined to learn. I hate not being able to learn something once I put my mind to it.

It's beyond learning by watching because I can understand and adapt the why of the matter. I connect the dots from *A* to *Z* even if they're not explained or shown to me.

After watching Dario for years, I started cooking school to pursue my hobby, but eventually I fell out of love with the operating room and in love with the kitchen.

Okay, maybe my mentor and best friend had a little to do with me falling in love, but I'd never tell Dario that. I've been in love with him since we were eight and he blew on my scraped knee and held my hand as our mothers cleaned it for me. I loved Ava too. It wasn't long after that day that she disappeared. It broke my heart. She was always so nice to me.

"I'm going to kill Gio," I hiss under my breath.

He recommended this guy when I asked for someone who wouldn't rip me off for being a single woman. I'd gone behind Dario's back to ask his brother because I know Dario. He would have taken on this entire task himself.

He has enough on his shoulders. My phone rings right as I get ready to lose my shit on this man standing in front of me.

"Hello."

"What's wrong?" Dario demands as soon as he hears the frustration in my voice.

I rub my temple. "Nothing. Are we still having lunch today?"

"Don't, Carleen. I'm not in the mood. What's wrong?"

I sigh and roll my eyes. This man has been my protector for over twenty-seven years. It's one of the reasons I love him so much.

However, I hate to burden him with my problems. He carries so much responsibility with running our restaurant and training other chefs for his family's locations throughout New York and New Jersey.

Suddenly, the weight of it all settles on my shoulders. The pressure is mounting, and the panic rises. It's all too much.

I don't want to fail Dario and his family's legacy. I never should have spent all this money on this place and now I can't even live in it. I burst into tears as the frustration of my situation comes to a peak. I hate crying, I always have.

"Where are you? I'm on my way."

"Don't. I'll meet you at the restaurant. I need to get out of here." I sniffle.

"What's going on, Car? Talk to me."

"It's everything. My place is a mess. They've demoed everything. I'm going to have to find someplace to stay. Damnit, I don't want to go stay with my parents. If I have to listen to one more rant about the career I ruined, I'm going to jump off this damn building."

"Slow down. You can stay at my place."

"No, I can't. You're leaving at the end of the year. I don't know how long this will take."

"Exactly why you can stay at my place. You can have it to yourself once I'm gone. There's security and a concierge, you won't have to worry about a thing."

"Are you sure about this? I don't want to be in your way or cramp your style."

"You can have one of the guest rooms all to yourself. I don't even have to know you're there. Come on, with all the money you're spending on renovating that place you don't need to pay to stay somewhere, and you already said staying with your parents is off the table."

"You hate Blake's husband and you and Toni would kill each other. I'm your best option. This will keep you close to the restaurant so you're not driving across town in the middle of the night when inspiration hits you and you want to cook in the kitchen. Come on, Car. I've got you."

I sigh, knowing every word spoken is the truth. Against my better judgment, I bite the bullet and agree.

"Okay, but I need to pack. Can we push lunch back?"

"I'm coming to you. I'll have lunch with me. My car has more space. I'll help you move before our shift. Apollo can handle prep for service."

"Thanks, Rio. You don't know how much pressure you just took off my shoulders."

"Anytime, I'll see you in a bit."

CHAPTER TWO

The Packing

Dario

I enter Carleen's place and it's a fucking wreck. They've pulled this place apart to the studs. I'm surprised because she was supposed to be able to live through this.

I get pissed and head for the contractor right away to find out what the fuck happened. Arms wrap my waist and my body hums. I know it's Carleen instantly.

"Oh, no you don't, Rio. Come with me," she says as she starts to tug me in the other direction.

"How the fuck did this happen?" I ask as she tugs me into the garage.

I turn to look at her as I place the food on the folding table she has a suitcase sitting open on. She blows out a breath and rubs her forehead. There's so much frustration on her face.

It broke my heart to hear her crying earlier. I know how much she wants this place done. It's been her first big purchase since we opened the restaurant five years ago.

"I went on that girls' trip so I wouldn't be in anyone's way. I didn't think I needed to babysit these guys. This morning, I walked into this. Like, I don't understand. The movers weren't even supposed to empty every room. I still don't know who told them to do this. If they hadn't emptied the place, they wouldn't have been able to do this."

I blow out a breath and pull her into my arms. "Forget about it. It will work out. Remember when we were in high school, and we talked about getting a place together to become roommates?"

She laughs a little. "Yeah, my dad wasn't having that and then you went off with Dante to travel the world when I was old enough to do whatever I wanted."

I don't tell her I purposely spilled and told her dad our plans because I knew I couldn't live with her. Carleen came into full bloom senior year, gone was the skinny, lanky teenage girl I called a friend. She has one of those bodies that's a showstopper.

Medium-sized breasts and an ass that won't quit. Her long legs are shapely and speak of the workouts she's religious to.

I've wanted to fuck Carleen since we were sixteen and Dante soaked her with a water gun. The pink bikini she revealed in our pool house that day when she took her white T-shirt off had me so hard, I took off for the house to get my shit under control.

That was the first of many times I rubbed one out to thoughts of her and her sexy, deep-brown skin. I knew I was in love with her when someone else asked her to prom senior year.

I broke his arm after she said yes, his ass had the right mind to tell her he wasn't going after. She cried in my arms because she didn't think anyone else would ask her. Not because of me—she had no idea what I had done—but because she was never treated like the other girls. Being darker, Carleen felt like she wasn't as desirable as all the others. I call bullshit.

She was the prettiest girl in our school. The only reason I hadn't asked her was because I knew I couldn't have her, and it was wrong to get our hopes up, no matter how much I wanted her. However, in the end, to dry her tears I did take her.

"Yeah, well, we can finally be roommates. It will be fun."

She looks up at me with a small smile.

"Do you still walk around naked?"

I grin. "I have that robe you bought me for Christmas."

"Ha!"

"I could ask you the same thing. I've heard Toni complaining about you in your panties and bra all the time."

"Yeah, but Dario. You've never walked in on me butt-ass naked in the middle of the day."

"To be fair, I thought I had more time. You were an hour early."

"Ugh, I haven't used my key to your place since."

I laugh. "What? I didn't give you a good show?"

I swear, I see lust fill her eyes. I release her and take a step back. The last thing I need is to add to the complications in my life.

I have never dated a Black woman, not because I'm not attracted to them. I actually love looking at them, but Carleen is the only one I want. I'd rather date the total opposite of her if I can't have her.

For me, it's understood no woman will ever measure up to her. How could they? In another life, I would have married this woman years ago. She's everything I want.

"Whatever, Dario. I better not see your ass cheeks or anything else."

"I make no promises." I wink and clap my hands. "Okay, let's eat and then you can tell me where you need me."

Carleen

I never should have mentioned seeing him naked. I will never in my life forget that day. I almost slipped in my own drool. Dario is hung like a motherfucker and then he has the nerve to have an upturned bend in it.

It's almost a shame he's not into Black women. All I want is one experience, just one. My pussy pulses from the memory of the delicious sight.

The view is just as nice from the back as it is from the front. Dario has a nice, tight, hard-looking ass. Who am I kidding? The Di Lorenzo men were bathed in beauty and dipped in sin. I envy any woman who gets to spend a night in one of their beds.

"What are you thinking about?" Dario asks as he dips his grilled cheese into his tomato and basil soup. It's from one of our favorite spots.

"I'm working out a new recipe," I lie.

"Oh really? For what?"

"It's a pasta dish. I'm thinking citrus and seafood."

"Mm, sounds good. You go with herbs, that's going to be nice. Maybe you can make it for me before I leave. I'll help you tweak it. Are you thinking of adding it at the restaurant?"

I blush. I've never added one of my main courses to the menu. I'm terrified to. Dario is a master in the kitchen. I don't even think he would be in business with me if we weren't best friends.

I still have so much to learn. I work hard to improve, but I don't think I'm there yet.

He points his half-eaten sandwich at me. "*Marone.* I can see your thoughts. Before you start that bullshit. You're one of the best chefs I've ever worked with.

"You're a natural, the speed you learn at is crazy. Your flavor profiles are amazing, and your knife skills are unmatched. It wasn't my cook that got us that James Beer award—I wasn't in the kitchen, you were a major part in the acquisition of our three Michelin stars.

"We've kept them because of you. You're on that cookbook cover right along with me. A million copies sold. You're a part of that."

"All a part of being in the right place at the right time."

"Fuck outta here." He tosses the rest of his sandwich down and sits back as he folds his arms over his chest.

I look away as his muscles stretch his polo. I've been doing my best not to stare. Dario is about half an inch shy of six-six. While the leaner of the twins, he's still a bulky man. Every inch of him is sexy, especially the *kiss the chef* tat on his neck. I know for a fact he has other distracting tats along his ribs and across his pelvis.

For years, Dario has spent time in the gym with me. Because of him, I've continued kickboxing and started lifting. I've sculpted this body with him at my side, pushing me to be my best, even on the days I've wanted to give up. Most times in hope that our sweaty workouts would turn into more.

Someday.

Heck, a girl can hope, and dream, can't she?

"You know, you annoy me sometimes."

I tilt my head to the side and laugh. "Really? Wow, and I thought we were best friends."

"And that's exactly why. I know you can't believe the crap that comes out of your mouth, but I also know you're not the type to fish for compliments. So, I'm still trying to figure out where this all comes from."

I mirror his posture. "Not everyone is as confident as you are. People put on a brave face, but most are faking it until they make it."

"Please, miss me with that shit. You know how my family is about our legacy. You would never have been granted a position, least of all a restaurant, if you didn't have the skills. With me or without me, you needed the talent, and you have it."

"Can we change the subject?"

He snorts. "Want to talk about that first steak you made for me? Now that was pure shit, and I think I had the shits for a week after."

I burst into laughter and toss my paper napkin at him. He's not lying. I was so nervous to cook for him and I choked so bad. It's like I forgot everything I learned. It was horrible.

"You still suck as a pastry chef."

He shrugs and winks. "But my best friend is one of the best pastry chefs in New York so I'm safe."

I duck my head and blush. I am great with pastries, but I want to master savory cooking so bad. It's why I work so hard. I'll get there. I'll have my signature dish that I can duplicate to perfection every time. I know I will.

"That was perfect as always," he says as he finishes his food. "So where do we start?"

"What, you have some hot date?" I tease.

He frowns at me. "No, *we* have to get to work. That reminds me. Keep that asshole out of my place."

I groan. I should have known this was coming. I started dating a few months ago and Dario hates Lou with a passion. I still don't know why, they've hardly met.

Lou is a pretty nice guy. We met on a dating app. It's not that serious, but I'm tired of trying to explain that to Dario. If it were up to him, I would never talk, text, or go on another date with Lou.

Honestly, Lou checks off most of the boxes. All except being Dario Di Lorenzo. He owns a successful real estate company and he's been a total sweetheart.

"Dario, see, now this is why I should find someplace else to stay. Trust me, I don't want to listen to you fucking any more than you want me to have someone in your place."

"So, you're fucking him now?"

"No, but that's none of your business."

He snorts and shrugs. "You don't have to worry about listening to me fuck. I've been celibate."

I scoff. "Bullshit. Since when?"

"You make me sound like some manwhore. Is that how you see me?" He pulls a face, looking truly hurt.

"The Fleming twins, Natale Hearth, your professor your senior year in culinary school, shall I go on?"

"I was in a monogamous relationship with each of them."

I laugh so hard I have to hold my stomach. He was not monogamous to the twins. He was screwing one and dating the other. They just didn't seem to care.

"Whatever, I haven't been dating because I know I'm not going to find what I want. You won't hear a peep out of me unless my hand grows lips."

"Fine. I won't have Lou over."

I don't say out loud I think that's coming to an end. Lou wants things I don't want with him. I think I might be wasting his time.

"Good. Now let's get this stuff to my place. Time is ticking."

CHAPTER THREE

Be My Date

Dario

"That looks great," I say as I place my palms down on either side of Carleen at the station she's working at, caging her in.

She turns her face up and smiles at me. "Tell me what you think. Be honest."

She quickly sidesteps me, but I place a hand on her back before she can get too far away. This may have been a bad idea. I love having Carleen living with me. That's not the problem. The issue is I feel our bond deepening.

It's not limited to my place either. Like now, we're still at the restaurant after hours, working on the new menu for next week. I'm not going to lie and say I don't feel the chemistry flowing between us.

I get a pang in my heart every time I think of having to go to Italy where my life will change forever, there will be no turning back.

I take a bite of the pasta and scallop dish she has prepared. The flavor is magnificent. The lemon and the herbs are the perfect pairing, and the pasta is cooked to perfection.

"It's delicious. I'd add a little black pepper and maybe zest some lemon. This is going on the menu, Car."

"No, it's not ready. I was thinking of doing a cream sauce or something."

"It's perfect. You're overthinking. I'm telling you, this is going to be a hit. Look at the sear you have on these scallops. A few simple edits and this is it. The cream sauce will drown out the crispiness of the sear and ruin the pasta. This butter sauce you have here is nice. Leave it."

She looks at me with wide eyes. I can't help tugging her into me with an arm wrapped around her head. I kiss her forehead.

It's only been three days and I want things we can never have. We've laughed and talked late into the night every night since she's been with me.

It doesn't matter if we've gotten home late and are exhausted from closing. We go to our rooms and shower the day away, then end up on my couch fighting to stay up to spend stolen time together.

She's become more of a magnet. I can't stay away from her. I've questioned why I'm going through with this family promotion. Gio would be the better fit. I've never understood why I'm being groomed for it. Hell, Dante would be even better.

Don't get me wrong, I've earned the name *Rio the Butcher*— not from the kitchen either. While I'm not as brutal as Dante, I can be just as vicious when provoked. I haven't had to show that side since I was a Capo. Man, the shit I did when I was twenty.

To this day, I think it was the actions of some shit Dante and I pulled that got the books open. All three of us were made at the same time. Both my grandfathers were proud—Grandpa Esposito more so of me. I don't think he much liked the fact that Gio was made at all.

Now, as an underboss, I haven't had to prove myself. My name travels for me. Although, I get the feeling this trip is about to change all of that.

"Where'd you go?" Carleen says in that soft, raspy voice of hers.

"Just thinking. Hey, so Dante and I decided to go to the company Halloween party as 1920s gangsters." I pause, knowing this is stupid of me, but we're both going so here goes. "I was wondering if you would be my Bonnie. You know, come with me as Bonnie and Clyde."

She bites her lip. "Um, that only gives me two days to find a costume."

"I sort of got it for you."

She lifts a brow at me. I give her my best smile. "Oh, come on. It's much better than showing up in a chef's coat. That idea is so lame. You're not even trying. It will be fun. The pictures alone will be worth it."

She frowns. "I was not going in a chef's coat." She pouts.

"Oh wait, you were going with the scrubs." I laugh.

"Ugh, you don't know me as well as you think. Let's clean up and get out of here."

"No, wait. I want you to taste this," I say as I push the dish she made toward her.

I hold the fork out and watch that gorgeous mouth as she wraps her full lips around the fork as she closes her amber eyes. She hums and I grow hard from the sound.

When she opens her eyes, the smile on her lips is priceless. Her entire face is lit with excitement. Now this is the Carleen I watched fall in love with the kitchen.

"Oh my God that *is* divine."

I wink at her. "See, I told you."

"Okay, okay, but I couldn't have done this without you, Rio. You could have told me to get out of your kitchen and find something else to do with my life, but you have been supportive from the beginning. You will never understand how much that means to me."

"You have the chops, baby. You did all the real work. It's been an honor to watch you find your wings."

"Ah, let's not push it. I have to be able to repeat that same dish a thousand more times before I start patting myself on the back."

I frown. "Whatever. I'm boxing this up to take home." I point at the dish.

Carleen

I'm bursting at the seams as we push into Dante's apartment. He loved the dish. His edits were good ideas. I can't wait to try them to see if I can do it all again.

Dario thinks I'm not confident in my skills. That's not it. I'm a perfectionist. I was at the top of my class and a damn good surgeon. I left all that time and skill behind, so I want to be the best as a chef.

I need to be able to show my father that my happiness didn't come with the price of failure. I just found a path to success *and* happiness. I need him to see this wasn't about Dario. I love to cook.

"You want to watch a movie?" Dario asks as he pulls his shirt off.

I drop my gaze to his chest. I've learned to appreciate so many things about this man in the last three days. His right side is covered in words and little, tiny butterflies. It's like they swarm down toward where his happy trail should be and disappear into his jeans, sweats, or whatever. I've seen each look.

It's not like I haven't seen the tats before, I just have a new appreciation for the view. I look forward to coming home after work to be treated to this. Shirtless Dario is a gift in itself.

"I, um, I was going to do some writing in my journal and get that recipe down while it's still fresh."

"Cool, I'm going to shower and make a few calls. I'll be waiting when you're ready. We can sleep in tomorrow."

"I have a hair appointment in the morning," I say.

I plan to get a wash and set. The kitchen can be hell on my hair. All the sweating and steam and heat of the kitchen sends me to the salon twice a week to keep my shoulder-blade length hair looking decent.

I don't miss the look of disappointment on his face. In all honesty, I've loved our nights together, but they're breaking my heart. I'm in love with this man and being with him feels so natural. I need a little space to tighten the lid on my feelings.

Maybe some time writing how I feel in my journal will help me get my head back on straight. Dario and I will never be a thing. I have never even seen him with a woman of color.

I once had a little hope when Dante started dating Bethany, but the twins aren't alike in everything.

"No worries. If you change your mind, text me. Have a good night, Carleen."

"Good night, Dario."

I move across the apartment to the room I've been calling my own. My lids are growing heavy as the exhaustion of the day kicks in. I strip down out of my jeans and tank top and head into the shower.

My mind turns to when Dario walked up behind me in the kitchen tonight. My pulse raced and I wanted to lean back into him. I always feel so safe around him. I couldn't help wanting him to fold me into his embrace.

While the shower rains down on me, I reach between my legs to relieve this ache. Closing my eyes, I press a palm and my forehead to the shower wall and pull up images of Dario's hard body and that anaconda.

I pretend it's his big hand running through my pussy lips. I'm a panting mess as I bring myself to climax. This is why staying here was a bad idea. I know how I feel about this man.

Why am I putting myself through this torture?

I finish my shower after I'm done and pull on some shorts and a tank top. Picking up the two notebooks on the desk, I start with the recipe.

My phone rings and I pick it up to see it's Lou. After what just happened in the shower, I think it's best to let this situation go. I've never been one to string someone along.

"Hello."

"Hey, gorgeous. I've been thinking about you all day."

"How sweet. How are you, Lou?"

"I'm a hundred-percent better now that I'm talking to you. Listen, I was thinking. It's been a while since we've been able to make time for each other. How about I come over and we have a bottle of wine together?"

"Oh, we haven't spoken in a few days. The reno has turned into a disaster. I'm not staying at my place."

"Well, where are you? You know you can always come stay with me or in one of my rentals."

I don't miss the excitement in his voice. I know Lou wants to be more intimate. I just haven't felt it with him.

"Thank you, that's so sweet of you, but I'm staying with Dario for now."

"The best friend?"

"Yes."

"He's a Di Lorenzo, isn't he?"

"Yes."

I don't know why my hackles go up. It's the way he asks the question. It's not the first time he has asked questions about Dario. However, this time rubs me some way. I don't like it.

"They're of Italian descent, right? From the old country."

"Di Lorenzo. That should tell you all you need to know."

Lou clears his throat. "Well, does he mind me coming there? I want to spend some time with you."

"Actually, this is his space, I would never invite someone here."

It's the truth even if Dario didn't say to keep Lou out of his home. Besides, Dario may not like to talk about his family, but I've grown up around him enough to know they have secrets, and I wouldn't want to invite someone into his life, not fully understanding them.

This trip to Italy is about to change something for Dario. I've feared that his family wants him to take over *Amore Domestico,* the family's first restaurant in Italy. I mean, it is his legacy. However, that would leave me here in New York without my best friend and with a restaurant to run all on my own.

I've been feeling like I'm about to lose him. As hard as I've tried to ignore it, it's been like an eerie feeling circling my thoughts.

I snort to myself. If I'm honest, Dario has become more than a best friend since we've been working together. We breathe each other's next move. The way we work in the kitchen is magic. I'm going to miss him while he's gone.

"Carleen?" Lou calls my attention back to the phone. I run my hand into the front of my hair, knowing I should end this conversation now.

"Sorry, what was that?"

"If I can't come see you tonight. I want you to come spend a weekend with me and my family. I want them to get to meet you."

"Oh, Lou. I'm sorry. I'm not ready for something like that. Actually, I was thinking we should take a break. I think we want different things, and I don't want to string you along."

He's silent for a moment. Suddenly, I hear him curse away from the phone. "Listen, maybe I'm moving too fast, but I don't think that means we should end things. How about we do take a break. I'll give you a month or two and then we can try things again."

"I don't know, Lou."

"Just think about it. Text me anytime you want to talk. I'll be here whenever you want, but I'll give you some space."

"Okay," I say because at this point, I just want off this call.

"You have a good night."

"You too."

I hang up, finish jutting down the recipe and pick up my other journal to write how this day has left me feeling. An hour later, I pass out with a ton of thoughts on my mind.

CHAPTER FOUR

Work Marriage

Carleen

"Amazing, right?" Dario croons as I pull into my mouth the slice of cheese he has held up to my lips.

"Oh my God. It's so fresh," I reply. "That hint of spice is everything."

"Here, *mangiare*," he says as he shaves some of the cheese into a bowl of crab ravioli and marinara sauce. "I went old school. This is my great-great-grandfather's gravy with a little Dario flair."

I smile as he calls the sauce gravy. I don't think he realizes it, but Dario's Italian American culture slips through so often, always carrying that Jersey flair. It's endearing.

I open my mouth and take in the bite he offers. It's fucking orgasmic. This is so natural for him. Dario's love for food comes through in his cooking.

"Wow," I say after I finish chewing.

"You like? I used the wine from the Di Lorenzo vineyards. Its earthy notes are perfect. I can't wait to make this for *Nonno.*"

My shoulders sag a little from the reminder that he's leaving. I don't know what I'll do if he has to stay in Italy to run the restaurant there. Dario has been there for me for so much in my life.

I've always imagined him as my children's godfather. There may be no chance of him ever being the father of my children and I'm learning to be okay with him never knowing how in love with him I am, but I still want him in my children's lives.

"Do you know how long you will be?" I ask the question I've been avoiding.

A sad look comes to his face. "I'm not sure. You're welcome to stay at my place as long as you need to though."

Just not welcome to come along. I nod and turn away to busy myself with wiping the spotless counter.

"Hey, bosses." Apollo walks over and saves me. "We're ready to go live on the line when you guys are."

"Good, I want you to stay after service. This dish will be going on the menu. I need you to learn it as well as Carleen knows it. You guys will be running things together while I'm gone."

"Cool, I don't think we'll have the work marriage you two have, but I'll do my best," Apollo says.

"Work what?" Rio asks.

"Work marriage. You two are definitely work husband and wife. It's amazing to watch. You two move around each other like a dance. I think that's what gives the food that extra *muah.*" He kisses his fingers with the last word.

Dario chuckles and looks at me. "You hear that? You're my work wife."

He takes the towel out of his back pocket and snaps it at my ass. I yelp and scowl at him. As payback, I dip my fingers in a nearby glass of water and flick it at him.

"Some work husband you are. Abusing me in front of the employees."

Dario wraps an arm around my waist and tugs me closer. He leans into my ear. "I'd never hurt you."

He taps my ass and turns to head to his station for the night. I stand stunned and thoroughly turned on. I really don't think he understands what he does to my body. I blink after him like I'm lost.

"All right, chefs, we're live," Dario calls out, snapping me out of my fog.

Dario

Another amazing service. I'm going to miss this. While Papa Riccardo has kept me close, always in my ear about my life as a Di Lorenzo and what the name means on the other side, my *nonno* is the one who has encouraged my love of the culinary arts. You would think it would have been the other way around.

Nonno takes pride in his bloodline, but for him it started with *Amore Domestico* so to be a Di Lorenzo, first starts with the business. Then we have this thing of ours. The part of my life that's pulling me away from all that's familiar. The dragons and their world.

Growing up and learning those dragons were *la cosa nostra*, our thing, the other crime families—has made me want to shield Carleen even more. Which is why I stand here, propped against the wall while watching her jot down notes in her recipe journal. She always has that thing with her.

I'm trying to anchor myself, so I don't do something stupid like go over there, wrap her in my arms, and tell her I love her. It takes more of a man to walk away in order to keep her safe, than it does to be selfish and give in. This is what I've been telling myself for years.

Although, I'm starting to wonder if this is true. A pat on my shoulder causes me to turn to look over it. Pauly, one of our older line cooks has his eyes on me.

He gives my shoulder a squeeze. "You've been in love with her for as long as I've worked for you. *Che problema c'è?* Why waste time, tell her how you feel," he says with a knowing look in his eyes.

I shake my head. "She's too good for me. My life would eat her alive. We need to stay who we are."

"*Marone.* Suit yourself. I'll never understand this generation. In my day, you found your soul mate, you married them, and lived a good life. I miss my Anna. What I'd give for a few more moments, but what do I know?" He shrugs. "Good night, Dario."

"Good night, Pauly."

I push off the wall and stroll over to Carleen. She looks up from the pages of her journal and gives me a smile.

"Is that the recipe you wanted me to make?"

"Yeah, you don't mind, do you?"

"No, but not here. Let's get out of here and I'll make it at home."

"Okay."

She gathers her stuff and places it in her backpack, as I get our coats. Taking the backpack from her, I place a hand on her back as we move to turn the rest of the lights out and lock the place down for the night.

Thoughts of doing this together for the rest of our lives dance in my head. I ache to be going home to our little family. A house filled with love and laughter. If Carleen knew how much blood I have on my hands, she'd probably run screaming.

I wouldn't have to worry about her not fitting into my world or her safety. She'd probably look at me with such disgust and disdain, it would be enough to break my heart.

I'm not ashamed of what I've had to do. It's always been to keep my family safe. There's always someone out there who feels what's ours should be theirs.

"You look so stressed out and tired," Carleen says as I open the door to my car for her to get in. She cups my face and looks up into my eyes.

I clasp her hand in mine and turn to kiss her palm. Dropping our hands to our sides, with hers still in mine, I make circles in her palm with my thumb.

"Promise me something."

"Okay," she says, looking up at me nervously.

"No matter who I become, always remember how much I care about you as a friend. Remember the boy you played with on that playground."

"Hey, Dario, is everything all right?"

"Yeah, just promise me."

"Um, okay. I promise." She wraps her arms around my neck and pulls me into a hug.

I embrace her tightly and bury my face in her neck. Carleen's five-eight frame is swallowed in my arms as I'm comforted by her subtle scent, a soft vanilla and coconut.

"Come on, let's get out of here," I say and kiss the top of her head.

Carleen

I finish my shower and pull on a pair of sweats and a T-shirt. I haven't been able to stop thinking about Dario's mood and words back at the restaurant.

Something is going on with him. I'm becoming more afraid that he's not coming back from Italy. I'm losing my friend.

All our lives, I've known something was different about Dario and his family. What I think is going on is something you don't just come out and ask about.

I heard the rumors in high school. There was a reason everyone feared the twins and it wasn't their massive size. I've seen the movies; I know the less I know the better. Plausible deniability. Yeah, I know nothing, I see nothing. My nice Italian friends are in the food industry, nothing more.

Yet, Dario made it sound like this trip is about to turn him into Michael Corleone. *No matter who I become, always remember how much I care about you as a friend. Remember the boy you played with on that playground.* Ugh, my brain is tired and running away from me.

With a sigh, I go to pick up my journal to write my thoughts down before I go out to see if Dario is done with the food he's making.

A frown comes to my face. My diary and my food journal look almost identical. I've never thought of that before. I've always lived alone so it's never been a thought. However, at the moment, when Dario has my recipe journal while I sit with this one, it's a nagging thought.

"Best be hiding this thing," I mutter to myself.

Oh lord, if Dario ever saw the things I've written in here about him, I'd die a slow death. All my fantasies and dreams line these pages. From what I think he's going to Italy for to the fact that I dream of one single night in his arms. I've even written all the things I would do to him on said night.

"He definitely never needs to see this."

I finish my entry and go in search of Dario. The first thing I notice when I get closer to the kitchen is that I don't smell anything cooking.

A smile breaks out on my face as Dario comes into view passed out on the couch. His snoring is the next thing that hits me. His chest is bare, and he has on sweats. I grab a throw and toss it over him. Feeling as exhausted as he looks, I turn and head back to my bedroom.

CHAPTER FIVE

Halloween

Dario

Carleen makes one sexy Bonnie. She has on a wig that's cut into a wavy bob, framing her gorgeous face. Though I love her natural, long, dark hair, she's pulling off the blonde. It's making her amber eyes pop against that deep, dark skin of hers that seems to be glowing tonight.

The flapper-style dress is fitted snuggly to her breasts. I've been trying not to stare at them or how the dress fits across her ass.

I couldn't help comparing my brother's cute little assistant to Carleen. While Lizzy is pretty and a few shades lighter than Carleen, she's no Car. Carleen is closer to an umber complexion while Lizzy is more chocolate. Still brown and pretty, but nowhere as gorgeous as my Carleen.

When I had those thoughts earlier, I dropped my eyes down to Lizzy's breasts with a smile on my lips. Carleen's cleavage definitely makes Lizzy's pale in comparison. Don't get me wrong, she has a cute pair. They're just not like Carleen's full, ripe breasts.

"You okay?" I ask Carleen for the millionth time since my twin left with his family.

Something has changed tonight. There's been a bit of a distance between us. My mind races. I don't think Carleen let Bethany rub her the wrong way. She's not that sensitive.

"Yeah, I'm fine."

"You sure?" I go to press, but Gio catches my attention from across the room and gestures with his head for me to follow him. I pause and frown. "Hold that thought. I'll be right back."

"Take your time."

My frown deepens. I don't like her tone. I wish I knew what she's thinking. Her body is so tense and she's giving off a standoffish vibe. I run a hand down her arm and give her wrist a gentle squeeze before I turn to cross the room to my brother.

Carleen

I wipe the back of my hand across my mouth as I finish my third fruity drink. I've been sulking since catching Dario staring at Lizzy's breasts. I cup the sides of my boobs and adjust them in my dress.

"Mine are bigger than hers," I mutter to myself.

I'm pissed because I've never seen Dario look at a Black woman before. Why her? Sure, Lizzy is gorgeous. I think this was the first time I've seen her without her glasses or dressed in some black-on-black, Goth-looking outfit, which definitely has brought out all her stunning features.

I toss back another drink. "But why her?"

"Why who?" Jace asks as he appears at my side.

"Oh, hey, Jace."

"Whoa. You might want to slow down on the drinks. You're sounding a bit slurred there."

I frown. "Listen, you can go back to the silent killer shit. My father isn't here tonight," I grumble.

He snorts a chuckle and holds up his hands. "I'm not your enemy."

"No, Lizzy is," I bite out before my brain can tell me to shut the hell up.

"Lizzy?" he says, and something crosses his face. "What makes you say that?"

"I've never, and I mean never, seen Dario look at a Black woman before. What was that about? He was totally checking her out. My boobs are bigger than hers. She doesn't look like she's willing to do half the shit I am." I pause with my chest heaving. "Oh God, I have had too much to drink. I'm just tired. I love him so much, but I know nothing will ever happen."

Jace places a hand on my shoulder and gives a gentle squeeze. "Take it from me. You can think someone doesn't see you when all they see *is* you. There are just other things keeping them from you.

"You're gorgeous, Carleen. I came over here because I don't want Dario to lose his shit on that guy who was heading over here to try to talk to you."

He winks down at me, and I take a cleansing breath. I try to put his words together in my head, but nothing makes sense. Looking up into his eyes, I search them, trying to make my brain clear.

"What guy? Why would Dario lose his shit?"

Jace shakes his head at me. In the most brotherly way, he scoops his arm around my waist. I lean into his side.

"I'll get you home. Dario may be a while."

"You better not be trying to cover for him while he gets in Lizzy's pants."

"Lizzy is not for him. She already belongs to someone else. I'm protecting what's Dario's," he says.

I bank those words for later as my stomach reels. I may have had too much to drink.

Dario

I catch up to my brother and look around as we head toward his office. No Jace, interesting. The two are joined at the hip. They have been since we were younger. Jace and Gio were born a day apart. They have grown up like brothers. Jace has looked out for me and Dante as much as Gio has.

"Is it me or is Bethany getting worse?"

"She's definitely smelling herself. Don't worry about her. Time is ticking on that clock," Gio replies as we enter his office.

"Yeah, but is he listening to you?"

"Dante will hear me when I start to speak his language. I'm not worried about that. She's the one who should be worried. Do you have those photos I asked for?"

He sits behind his desk, and I take one of the seats in front of it. Dante's wife is fucking around behind his back. I almost butchered the motherfucker's ass myself, but Gio told me to wait, he had it covered. All he needed was a picture of the guy's face.

"Yeah, the guy has been around the restaurant every day this week. He's too busy watching me to notice Apollo taking pictures of him. I have Salvatore following him as well."

"Good. Sal knows not to get too close." It's a statement, not a question.

"Who is this guy? I get the feeling there's more to it than him fucking Bethany. And why am I so interesting to him?"

"To ask questions is to get answers you may not want. I'll take care of this. You focus on your trip."

I grunt and pull a face. I hate when he's like this. I know he does it to protect me and my twin, but it's starting to feel like Gio has this looking glass I want to be able to see into. I always feel like I'm going to be blindsided by what he knows.

I shrug the feeling off. "Did you see the way he looked at Lizzy?"

"Yeah, but we're not here to talk about that." I sigh. I figured that. "*Nonno* will be here in a few days," Gio says.

I inhale deeply. "What? He thinks I won't show up. He's coming to get me himself?"

Gio frowns at me. "You underestimate our grandfather. You might want to check that."

For once in my life, I hold my words in. I know Gio isn't my enemy, nor is Nonno. If anything, Gio has always been the one to help me balance this world and Nonno has always been there to encourage my normal life.

"He's doing this to make things easier for you. You won't be walking into all of this blindly. He's coming to be in your corner."

"Yeah, I know. Do you think that's why Papa Esposito keeps blowing up my phone?"

"He's been calling you?" Gio seethes.

"Yeah, four or five times a day. I haven't been answering. Shit's getting annoying though."

Gio works his jaw. The amount of rage I see in his eyes nags at me. Papa Esposito pulled me in right after my mother disappeared. I craved the attention I lost from Ma. She was patient with my questions and curiosity. My grandfather filled that void.

I get Dante hates the man for trying to have him placed in a straitjacket. However, Gio's anger is because of something else. My thoughts go to the things I overheard the day my mother left.

"Dario, I need you to trust me. In the end, you will understand everything and why it was necessary. Let him call. What you're doing is none of his business," Gio says, pulling me from my thoughts before I can get too lost in them.

He stands and walks over to the hidden bar in his office. His words leave me with an eerie feeling. My curiosity kicks in and my lips move before I can trap the words in.

"Do you believe she left us? Something else had to happen. Is that why you hate Papa Esposito so much?"

"More questions," he replies and walks over with a tumbler to hand me. I take the glass, but only stare down into it. "This is why *Nonno* wants you on the other side. To lead the future, you have to understand the past. Play your part, Dario and all your questions will find answers. Be who you are."

He places a hand on my shoulder and gives it a squeeze. My phone buzzes in my pocket. I pull it out and find a text from Carleen. She's left.

Gio grunts at his phone, grabbing my attention. "Jace will get her home safe."

"I'm leaving her. I've never not been there for her."

Gio smiles at me. It's that knowing smile of his that says he's looking into that crystal ball again.

"I'll finish what was started," he says and drains his glass.

I narrow my eyes at him. His phone rings and he holds up a finger. I nod and turn my attention back to my phone. Something about the text makes me furrow my brows.

Car: *I left. Don't want to be in the way.*

CHAPTER SIX

Secrets and Wishes

Carleen

"Come on, I've got you," Jace says as he helps me into the apartment.

Those drinks packed a silent punch. They didn't taste as if they had that much alcohol in them. Now, my face is rocked, and I don't think I would have made it on my own. I'm grateful to Jace.

I would have been so embarrassed if Dario came home to find me sitting in front of the door trying to figure out how to get inside and probably in tears because I couldn't. I breathe a sigh of relief when Jace sets me on my bed after I point out which room I'm staying in.

He kneels before me and unfastens my shoes to pull them off my feet. I take him in. Jace is a gorgeous man. I've always been curious about him. His strong, handsome features are alluring and he's a huge guy.

"You're the only one who didn't wear a costume. Not your thing?" I slur as he gets my first shoe off.

He looks up at me and smiles. Using a tie that seems to come from nowhere, he pulls his long blond hair up into a man bun. I burst into laughter as the two bite marks and dripping blood come into view.

"So what? You were supposed to be Gio's blood slave?"

He shrugs. Jace has never been one for many words. I've mostly seen him whispering to Gio or murmuring to the twins. I've never had the privileged to hear his voice more than I have tonight. It's a nice, deep, almost gravelly voice.

I reach to twirl a loose strand of his hair around my finger. He looks up through his lashes to grin at me. His eyes are a light green at the moment, but I've seen them a few different colors before—gray and light brown, I believe.

Jace is no Italian. His strong narrow nose, square bearded jawline, and thick brow area speak more of Norse descent. His blond brows thread as he watches me study him.

"You hang with nothing but Italians, but you look like a big Viking to me." I drunkenly giggle.

"That's because I was raised by Italians, but my father was one-hundred-percent Danish, and my mother was Scandinavian and Italian."

I hold my breath, waiting for him to continue. I want to know more, but once again. I don't ask any questions when it comes to anything connected to the Di Lorenzos.

I wonder if that's my problem? I should know more about the people I'm in business with and my best friend for that matter.

I shove those thoughts away. Dario would have told me what he felt it was safe for me to know years ago. I trust my friend.

Jace says nothing else. He finishes with my shoes and stands. With a nod, he says, "I don't have permission to touch you any more than I already have, so I'm going to leave you to undress and climb into bed. Rest, I'll lock up. I'll tell Dario to check on you."

Then he leaves. I don't know if Dario will check on me when he gets in. Not after the drunken text I sent him to let him know I left the party to go home.

I stand and strip from my costume, then grab my journal. I'm still pissed. I think of calling one of my girls, but they'll only tell me to tell Dario how I feel. The man is my business partner and my best friend.

I'd be complicating a good thing. I don't want to lose my friend or the business we've built. My head full of thoughts and my stomach rumbling, I head to the kitchen to find something to eat.

I find some leftovers and pop them in the microwave. The chicken parmesan hits the spot. I probably shouldn't but I grab a bottle of wine and pour a glass.

"I'm turning into a lush," I murmur before taking a sip. I shake my head. "This isn't you, Carleen. You've never been this twisted over any man."

Except him.

The taunting thought makes me growl at myself. Aggravated and needing to vent, I open my notebook and start to write feverishly.

I just wish for one night I could show him how I feel. One night to get this all out of my system. I wish I could look him in the eyes and allow him to see what I've been hiding.

I wouldn't cling to him after. I'd take my one night and move on with my life. We could keep our friendship and I'd be able to move forward to find what's meant to be mine.

"That's my one wish." I sniffle and run my hand under my nose.

I refill my wineglass and stumble to my room. I'm going to have to figure something out. This is starting to hurt.

He's not against Black women. So, it's me.

Dario

I push my way into my apartment as my stomach growls. Jace returned to the office as I was leaving out. Gio had more he wanted to say before I could leave and come check on Carleen. I enter the kitchen to find a plate on the island next to a bottle of wine and Carleen's recipe journal. I smile to myself. She must have been working on a new recipe.

I cork the wine, then clear her dishes and wash them before I search for something to eat. The chicken parm I'm looking for is gone. My stomach protests loudly.

I never did get to make that recipe Carleen wanted me to make. I passed out last night. When she drinks, she usually wakes hungry. I could make the dish and leave it for her in the warmer with a note.

I turn for her recipe journal and flip it open to the page she has a pen shoved in. I notice right away this isn't her recipe book. I should shut it and walk away, but my name is all over the page I'm staring down at. When it sinks in this is her diary, my mind screams for me to close it, but that curiosity that has burned within me since I was a boy causes me to keep reading.

I groan and pull a hand down my face. "Damn, that's why she was pissed?"

She thought I was checking Lizzy out. Carleen thinks I'm not attracted to her or Black women. At least she thought I wasn't attracted to Black women. Now she thinks it's her.

Against my better judgment, I keep reading and the wheels in my drunken mind start to turn. I run my fingers over the page and the few wet spots, as if she was crying as she wrote this.

I have one wish. That's all. Why can't there be an alternate universe where for one night Dario could be mine? A night where he'd make love to me, and I could show him how much I love him and have always loved him.

I wouldn't ask for more than one night. I'd take it and be happy that I don't have to hold these feelings so deep inside. For one night, I'd get to feel him inside me and call his name as if we could be more.

I'm tired of masturbating to my thoughts of him. Now, I know he's not against Black women and I can't shove this hurt away. I wish I could rid this ache from my body. I've never wanted anything so badly in my life. I know he's keeping something from me, but I don't even care. One night, that's all I ask. It would be my one and only one-night stand. Surely, my future husband can't begrudge me that.

I would give Dario my all in that one night. I'd show him how much I care for him with my body and then…In the morning, I'd breathe and act like it never happened. I'd hold it in my heart like I've held all my feelings for him.

That's my one wish.

I look up and stare into space. I work my jaw as I try to filter through my thoughts. There's a part of me that knows I should go to my room, shower, and forget what I've read. Then there's the part of me that wants to grant her wish.

I just don't know if I can. Can I have Carleen and walk away for her to find someone else and forget about me? I don't think I have that in me. However, she's going to marry someone someday and I'll be forgotten.

Just the thought of it makes me sick to my stomach. Images of her body covered in oil as I run my palms over her skin fill my head—but it looks like she's in love with me as much as I'm in love with her—this would be a fucked-up thing to do.

I grab the bottle of wine and uncork it. Walking to my room, I drain the rest of the bottle as I try to forget what I've read.

Fuck me.

CHAPTER SEVEN

What We Want

Carleen

The bed dips and I groan. Rolling onto my other side, I'm faced with the scent of alcohol and Dario. I would know his scent anywhere. It's subtle because we work in a kitchen, but it still clings to his skin in a fresh way.

I go to burrow into the scent when I realize it shouldn't be in my bed. I open my eyes to find his hazel gaze locked on mine. Before I can say a word, he captures my lips and kisses me deeply.

I moan into his mouth and lock my fingers in his hair. My senses kick in when he reaches to palm my ass, rolls me onto my back, and settles between my legs. I wrap my bare legs around his waist and his naked skin is the first thing I register.

I have to be dreaming. He groans as his thick erection pokes into me. My eyes fly open, and I break the kiss. Dario starts to kiss his way down my neck to my collarbone. My skin feels like it's sizzling with each press of his lips.

"You're so beautiful. I've always thought you were gorgeous. I've wanted this body since I was sixteen. If things were different...I do care about you, Carleen."

He says all this while caressing my body and moving lower. I fell asleep in my panties and bra, leaving me bare to him as he pulls the covers back and settles on his stomach with his face in my core. My brain still hasn't kicked in yet.

I hold my breath as he licks my inner thigh. Lifting to his knees, he peels my panties down my legs, then lifts my leg to drag his lips and tongue against my skin until he reaches my apex. Tossing my leg over his shoulder, he dives in for my honeypot.

I finally find my words. "Dario, what are you doing?"

He looks up at me as he slowly licks through my folds. His hazel eyes blazing with desire. My heart skips a beat. He kisses my inner thigh once more.

"I'm giving you your wish and putting us both out of our misery," he murmurs and returns to feasting on me.

I close my eyes and fist the sheets. Oh God, am I dreaming? I have to be dreaming. His mouth is a work of art. I normally hate receiving oral sex, but Dario has the right amount of skill and patience to allow me to enjoy this experience. Or at least, that's what I think until he intensifies things and I have to try to crawl away from him.

He looks me in the eyes and smiles. I bow off the mattress, pleading with him for mercy. He reaches for my hand and pries it from the sheet to link our fingers together as he continues to eat my pussy like the special of the day.

"Fuck," I sob.

He hums and backs off to lick his fingers before playing with my pussy with his hand. My eyes roll into the back of my head. My heart is hammering.

The feel of his tongue and lips dragging up my stomach causes me to open my eyes again. He's moving up my body at a torturously slow speed.

When he gets to my lips and kisses me again, it clicks that this isn't a dream at all. The moment I feel him bump up against my sex with his huge penis, I start to pant. This can't be happening.

"Dario," I cry out as he slips inside me, his hand fisted tightly on mine.

With my free hand, I cling to his broad back. My toes curl as he works his hips, pushing into me. Tears fill my eyes and roll back into my ears. He cups my face with his free hand.

"Carleen," he whispers against my lips. He throws his head back and groans. I snap out of my shock and start to work my hips. "Oh God, baby. You feel so good. You're killing me."

I pull my legs back and spread them for him. He growls and palms my thighs as he starts to drill into me. I'm so wet for him.

"Yes, yes," I cry out.

He covers my mouth and kisses me deeply. It's like he's trying to tell me something through our sealed lips. Damn, I knew sex with Dario would be good, but this is amazing. I drink him in and get drunk all over again.

Dario

"Yes, come for me," I groan.

I don't want this to stop. She feels so fucking good. My heart feels like it's going to come out of my chest. This was a big mistake. I reach for her hands and bring them up over her head.

I'm not fucking, I'm making love to her. The deeper I go, the more I know I'm not going to give her up. One night isn't happening.

"Dario," she cries as I take one of her nipples into my mouth.

I suck on the dark-berry tip and groan as she ripples around me. Her body convulses as she soaks my shaft. I'm not ready to come, but I don't think I have a choice. I try to hold on, but the moment she latches her lips onto my neck, I spill inside her.

It's then I know I've fucked up. I'm so damn drunk, I forgot to put on a condom. I've been through three bottles of wine since I read her journal.

I pull out and kiss all over her face. Almost as if I'm apologizing for dragging her into my life. I wish things were different.

I wish I could roll onto my back and wait for round two, but I shouldn't be here in the first place. When I do roll onto my back, I lie staring at the ceiling. There has to be a way to have her, keep her safe, and still do as my family needs.

I'll go to Italy, check the climate of things, and when I return, I can claim what's always been mine. As I have those thoughts, Carleen moves down my body and settles between my legs. I suck in a breath when she pulls my still soft cock into her mouth.

"Fuck," I groan as I start to grow hard again. "Baby, you don't have to."

She takes me all the way down her throat, before lifting her head. She sucks the moisture back into her mouth. "But I want to."

She then proceeds to give me the best head of my life. I mean that nasty, deep throat, slurping, spitting, toe-curling, ball-sucking porn-star shit you never think you'll find in real life.

Yeah, there's no fucking way I'm giving her up. Not in this life or the next. I just have to make things right to have her in my world. I need her.

CHAPTER EIGHT

Good Morning

Carleen

I wake with a strong arm wrapped around me and a warm, hard chest pressed to my back. The soreness between my legs tells me the images floating through my brain aren't from a dream at all. Dario's scent surrounding me confirms what I already know. I slept with my best friend, and it was the best sex of my life.

He takes in a sharp intake of air behind me and kisses the side of my neck and then my shoulder. Next, he palms my breast in his large hand, kneading it, while he runs his long leg up and down mine.

"Good morning," he murmurs against my neck as he slides his hand down between my legs, cupping my sex before slipping two fingers inside me.

"Mm," I murmur back, not wanting to share my morning breath, but unable to remain silent.

He locks his leg around mine, using it to pull my legs apart. I roll onto my back and look up into his intense gaze as he works my body to climax. I toss an arm over my face as my cheeks flush.

Dario chuckles and nudges my arm with his nose. "I like to fuck first thing in the morning. Get used to it," he says.

I remove my arm and look up at him with wide eyes as my orgasm hits in that exact moment. It takes a moment for me to recover. When I do, I lift onto my elbows and stare at him.

"What?" he asks, lifting a brow.

My thoughts are racing. Clearly, he read my journal. I'm still trying to understand how. Then it clicks.

I palm my forehead and groan. I was so focused on my glass of wine. I left the journal on the kitchen island.

"Come shower with me. Then we can have a talk," he says.

I go to wrap the sheet around me to stand. He snorts and snatches it away. I look at him with a scowl.

"Carleen, I don't know what's going on in your head, but neither of us will be forgetting what happened last night."

I roll my eyes and stomp my way into the bathroom to brush my teeth. I feel him hot on my heels. When I look over my shoulder, he's right behind me in all his naked glory.

I nearly trip over my feet as I try to put distance between us. Damn pigeon toes, it's how I fell on the playground all those years ago when I realized I was totally in love with him. Frowning at the thought, I turn to keep my focus on grabbing my toothbrush.

Dario palms my breasts as he stares into my eyes through our reflection. As tall as I am, I still look so small standing before him. I won't even dare to think of how good we look together.

I thought this day would bring me so much joy, but I feel like I'm going to lose my friend even sooner than I thought. I can't help feeling like we've doomed our relationship.

I rinse my mouth out and straighten to turn to Dario. He locks eyes with me and says so much in his stare. My belly grows warm with uncertainty.

"You read my diary?" I ask with my brows furrowed.

He brushes his thumb against the corner of my mouth. The simple gesture softens any anger I have rising. I shake my head and go to step around him to head for the shower.

A yelp leaves my mouth when he tugs me back to him and tosses me over his shoulder. Another yelp escapes my lips as he slaps my ass, then bites it before kissing the sting away.

"My shower is bigger," he says as he laughs.

"I'm going to kick your ass," I growl.

He kneads the cheek he slapped. My brain is still trying to catch up with this morning and last night. What does all this mean?

"Stop thinking so much. I'd rather my eggs fry in a pan," he rumbles.

"Ha ha."

When we get to his room, he moves to the master bath and places me in the shower. He then turns to walk back out to the sink to brush his teeth. I take the time to stare at his body, taking in every detail of his muscled frame.

Dario has been into kickboxing for as long as I have. We started together as kids. However, I've stuck to it because it's been more time we get to spend together, and it doesn't hurt that I've gotten to ogle him all sweaty and worked up.

In this moment, I marvel at his chiseled back and tight, firm ass. At almost six-six, Dario is a work of art. His back is broad, his arms are huge, and his legs are thick. Swole is the word that comes to mind as I watch him move. Although slightly leaner than Dante, it's not by much. The Di Lorenzo brothers are not small men.

He rinses his mouth out and reaches for something in one of the drawers before he turns to face me with a smile on his face. I fold my arms under my breasts as I watch him saunter back toward me. I try not to look down at his erection. It's completely distracting.

He enters the shower and crowds me up against the wall behind me. I place my hands on his ribs, trying to hold on to the tiny space separating us. That doesn't stop him. Dario dips his head and kisses me with so much passion, I forget all my thoughts.

"I remember that guy you ghosted over morning breath. There's no way you're ghosting me, but I don't want to give you a reason to either," he says against my lips.

I burst into laughter. I did tell him about Sean. God, he had bad morning breath and always wanted to talk first thing. It pissed me off. He had great dick and was convenient at the time because he worked at the hospital too, but that breath was too much.

"Oh my God, you remember that? That had to be like ten years ago."

"I remember everything about you. I wanted to drag his ass behind my car for touching you."

I snort. "You were dating someone at the time." I snap my fingers. "Addison or Allison. Something like that."

"But Carleen was what I wanted her name to be, and whoever she was her memory doesn't matter."

I lower my lashes and blush. He palms my ass and tugs me into him as he takes my lips again. I'm breathless when he pulls away and backs up. Turning the water on, he stands under the spray and allows the water to cascade over him.

I can't take my eyes off him as the water causes his hair to fall into his face. He runs a hand through the front, pushing it out of his eyes. I bite my lip nervously.

"Wh…what happened last night, Dario?"

He shrugs. "I was drunk and hungry when I came home. There was nothing to eat. I think someone ate my chicken parm." He gives me a knowing smile and lifts a brow. "I know you wake hungry when you've been drinking. I saw the notebook thinking it was your recipe book. I was going to make the dish you wanted me to try and leave it for you.

"I know I should have closed it the moment I saw what it really was, but I couldn't stop reading." He pauses as he strolls back toward me. Placing his palms against the wall behind me, he dips his head until we're nose to nose. "I've wanted you all my life, Car. I thought I could ignore what I read and drink myself to sleep, but the more I drank, the more I wanted to give you that wish."

"My one night," I whisper.

He kisses me again and lifts me onto his waist. I wrap my arms around his neck and get lost in the heated kiss. Whimpering when he breaks it and presses his forehead to mine, I find myself breathless.

He lifts his hand and the foil packet he's been palming comes into view. He bites into it while holding my gaze as he reaches to slip the condom on.

I try not to think about the others he has fucked in this shower. I'm sure there have been others. I just don't want to know about them.

I cry out when he slides smoothly into my body. I'm so confused. I only asked for one night and if I remember right, I made it clear I'd take that one night and never look back. This, this is more than a night of bliss and there are so many feelings involved as he strokes in and out of me—not all from my side either.

"Carleen," he groans my name. "I've wanted to make you mine for so long. Now, I have you, I'm not walking away. All I want is you."

"Don't, Dario, please don't."

He grasps my face and looks into my eyes, then growls and starts to pound me into the wall behind me. "Don't what? Claim you? Show you, you belong to me? Fuck you like I want you? Don't what? Need you?"

"Oh. My. God." I pant.

"Yeah, that's what I thought." He kisses me hard as he continues to fuck me senseless.

I'm so lost in him, when he slips a finger in my ass, I take it and start to keen and whimper his name. My eyes roll into the back of my head. I've never felt so wet in my life. I almost ask him if the condom came off and he spilled inside me.

However, I don't get to as it feels like my soul is sucked out of my body and dropped back in as he pulls away from the wall, locks his hands beneath my ass, and bounces me effortlessly on his shaft.

"Dario," I whimper. "I can't breathe."

"Then take my breath," he says and kisses me.

I clench around him, soaking his length and balls as I come again and pass out.

He's going to break my heart. I know he is.

Dario

"Hey," Carleen says as she looks up at me from lying on my chest.

"Hey, gorgeous. Ready to eat something?"

She laughs. "I'm actually starving."

I pull her to me by the back of her neck and kiss her. Her full lips are so welcoming. I could lie in bed kissing her all day. However, her stomach protests and ends the kiss. I nip her lower lip and move to climb from the bed.

I had to carry her wet, naked body to bed after our lovemaking in the shower. I've never had a woman respond to me the way she does. Yeah, I've left everyone I've been with satisfied, but Carleen takes to my touch like breathing.

I toss one of my shirts on the bed for her before I tug on a pair of gym shorts. I can't take my eyes off her smooth dark skin as she pulls the shirt over her head. When she stands, my shirt swallows her body, but her long legs peek out, tempting me.

I reach for her hand and lace our fingers together as I lead her out to the kitchen. This feels so right, like this is how things should be. I double down on my determination to figure out how to keep both of my worlds and make sure she's always safe.

"What are you thinking?" she asks nervously.

I lift our joined hands to kiss her fingers. "I still have to go to Italy in two months. I can't change that, but I want to spend every moment I can with you before I go."

"You still don't know how long you'll be there?"

I frown and shake my head. "No."

"What are you going for?"

My entire body stiffens. This is why I should have kept my distance. I don't want to lie to her, but I can't be completely honest either.

"Oh, I'm sorry. I shouldn't have asked."

I stop and spin her into me, pinching her chin between my fingertips. I look into her eyes and see the love I have for her reflected. I'll always protect her from my world. We've been smart in business. As long as I continue to be smart, I can do this.

"My grandfather needs me to be with him for a while," I reply and kiss her with a promise I can't make out loud. Instead, I think the words as I pour them into her lips.

I'll always keep you safe. I love you.

CHAPTER NINE

Brotherly Meeting

Dario

I take a sip of the brandy Dante hands me. My mind has been on Carleen since I had to slip out of the restaurant to come for this after-hours meeting with Gio and Dante. I wouldn't normally sit in on a two-hour Capo meeting, but I want to have my ear in on everything before I leave for Italy.

Gio keeps things running smoothly, but I don't want to come off as incompetent. I need to have a finger on the pulse of the operation. This is my responsibility.

"The union workers in New York are starting to complain about a few of the restaurants over there cutting hours to prevent having to pay the proper wages," Jace says as we sit in Dante's office.

"Yeah, I'm hearing the same thing from Mitch about a few of the Jersey restaurants. It's bullshit. Those guys can afford the wages. It's all those cheap bastards with the gaudy front of house and A-list clientele but shittily-run kitchens," Dante mutters as he sips at his own drink.

"Exactly, I know some of the chefs. Those guys bust their asses for the owners to shit on their best workers and fuck up the flow of the kitchens," I say.

"We'll fuck with their pockets then," Gio says. "Do we control any of their suppliers?"

Jace nods. "We do."

"Good, I'm sure I can redirect some of their patrons for a while. Dante, you have the inspectors start paying random visits. That should get the point across."

"No problem," Dante says to Gio. "But I wanted to ask you something. This Jacob guy from earlier, what exactly was the problem between him and Bethany?"

Gio lifts his tie as if examining some nonexistent stain, then smooths it back down against his chest. "Your wife had one of her tantrums and cost the guy his job. I already had an eye on him. She actually opened the door for me," Gio says nonchalantly. "Anyway. The senator wants you guys to cater his holiday party, Dario."

I narrow my eyes. I know right away Gio is hiding something. I don't call him on it because I don't know if it has anything to do with the Bethany situation on the whole. I'll get to meet this Jacob guy soon enough. I meet and train all the New Jersey and New York chefs, something I've been thinking of handing over to Carleen in my absence.

"Carleen told me. She turned him down already about a week ago."

"Her beef with her uncle is her own. These are friends of ours. I need you to cater the party."

I snort. "You know, I'm not going to be taking shit from you once I'm boss," I say with a teasing smile.

"Nothing around here will change, little brother. I always have what's best in mind at all times."

"I hear you. Her beef isn't with the senator. It's with her dad who will be attending the event. She's still avoiding him."

Gio waves me off. "I'll let him know *you* will be catering."

I sigh. In Gio fashion, this means the end of the conversation. I still wonder why Nonno hasn't chosen him to be Don. If I didn't need answers, I'd push the issue.

"Anything else for me?" I ask, ready to head out to get back to the restaurant before Carleen closes. I want to see her home.

"Silvio is late with his payments again," Jace says.

"What's going on over there? We know it's not out of disrespect. He's a friend of ours. How can we help?"

"It's not Silvio. It's Silvio Jr. He has a coke problem and he's fucking up his father's business. He sells goods and supplies out the back of the place and he's skimming from the register. Silvio doesn't know what to do with the kid," Jace replies.

"I'll send one of my guys for this one. That's my side of town," I say and stand.

"Is Apollo ready to step up while you're away?" Gio asks.

I nod. "On all fronts. He'll run the business and watch out for Carleen. I talked to him today."

Gio nods. "Good. I'll keep an eye on everything as well. You don't have to worry."

"I'm not. I want to get this over with. I have things here I need to settle."

"Mm," Gio hums as a light fills his eyes while he looks at me over his tumbler.

That's my cue. He's in that crystal ball of his. I don't need Gio digging into my plans with Carleen. I don't want my family life anywhere near her. He doesn't need to finesse my love life.

"Call me if you need me," I call over my shoulder.

"Dario," Dante calls.

"Ha ha, very funny."

"I love you too," he croons.

I look over my shoulder. "Yeah, yeah, I love you guys too."

I look to Jace and give him a nod. He's like another big brother. I don't think I have to voice how much he means to me.

He's saved my life more than once. I'd die for any one of the men in this room. All they need is to call and I'm there.

Carleen

I need to go home and take a nice, long bath. This day has been hell on my body. After sex with Dario last night and this morning, everything hurts.

The delicious soreness has turned into something else after a full night's service. Dario had to step out in the middle of the dinner shift, and it seemed like all hell broke loose. One of our line cooks took ill and I had to step in for her. On beef, nonetheless.

When that one couple asked for me to come out, I thought I was going to be sick. In one night, I ruined the restaurant. However, they wanted to compliment the chef who cooked them the perfect steaks. I gained a little more confidence after that.

However, it was like every ticket that came in from then was a steak. Medium rare, rare, well done, my head was spinning. My normal station during service is usually desserts or seafood, chicken, and sides. That's when I'm cooking.

I'd thought I'd be calling tickets tonight. It's why I opted not to take a bath before heading into the restaurant this evening. We were already running late.

I moan as strong hands settle on my shoulders and begin to knead as I have the top part of my body stretched out over the prep top. I relax and sigh. This is the life. A glass of wine and a bath and I'd be a happy woman.

"You look exhausted, baby. This place looks done. Let me take you home," Dario rumbles.

"But I don't even want to move," I almost whine.

He chuckles. "I'll carry you, but you have to hold the flowers."

I look up with a frown. "What flowers?" I gasp when I see the huge bouquet resting on the steel tabletop.

Straightening, I look over my shoulder as Dario reaches around me to unbutton my chef's coat. He has a smile on his lips and his eyes twinkle. I reach to cup his face and he dips in for a kiss.

"Flowers, Di Lorenzo. I'm liking this side of you."

He pulls my coat from my shoulders and kisses one exposed by my tank top. My entire body ignites. All the aches and pains pale next to the ache of wanting him.

"I've wanted to treat you like my queen for years. I won't miss a single moment to place that smile on your face. Let's get out of here. I have candles and bubble bath out in the car. Tonight, I plan to spoil you."

"Wow, if I'm dreaming leave me alone," I sing in my best Christopher Williams voice.

"Come here." Dario laughs and places me in a headlock to tug me into his body as he kisses my forehead. "How was service?"

"Ugh, I don't know what I'm going to do when you're gone."

"You're going to be fine."

He hangs my chef's coat with the others that will go out to the dry cleaners first thing in the morning and grabs my coat to help me place it on. He then wraps an arm around my waist, shoving his hand into the back pocket of my jeans.

I can't help smiling as we leave the restaurant locked together. "My uncle called," I say cautiously.

He groans. "Listen, baby. I spoke to Gio. I understand your position but—"

"Dario, it's fine. It's business. My uncle is a huge client. I get it and I need to face my father at some point. Mommy has been asking me to start coming back to Sunday dinners."

"You don't have to be involved if you don't want. I can do the event. You can help at the restaurant, but you don't have to attend the service."

"We'll be closed that night. It will look odd if I'm not there. Don't worry about it."

He opens the back door to his X4 truck and takes the flowers to place them in the car and then opens the door for me. Before I can climb in, he grasps the back of my neck and kisses me so passionately, my toes curl in my Crocs.

He places his forehead to mine. The air seems to shift as he takes on the serious air from a few nights ago. "Trust me, Carleen. I need you to trust me."

I lift on my toes and kiss his lips as he tries to back away. "I've trusted you all my life, Rio."

He pecks my lips, then nods to himself. I get into the car and settle into the seat. Again, I note that something is changing. I know my best friend. However, I don't want to push. If he wants me to know, he'll tell me.

CHAPTER TEN

Remember When

Dario

This bathwater is roasting my nuts, but I grin and bear it. The things I'm willing to do for this woman. I sit back against the tub, waiting for the water to cool with my eyes closed.

Carleen sits between my legs with her back to my front and her head back against my chest. She's so relaxed. I felt the moment she released the stress of the day.

I pray with all that I am that the answers I find in Italy won't take this away from me. Whatever I find, I'm coming back to my woman. I furrow my brows as something dawns on me.

"What's on your mind, Dario? You've grunted like three times already," Carleen's sweet voice cuts through my thoughts.

"Papa Riccardo is racist," I reply absently.

She snorts. "No shit. You're just figuring that out? That man is the embodiment of all the bigot Italian stereotypes I've seen in the movies and on TV. If I didn't know the rest of your family, I'd think everything on the TV was true."

I shift a bit behind her to look into her face. Anger seizes me as I wonder if he's ever done some shit to her behind my back. She turns to face me and places a hand on my chest.

"Calm down, killer. He's never stepped out of line with me. It's just the way he says things and how he looks at me. I've heard him call others names and make remarks, but never to me."

"You know we don't think like that and *Nonno* has never shown that type of behavior. Yeah, I know it happens in our culture, but never in my home. Not even from my dad."

"Relax, Rio, I've never felt unsafe around you or your brothers. *Nonno* is a sweetheart. I…I never saw you interested in a Black woman, but I thought that was preference."

"You're the only Black woman I've ever wanted. If I couldn't have you, I didn't want any, not because I'm not attracted.

"To be honest, I already know our children together could never follow in my footsteps, but that doesn't matter to me. That might be a good thing."

She knits her brows. "How so?"

I thin my lips and think about my next words. I don't know how much I want to tell her about my family's real life. For years, I've had to think twice when having her over if Nonno was in town.

My father was never brought into the life. Not on the level my brothers and I have. His places of business and our home have always been safe and as close to civilian as you can get. However, Nonno's presence always changes things.

"It's a blood thing. Our children wouldn't be considered for a lot because you're not Italian. Your family can't be traced back to the other side."

"You mean, they could never be made? Dario, are you telling me you're a *made* man?"

I kiss her forehead and remind myself I've fallen in love with a brilliant woman and keeping her out of my world will be harder than I thought. She's smart and observant. Carleen could never be oblivious.

She's called out her own family members for dealings not so above the board. While I know the truth, I've never confirmed or denied her suspicions.

"I'm not telling you anything. I'm a chef and I run a restaurant with my future wife," I murmur against her skin.

"Your what?"

"You heard me. Remember our wedding?"

She bursts into laughter. I remember it like it was yesterday. I was so proud and happy. I even bought her candy as a wedding gift.

"Oh, my God. I had a tummy ache from all that candy," she groans.

"I told you not to eat it all in one day."

"Yeah, but I thought you just wanted me to share with you."

"So you ate it all?" I chuckle.

"Well, yeah, I was eight and I thought my mom was going to throw it away. It was better I ate it all than no one get to eat any."

"Your logic is fucked up, baby. I was your husband."

She laughs harder. "It made sense back then."

I kiss her shoulder. "How could you not know I've been crazy about you?" I murmur against her shoulder.

"We were kids. We were playing. You couldn't have known I had a real wedding planned with a dog and four kids of our own."

"Best day of my life."

"It was a highlight in mine too," she says with a smile in her voice. "You were so cute. You had gelled your hair for the first time, and you were dressed up in a suit. I still have that little dress."

She pauses in thought for a moment and peeks over her shoulder at me. "Although, that's when I knew your grandfather hated me."

I wrinkle my brows. "My grandfather?"

We had our wedding on the playground. My grandfathers weren't there. I know Papa Esposito pulled me aside a few days later to tell me how important it was for me to marry an Italian woman, but I never gave any of that much thought.

I never thought I'd marry anyone. Carleen has been it for me for a very long time as far as true commitment goes.

"Yes, I don't know how he knew. Your mom and mine were the only ones at the playground, but the next day he appeared at our school. I thought he was there to pick you up.

"He stopped me and told me I'd never be the type of woman you would marry. He said to stick to my own kind."

I almost explode. I stand up so fast my head spins. "I thought you said he never said anything to you. That's a whole lot of something to me."

"I forgot about it until just now. My memory and the fall, you know. Besides, we were eight, Dario. I went home and cried to my mother about it and forgot it after she made me feel better."

I run a hand through my hair as I vibrate with rage. I try to calm down as I remember her accident. It's so easy to assume she's recovered all her memories. Every now and then, it becomes clear that's not the case.

"Babe," she calls as I stare into space. I look down as she palms my shaft. "Forget about it. I have. Let me help you relax."

She takes me into her mouth, and I have to reach out to place my palm against the wall. This isn't over, but she doesn't need to know that. I have a conversation for my grandfather. I'm starting to see why my brothers hate him.

"Fuck," I groan as Carleen pulls my full attention.

CHAPTER ELEVEN

What We See

Carleen

Dario wraps his sweaty arms around me as I towel off. We've been in the training gym for the last hour. Fraya, my trainer, has been kicking my ass.

Dario kisses my sweaty shoulder. "You're revealing your left side too much. Fraya is taking advantage of that," he murmurs.

"You want to spar with me instead?"

He turns me in his arms and looks down at me. I give him a teasing smile. Dario and I stopped sparring when I turned nineteen. He'll watch and bark orders, making sure I push to my limits, but he hasn't been in the ring with me in years.

"If that's what it takes. Let's go."

I tilt my head at him. "What has changed to get you in the ring with me now?"

He frowns. "One, I won't be distracted by wanting to fuck you because I plan to as soon as we shower to get out of here. Two,

I'm leaving. This is the one thing I know you have to protect yourself while I'm gone."

I lift a brow. "You say that like I'm in some type of danger," I say and search his eyes.

He purses his lips but doesn't say more. I can see the wheels turning in his head. I wrap my arms around his waist and look up into his eyes. As much as I don't what to pry, I don't like to see him stressed more.

"Rio, it's me. What's going on?"

"If anyone ever wanted to hurt me, you would be the way to do it. Women and children aren't off-limits to everyone." He pauses and kisses my forehead. "You know what, never mind. We can spar another day. Are we still going to your parents'?"

I groan. "Do we have to?"

He chuckles. "I told you I'd go for moral support. I need to go to my father's after. *Nonno* is in town."

"Oh, man. I'm having lunch with Antonia and Blake. Maybe I can cancel or reschedule."

"Don't worry about it. I need to spend some time alone with *Nonno* anyway."

"Oh."

"Don't make it sound like that," he says and palms my ass, drawing me into his body. "My grandfather wants to get me up to speed with what he wants me to do while in Italy. It will be boring, and he'll probably start with the old stories. Go have lunch with your cousin and friend. Enjoy yourself.

"I promise when I get home, we can spend our night off together, doing anything you want. Just the two of us."

"Um, I like the sound of that. Movie night."

He slaps my ass, causing me to yelp. I dance back and take a stance to slap box him. I catch him quick with an open hand to his shoulder and ribs.

"Come here," he croons, palming my head and pulling me into his chest. "My little fighter, I always knew from our first playground fight when you beat up Pauly Vitelli you could take anything on."

I smile. "He called you a punk. He had it coming."

"I was twice your size. I could have handled it on my own."

"You did. You think I don't know it was you who broke his cheek the next day?"

Dario roars with laughter. "I saw him whisper something to you by the seesaws. He was trying to provoke me."

"We were six. What do you mean, provoke you?"

"That little shit knew what he was doing. I hated him."

I stifle my laugh as he scowls. Dario has always been so overprotective when it comes to me. Which is why I shake off my concern about his earlier comments. I don't want him to go, and I guess I'm looking for reasons to panic about it.

"If we're going to make my parents', we better hit the shower. You know how my father can get."

"You're right. I want to take my time with that shower."

"Rio," I squeal.

He tosses me over his shoulder and moves for the private locker room. I bounce on his shoulder with a smile on my lips. Having a man tall enough to not only lift me but carry me around is sort of hot.

I finally admit to myself that I'm happy and this relationship is happening. This man knows me better than anyone. This is Dario, my best friend, what could be wrong about us?

***

I ring the bell to my parents' home and try my best to hold in my disappointment. Nonno called and Dario had to meet with him sooner. I thought I'd have his strength to get through this.

It's probably better he's not here with me. I'm not so sure I'm ready for my father to know we're dating. My father has hinted more than once—he believes I threw away my career because of Dario.

Did I find my passion for cooking in one of Dario's kitchens? Yes, but I'd already been unhappy. I couldn't breathe to enjoy and love my work. My father was always pushing for me to be a step ahead of everyone else.

I had to do better than the three generations of surgeons before me. However, my father and mother, grandfather and great grandfather are all amazingly accomplished. I don't know if there was ever room for me to do better.

"Carleen," my mother sings in that Bajan way—that's been passed down from her parents—as she opens the door.

"Hey, Mommy."

She pulls me into her embrace, and I return it while absorbing her comforting presence. My mother is a surgeon, just like my dad, but she's never been as hard on me as he has. I've always felt like my mother has been proud of me no matter what I do.

She releases me and looks me over with a smile on her lips. "Look at you. You're glowing. You look good, Carleen. Happy."

"Thanks, Mommy. I am."

"Good. Them thighs are thick though, you better watch that. Come on in here."

I ignore the thigh comment. She means well. In my family, you grow up and get used to comments like that. I try not to take them to heart.

She ushers me inside and I'm greeted by the sound of a full house. I'm surprised. I thought it would only be me and my parents.

As we enter the sitting room, I find three of my mother's siblings and a few of my cousins sitting around. This should be interesting.

While my mother fell into medicine, her family has a heavy background in politics and law enforcement. With the exception of my oldest uncle, who's a mortician and has a chain of parlors throughout Brooklyn, Harlem, New Orleans, and back in St. Kitts where my grandparents settled after growing up and marrying in Barbados.

Uncle Kington remains in St. Kitts. I know him the least of my uncles. Although, I get the feeling Uncle Kington is not the one you want to make angry.

Here in the States, I have an uncle in the FBI, one in the Senate, and another in the judicial system and that's just Mommy's older brothers. She's the only girl out of eight children. We have several other well-positioned relatives by blood and marriage.

My cousin Antonia is a federal prosecutor with her crazy ass. She has had her eye on a judicial seat since we were little. I'm so proud of her and all she's overcome to be where she is.

Justin is my other cousin. He just made detective on the force.

"Car, thank God. These old folks are in here tripping. If you didn't get here soon, I was about to shove some biscuits in my purse and cut my losses," Toni says.

"Antonia, keep playing with me, eh? I'm not too old to bop your ass with that mouth of yours. I don't know why your mother and I allowed you to be so outspoken," Uncle Rick says and sucks his teeth as he glares at Toni.

Toni rolls her eyes. "It's this mouth that got Stephan junior out of his little situation last week and this same mouth helped Augustus keep his wife from leaving him and taking that baby with her."

Justin and I groan. This is why everyone runs from Toni. She means it with love, but she's not going to allow anyone to forget how much they use her—I can't blame her though.

Some of my mother's family can try to look down their noses and act like their shit doesn't stink, but when they need something, Toni is the first one they call to clean things up for them.

I learned a long time ago; money doesn't exclude messy. Anyone who says otherwise hasn't experienced real life and wealth, they're just running their gums. The only difference is the ability to pay the price to hide the mess. My family is extremely good at that.

"Toni," Uncle Rick warns.

Toni pinches her lips and rolls her eyes. Oh, lunch after this is going to be interesting. Toni is already on one and Blake is always good for a laugh. She's sure to match Toni's energy. I try not to laugh at my cousin.

Uncle Rick comes over and kisses my forehead before he pulls me into a tight hug. Of all my uncles I'm probably closest to Uncle Rick. He's the judge in the family and the youngest brother of the older four.

"Oopies," he croons with his gravelly voice. I can't help smiling at the old nickname. As a young girl I always tripped over my own feet. The name Oopies just stuck, don't ask. "You look well. Getting a little thick and things. You still going to the gym?" He releases me and holds me out at arm's length.

"Yes, religiously, Uncle Rick." I pat his belly. "You need to come to the restaurant so I can feed you. I can't have you out here looking this fine. My friends are already lined up to make you their sugar daddy," I tease.

"Oopies, I'm not interested in none of them pissing-tail little girls you and Toni call friends. Like I haven't noticed their fast asses joining my gym. If I would have known what the dating scene had to offer once I got out there, I would have worked harder to work things out with my wife."

I laugh and look to Toni. She has a scowl on her face. We both know which friends he's talking about. My uncles are handsome, wealthy men with their dark-brown skin, silky curly hair and honey-amber eyes. Uncle Rick is a catch, he's just not with the bullshit.

"Where's Dario?" My Uncle Talon asks as he types on his phone before he puts it away. This is my FBI uncle. Justin's father.

"Wow, Uncle T, and here I thought I was one of your favorites."

"You are, Oopies." He smiles at me as he calls me by my nickname. "You two are always attached at the hip and I wanted to talk to him. I thought I'd see him here today."

"He was coming but was called away at the last minute."

My father scoffs, drawing my attention. I can no longer ignore his glare as he sits in his favorite chair watching me. I turn to him and give a wobbly smile.

"Hey, Daddy."

He stands. "We can eat now," he says and turns for the dining room.

I look to my mother with pleading in my eyes. I don't want to be here. It's been five years and he's still not over my decision for *my* life.

The last time we fell out over the topic was bad, really bad. That was six months ago, I haven't come back since. I thought it best to agree to disagree.

"He's stubborn, but he does miss you. He only wants the best for you," my mother says.

"Shouldn't that be my happiness?"

"Yes, but you don't know or see what we do." She runs a hand over my hair and tucks it behind my ear. "I believe we need to give you time to see it for yourself. Your father, on the other hand, wants to rush you to figure it out by telling you."

"Telling me what?"

She shakes her head. "Even if I tell you, you won't hear me. This is a lesson you're going to have to learn on your own. You're brilliant, Carleen, you come from my womb. The womb of a surgeon and scholar. You will figure it out in time."

I sag my shoulders. My head is starting to hurt. Mom wraps her arm around my shoulders and follows after everyone else.

"It will all work out," she whispers.

CHAPTER TWELVE

You Will Understand

Dario

I'm still seething from the conversation I walked in on earlier between Dante and our father. However, one thing in particular has been bouncing around in my head.

And why are you avoiding love?

I stand here with a drink in hand, watching my niece with the men in my family. If only my father knew, I'm no longer avoiding the inevitable and that's what's making me resentful. This burden shouldn't be mine.

Gio is well, competent, and alive. How is he being passed over for me? It's leaving a burning taste in my mouth. Having to leave Carleen earlier to come here already placed me in my feelings. I'm already being pulled from her and I've yet to step into this new role.

Bella's laugh rings out, grabbing my attention. My niece is the most adorable kid I've ever seen. Her little brown cheeks speak of her mother's African American and Asian Indian descent. I can't help thinking about what children with Carleen will look like.

No doubt her Bajan and African American heritage will make for gorgeous babies mixed with my Italian blood. My mistake the first night we slept together comes to mind. I know I should have told her I came inside her in my drunken state, but there's a part of me that wants nothing more than to be the father of a child with Carleen.

Would that stop all this and hand Gio his rightful seat?

"You're so funny, Uncle Lucas." Bella giggles.

I turn my attention back to all of my family again. They're laughing and smiling happily. We look so much like a normal family.

On the surface we are. If you don't count the men I've lost over the years or the occasional threat that needs to be silenced when someone grows enough balls to come for us, we are normal.

Dante has spent five years ignoring his position as Capo and it's been fine. I haven't had to chastise him for not covering his shit. He seems to have balance. That's all I ask.

Yet, deep down, I know if Dante were to stay with Bethany and have a son, my nephew would never be made, just as my sons would be passed over. That shit pisses me off and makes me wonder—why I'm changing my life around an oath that doesn't respect the things I love and hold dear.

This isn't the old country. To be honest, when listening to Nonno speak, I don't think we do shit the way it used to be done or the way it was meant to be done.

Most captains outside our family are greedy fucks with their hands so far in the drug business a jail cell awaits them with their names on it. If they're not selling the shit, they're using it. All nasty business.

Nonno has kept us smart and on our toes. Not one of us has allowed drugs to become a main earner. Pussy, booze, and gambling have done us well, especially with the age of the internet. It's growing too fast for the Feds to regulate what we can and can't do before the next loophole is created.

Dante was smart about the few relationships he made in the drug business and all with the understanding that he could pull out clean when needed. I frown and drain the glass of brandy I've been clutching.

"What's this look?" Nonno asks as he comes over and pats my cheek.

"Why me? Dante builds business and brings in earners. He always picks the right civilians to bring in—the ones who keep their mouths shut and get us our money. Gio is a master at keeping things in order and enforcing when needed. He keeps the peace. Either of them would be right for this. Why me?"

"Dario, I want you to look at the bible. When God picks a chosen one, He always picks the one who seems least likely. It's always the one who doesn't want it.

"I have a responsibility to our family. I will pass the family to the grandson I know is most capable of the storm I plan to leave in his lap. Before I can do that, I need to create a little storm of my own.

"Trust me, Dario. I've lived a long life and I have wisdom to share. When they look back on the Di Lorenzo legacy there will be no question that every Don chosen throughout our bloodline was one to be reckoned with. Not one weak head of the family ever.

"Be proud of the role you will play. I've designed it just for you, *mio nipote*."

"So this has nothing to do with Gio's lifestyle?"

"Gio's lifestyle. What lifestyle?" Nonno shakes his pinched fingers at me, his face turning red with anger. "What's this lifestyle everyone wants to tell me about? I don't have eyes? Gio hasn't live under my roof for years? What do you people think I don't know about *mio nipote*? His lifestyle." He snorts. "What do you know of his lifestyle? Do you understand this…this garbage you spread?

"Why does everyone speak of my Michelangelo as if they have some knowledge I don't? Lives have been ruined by jaws that just move. No facts, no understanding, no truth, just *bocche in movimento*. You watch your brother and learn."

I'm left standing feeling confused as Nonno storms off away from me. He has one thing right. I don't fully understand my brother's life. I've envied what I've suspected, but to be honest, I've never asked Gio about his dolls, his relationships, or what really happens at his parties.

He's never allowed me or Dante next to one of them. Papa Esposito is the one who told me what he assumes Gio is into and what Gio does at his parties in his free time. I've met a doll or two but as I think of it, I don't believe I would have assumed the nature of their relationship if not for the information already in my head.

"Well, fuck me," I breathe.

I might need to start asking Gio some questions. My curiosity is now burning. Dante comes over and pats my shoulder. I look into my twin's eyes with my brows furrowed.

"What was that about?" he asks.

"Man, I don't know. I mentioned Gio's lifestyle, and he blew up on me." I knit my brows farther. "Dante, have you ever asked Gio about his dolls?"

Dante searches my eyes for a second before a grin comes to his lips. He shrugs. "I never had to. I found out firsthand about them years ago."

"Fuck outta here. You…you cheated on Bethany?"

He roars with laughter. "You still don't get it. I thought you would be the first to figure it out."

He pats my cheek and walks away, leaving me more confused. I run a hand through my hair, loaded down with a hundred more questions than I had before.

Carleen

I smile down at my phone as Dario texts me. I'll be happy to get out of here for lunch with Toni and Blake, but I'm looking forward to my date with Dario tonight more.

"Oh, I know that look. *Ooh*, you nasty. You finally let Lou hit it. Now that's what I'm talking about. If you can't have the Italian dick you want, find the next one willing to smash them walls. Good for you."

"Girl, hush," I say, looking around to make sure no one hears her. "I am not sleeping with Lou. I'm not even dating him anymore."

"Wait, so who has that smile on your face? It says you're not just getting dick. You're getting some good good. That fight his mama, good shit."

"Why are you like this?" I groan and burst into laughter.

She shrugs. "I blame summer camp."

"This is true. You spent all your time with the camp counselors thinking you were so grown."

"I'm not even going to touch that one. I learned a lot." She has a sly smile on her lips.

"Yeah, like how to disappear with the male counselors for hours without getting caught."

"It was only one male counselor and that was when I turned sixteen. Don't try to make me sound like a bigger ho than I am. Besides, we're not talking about me. Nice try though. Who you texting, Oopies?"

"Noneya and Notchyo."

"Ha ha. I have your *none of your business* and *not your business*. Auntie Pat, Oopies has a boyfriend," she calls out.

"Oh, my God, how old are you? It's like you've never grown up. Are you like this at work?"

She rolls her eyes at me and sucks her teeth. "You know better than that. I stay with my heel on their balls. It's why you guys get all of the real me on the weekends."

"I don't want it." I pout.

She moves closer and wraps her arm around my shoulders as if to hug me. She holds me tight in her embrace and snatches my phone. I yelp and try to toss her off me to get my phone back.

It's locked, but just my luck, Dario texts me right as she holds the phone in her hand. My face heats. The last thing I said to Dario alluded to sex, I can only imagine what he has texted back.

Toni freezes and turns toward me slowly. Her mouth is hanging open. I groan.

"You're not just nasty, you're sneaky."

I almost burst into laughter from her facial expression as she says the words, looking like a Martin Lawrence character. She looks me up and down as she places her hands on her hips.

I snatch my phone back and read the text for myself.

Rio: *Baby, all you have to decide is if you want to ride my face or my cock. I'll do all the rest.*

I palm my face and groan again. When I peek through my fingers to look at Toni. She's glaring at me. I close my fingers and wish for the floor to open up and swallow me.

Toni moves to my side to hiss in my ear.

"You weren't even going to tell me. How long has this been happening, nasty butt?" She pinches my butt with her last words.

I go to answer her, but my father's presence traps the words in my throat. He appears out of nowhere and it dawns on me, he heard Toni calling out to my mother. I could kill her.

"You're seeing someone? Is it that real estate guy you said you weren't too into?"

"No," I nearly whisper.

"I hope whoever he is, he knows how to put you first."

"Oh, it sounds like he totally understands the assignment, Uncle Percy."

"Haven't you done enough?" I mutter toward Toni.

"Me?"

"Hush, we can talk at lunch," I bite out.

"What's all the commotion about?" My mother says as she enters the kitchen.

"Toni says Carleen is seeing someone."

"Toni needs to mind her business," I grumble.

"I'm sure if it's anything serious, Carleen will bring him by."

And this is why I love my mother. She ushers my father right out of the kitchen. I spin on Toni and mush her in the head.

"Why are you hiding this? You've been in love with that man since you had pigtails and couldn't walk without tripping over your own feet."

"It's new and I don't know if it will last. If things blow up in my face this could get awkward."

"More awkward than it already is? You do understand Dario is what your father is so pissed about?"

"Ugh, do I. I didn't leave medicine to chase after my childhood crush. I love what I do."

Toni scoffs. "Oh honey, this goes way deeper than that."

I look at her with my brows furrowed.

"Does everyone know something I don't?"

Toni holds her hands up in the air. She then taps my nose. "You're going to trip over this one on your own. We've been warned to stay out of it."

"By who?"

"The only person everyone around here is afraid of. Your mama. Anyway, are we doing some shopping? Sounds like you could use some new lingerie. Girl, you have to tell me everything. That's one big, fine-ass man. He looks like he puts it down...that walk." She sighs and fans herself.

I laugh. "I hate you."

"Tell me I'm lying though."

"What happened to that guy you were seeing?"

"Who? Old boy with the big dick and no skills?" She rolls her eyes. "I'll tell you about his non-fucking ass over lunch."

I laugh as she mocks convulsing. "Da...amn, baby, that was amazing." She rolls her eyes again and kisses her teeth hard. "For who? Girl, I wanted to burn his drawers and light his bed on fire. Waste of time."

I laugh so hard I have to hold my stomach. Toni is just what I need. A stress reliever.

CHAPTER THIRTEEN

Our First Real Date

Carleen

Exhausted and excited, I push my key into the lock of Dario's apartment with a smile on my face. I had such a good time with Blake and Toni, breakfast at my parents' was all but forgotten. However, when Dario texted that he'd be waiting for me at home for our first real date, I left them like my ass was on fire.

I know I'll have to hear about that tomorrow. My smile grows as the aromas of something delicious smelling hits me. The lights are dim, and candles are lit, leading the way into the apartment. My heart flutters.

I step through to the living area that opens to the kitchen and find Dario standing with his hands in his pockets. He's in a pair of black slacks with a white dress shirt that's rolled up to his elbows with a black vest over it.

He looks so sexy. It looks like he has been for a cut, and I know he's shaved again from this morning. He gives me a sexy smile and beckons me to him with two fingers.

I smile back at him as I notice the Franck Muller watch I bought him for Christmas last year on his wrist. It completes the look and makes me think he may have thought about me when he got dressed.

That watch had me thinking about my life after I purchased it. My father had a fit. I learned then never to exchange gifts with Dario in front of my father again.

I drop my bags, remove and hang my coat, and move forward. Dario tugs me into him and plants a hot kiss on my lips. I lift on my toes, trying to get closer to him.

"I missed you," I breathe when he breaks the kiss.

"Not as much as I missed you," he says as he massages my ass. "Go on and freshen up. I'm finishing dinner now."

"You cooked for me?"

He grasps my face and turns it up so he can nip at my lips. "Yes, and I plan to have you for dessert. I've wanted to see this sexy brown body covered in coconut oil for far too long. Tonight I'm living out my fantasies and more."

I grin and reach to palm the bulge in his pants. I bite my lip and squeeze. He returns his hands to my ass and tightens his hold this time as he pulls me flush to him. His voice comes out husky with his next words.

"Go freshen up before I toss all that shit off the table and fuck you on top. I'll make your sexy ass my four-course meal."

"I wouldn't mind," I breathe.

He chuckles. "We have all night for that. Let's have our first date. I need something normal in my life."

"Everything okay?"

"It will be." He swats my ass. "Get moving. You're about to make me burn the sauce for dinner."

I pout and turn for my bags before heading to his bedroom. Somehow, I've moved into his room and so have most of my things. I'm not complaining. I've loved waking in his arms.

I hum to myself as I strip from my clothes and head for the shower. I'm glad I listened to Toni and picked up something special. The dress I purchased is a knit illusion dress that makes it look like I'm not wearing anything beneath it, as the knit fabric creates a pattern to reveal what looks to be skin.

It has a handkerchief hem that stops midcalf, showcasing my long, toned legs. It's perfect to cover the bra and crotchless panty set I bought with thoughts of later tonight. I grin as I think of how this night is sure to end.

I shave and scrub down with some of the scented scrub I purchased. When I step out of the shower, I smell like a strawberry-mango treat. I lotion up in the same scent and dress in the lingerie.

The girls and I stopped for a quick wash and wrap. As quick as you're going to get in the Dominican hair salon. As I run a comb through my hair it bounces around my face and shoulders like fine silk. A little lip gloss and mascara and I'm ready to get dressed.

Slipping on a pair of heels, I turn in front of the mirror and grin. I put on the dress next and spray on some perfume, making the strawberry-mango scent a triple threat. The grin on my face comes from inside.

This is me. The real Carleen. I feel sexy and confident. I hadn't realized that was missing. Now, standing here, I get the sense I allowed myself to fall into a slump.

"Welcome back, Car." I wink at my reflection before I turn and head out to join Dario.

Dario

I smell her before I see her and I'm instantly semihard. There's not another woman in this world who can do this to me. When I turn to face Carleen, I'm frozen in place.

She's more beautiful than I've ever seen. I didn't think that was possible. Over the years, she's become more stunning with each day, every change, every phase. I remember them all and how I've fallen in love with her with each one.

Her braids in college. The ponytail and scrubs during her residency. The bob and hair clips when she first started culinary school. The long ponytail and chef's coat as we opened our own place five years ago.

"Why are you looking at me like that?" she asks as she comes over and wraps her arms around my waist.

As if having a mind of its own, my hand finds the seat of her ass. I palm it and pull her into my growing erection.

"I've been an idiot all my life. I truly thought I could live without you being mine."

She furrows her brows. "But why did you feel you had to?"

I'm saved by the ringing of my phone. I wanted to cut it off tonight, but I know I don't have that luxury. I answer and Apollo's voice comes through.

"Five."

I know he wants me to move to my burner for the week in five minutes. My frustration level shoots through the roof. This night was meant to be special. I wanted to end it with my face between Carleen's legs. However, I get the feeling in my bones this call is about to change my night or my mood at the very least.

I cup her face and crush my lips to hers. Before I can get fully carried away, I break the kiss and kiss the tip of her nose.

"I'm sorry, baby. I need to go take a call. Start on the wine and get comfortable. I'll be right back."

I frown as a look of disappointment covers her face. It burns me up that I'm being stolen away from her yet again. My phone goes off again and I growl at it as I see Papa Esposito is calling.

I don't have time for him and when I do talk to him it will be to check him for that shit he said to Carleen all those years ago. For now, he can fuck off.

I move to my home office where I keep my burner phone and slip inside, shutting the door behind me. The phone starts to ring as I get to the desk and put my hand on the drawer it's in.

"Yeah, what's going on?"

"You wanted to know if there was a change in that guy's pattern. He decided to stop just watching the place. He came into the restaurant before dinner service started and asked if we were hiring."

"You're shitting me."

"No, I'm not, he seemed antsy and get this. The guy has on fifteen-hundred-dollar loafers. What does he need with a busboy or dishwasher job?"

"*Marone.* What did you tell him?"

"I took his info and told him we'd be in touch. I figured you might want the number. What do you want me to do with this?"

"Sit on it for now. I'll talk to my brother in the morning. I don't want to make a move that will screw up whatever he has planned. Anything else?"

"Vito is asking for a sit-down."

Vito is a *stunad.* He never wants anything worth my time. All he does is fuck up. He's only still breathing because of his relations.

"Fuck him. Find out what he wants and tell him no. I don't give a fuck what it is. My answer is no."

"Got it."

"That it?"

"Yeah, boss. That's it for now."

I grunt and end the call. Throwing the phone back in the drawer, I note to toss it tomorrow. I shut the drawer firmly and head back out to my woman waiting for me. My personal phone rings and I'm almost a hundred-percent sure it's my grandfather again.

I check to make sure and snarl at my phone when I confirm it is. "The balls on this guy," I mutter as I ignore the call.

When I get back to the living area, I find Carleen sitting on the couch, nodding off. She jerks her head up and pushes a hand through her hair. She laughs and gives me a smile when she focuses her eyes on me.

"You want to rain check our date?"

"No, no, I just needed to rest my eyes for a second. You went through all this trouble."

"We need to eat, I planned to cook either way and it's just a few candles. I can blow them out and put the food away."

"It's fine. What did you make?"

"Pot stickers filled with Italian sausage and balsamic dipping sauce."

"Oh, that's going to be so amazing," she says as she stands up and rounds the couch to me.

I wrap my arms around her waist when she reaches me and dip my head to kiss her lips. This time I do linger and draw the kiss out.

"I'll plate. You can pour us some more wine. We'll eat at the coffee table and watch the movie."

"Sounds good to me."

She tilts her face up for another kiss, I don't deny her. I capture her lips in a deep kiss, gliding my hands up her sides. She smells outstanding.

This is something new, not her usual vanilla-and-coconut scent. Working in a kitchen, Carleen doesn't often wear strong fragrances. However, tonight I'm catching notes of strawberry and mango. She smells delicious. My mouth waters as I think about tasting her later.

I shake my head clear and move to the kitchen. The sound of her heels clicking behind me causes me to look over my shoulder. I allow my gaze to run over her.

I don't miss that something has changed. This is a side of Car I haven't seen in a while. She looks more confident and sure of herself. I can't help wondering what's brought on the change.

I get this ball in my stomach as I think the cause could be me. Something did change right before Carleen left her residency. At the time, I was more focused on the cage I felt I was in. While the head chef of a Di Lorenzo restaurant at the time, it still wasn't my own thing. I wanted control of at least one aspect of my life.

I was handed the title of underboss right around that time. Everything was changing in my life. I now see it was for her too. Something beyond her career.

"Hey, do you remember when we decided to open the restaurant?" I say as I plate our food and come out of my thoughts.

"Yeah, I do." She gets this distant look in her eyes. "That was such a weird time for me."

"Oh yeah. How so?"

"I was already having second thoughts and feeling suffocated by my dad. I didn't know what I wanted to do. Then one day, I was sitting in the coffee shop next to the hospital, making a pros-and-cons list.

"I was actually sitting and murmuring to myself. This gorgeous woman came and asked to sit with me. You know, the exotic beauty type? Green eyes, gorgeous mocha-brown skin, a real nice body, luscious dark curls."

Not my type, but I know what she means. Carleen has always been the perfect woman to me. However, I nod and listen.

She continues. "Well, we started talking. She told me her story of how she was in a terrible, abusive relationship. Then one day she was given a decision. Stay and die or leave, learn something new and live.

"I talked to that woman for an entire week. No matter when I showed up, she was there. Talking to her made me apply what I was going through to her story.

"I wasn't going through anything nearly as dangerous, but I felt abused by my father's expectations. I was dying inside. I had already learned something new. The only decision I needed to make was to live, you know?"

"Why didn't you ever tell me about her or express how you felt?"

"You had something going on. I could tell. You were always so distracted."

I narrow my eyes. "I always want to know what's going on with you."

"Well, it all worked out. She disappeared right after you asked me if I wanted to start the restaurant with you."

I rub my fingers across my lips. Our restaurant, *Anima Mias* was actually Gio's idea. He saw me struggling and suggested I open the restaurant with Carleen. I thought it was a great idea and approached her after she mentioned looking for a job in a kitchen. I give a small chuckle. "*Nonno* always talks about angels. How they show up in the forms of humans when you need them most. Those people who appear to step in for a short period of time and then poof, they're gone."

"Angels wear Prada?" She snorts. "Trust me, whatever she's doing in her new life, she's doing well, and I don't think it's the work of miracles. I had this feeling about her. I can't put my finger on it though."

I narrow my eyes. "And you haven't seen her since? You didn't feel like you were in danger, did you?"

"No, no. That's not it. I felt safe, but...like I said, I can't put my finger on it."

I shrug and pick up the plates as I start for the living room where we can kick back and relax while we eat, the table I set earlier is forgotten. Carleen follows with two wineglasses and the bottle.

I place our food on the coffee table and hold my hand out to help her have a seat after she kicks her heels off. Reaching for the remote, I then take a seat next to her in front of my plate.

Now this feels right. This is what I imagine our lives to be like. However, I find myself wondering for the millionth time if I can pull this off. Can I be a Di Lorenzo and have my happily ever after?

CHAPTER FOURTEEN

Scattered Dishes

Dario

"What do you want to watch?" I ask as I turn on the TV.

"Do you even need to ask?"

I laugh and pull up her favorite movie. "*Purple Rain* it is." I wink.

Carleen moans as she bites into the pot sticker after dipping it into the small ramekin of sauce with her chopsticks. I can't pull my eyes away from her lips as she chews.

Unable to have this distance between us, I shift and open my legs that are bent at the knees. I wave her over and she comes without hesitation. Once she's seated between my legs with her back to my chest, I pull her plate closer and shift again so we can both reach our food and see the screen.

"This is so good. The filling is so flavorful and lush. And the dumpling wrappers are cooked perfectly. That crispiness I love about pot stickers is there."

I wipe my mouth and kiss the top of her head. "There's more if you want. I made something light because you said you had a big lunch. But I made plenty just in case."

"Mm, no. This is perfect."

I reach to dip one in the sauce with my chopsticks and lift it to her lips. She takes a bit and moans. I bring the rest to my mouth and finish it.

As we sit, I try my best to focus on the movie, but her scent is driving me insane. I wrap my arms around her and hold her to my chest once she's finished eating. We're halfway through the movie when Car starts to squirm in my hold.

"Rio?"

"Yeah, baby."

"I've seen this a million times already."

"Thank fuck," I breathe, my palm beneath her chin to tip her head back to face me.

I capture her lips and drink from them in a deep, passionate kiss. All of my frustration from the day melts away. All I can focus on is the enticing scent of her body and the feel of her soft lips.

Not thinking, I swipe the dishes from the table. They clutter and thud against the rug. I break the kiss to turn Carleen and lift her to place her on the table. I lightly place a hand on her chest to push her down on her back. I scoot forward as if pulling up to a meal at my favorite Japanese spot.

With my hands on her thighs, I push her dress up to reveal my favorite place. When I zone in on her crotchless panties, I groan. I reach for her leg and bring her hot-pink toes to my lips.

She squeals and tries to pull her foot away, but I hold tight and kiss and lick at her soft skin. It's my plan to worship every inch of this body. I want to mark every inch as mine.

"Dario," she whimpers as I start to make my way up her leg with open-mouthed kisses, making sure to drag my lips against her skin.

Goose bumps rise. As I move my gaze to her core, I see her juices spill for me. If you told me a year ago, heck, a week ago, that I'd have my hands on this woman, I would have cursed you the fuck out and possibly put a bullet in your ass.

Now, I'm so consumed with the fact that I'm touching the love of my life, I can hardly compose myself. She wiggles and sits up on her elbows to look down her body at me.

We lock eyes right as I dive into her sweet-smelling pussy. I push her legs open and into her chest. Settling in to be here for a while.

I won't dare to say the words I feel aloud. Not before I know what's going to happen when I go to Italy, so I use my tongue to spell it out. I spell each letter into her folds.

I love you.

I do it repeatedly until I feel her juices rain down in my mouth. Not ready to move from my feast, I shift to my knees, wrap my arms around her thighs and lift her into my face.

Her shoulders balance her on the table as I have my way with her dripping-wet center. I devour her pussy as she calls out my name and cries for mercy.

Mercy I can't give. Not when I'm so lost in her pleasure. She starts to convulse, and her legs shake as I suck on her clit and rub my thumb against her puckered hole.

I back off and lower her body back down on the table. Dragging my palm down my face, I then lick it clean. I stand and give her a pointed stare to warn her not to move.

Working on the buttons of my vest, I quickly head to my room for the bottle of oil I had planned to use later. Tossing my vest on the bed and releasing the buttons on my dress shirt, I tear it off and toss it too.

Bare from the waist up, I kick off my shoes and tug off my socks before I grab the oil and a few condoms. I'm already hard and aching to be inside her. I chide myself for not being better prepared. I should have known we weren't going to make it to my bed.

I return to the living room and she's right where I left her. Her eyes are on the items in my hands. She bites her lip and runs a hand through her hair. Keeping my eyes on her, I sit on the couch, dropping the items in my hands beside me.

I look around the coffee table and laugh to myself. I'll have to have someone come in to clean the mess I've made. I may even need to replace the rug. Not caring much—I'd say it was well worth it—I lick my lips. Her flavor is still on them.

"Come here," I say, not able to wait a second longer to have her in my arms.

She stands shakily. I lean forward and place my hands on her hips, bringing her into me as I sit back. I love this dress on her. It makes her breasts look marvelous and shows off her curvy body.

She straddles my lap as I guide her. I reach behind her to unzip the dress. She tosses her head and her hair floats through the air, making her look like an angel, modeling for this mere mortal. The dress slips from her shoulders once I release the fastening.

She reaches to release her bra and her heavy breasts bounce free. I palm one and dip my head as I bring it to my lips. I draw her nipple into my mouth as I reach to knead her other mound.

"Yes, baby," she breathes.

I groan around her flesh. Reaching between us, Carleen frees me of my slacks. I'm so ready for her, I'm stiff as fuck in her palm when she pulls me free. I angle to kiss the side of her breast and then make a path down her ribs.

With impatience I can understand fully, she grabs a condom and brings it to her lips. Tearing open the packet, she then rolls it onto me as I watch. With her dress still around her waist, she lifts and slides down onto my length.

"Oh God," she breathes and blinks up at the ceiling.

I pulse inside her and wait for her to look me in the eyes. I can't keep my hands off her. They're everywhere as I'm unable to settle on one part of her body I want to touch most.

After a few beats, I palm her ass and begin to move her. She finally drops her gaze to mine. The desire I see in her amber eyes tells me all I need to know.

"Baby, you're so big," she whimpers. "You feel so good."

I groan and start to thrust up into her. I reach for the oil and push down to open the cap and pour it all over her chest. Like I knew it would, the liquid makes her skin shine and entice me. I'm a visual man. I'm turned on with my eyes. A plate has to look good to appeal to me, same with my women. Right now, Carleen's gorgeous oil-slick tits have me hard as a rock and if I'm not careful, I might blow.

Carleen doesn't help matters as she starts to ride me in earnest. She begins this lift-and-grind motion with her hips that's driving me crazy. It's like she lifts and then grinds her hips into me in a hooking motion as she takes me in deep.

"Yes, baby, just like that," I grunt through my teeth. I run my hands through the oil on her chest and drag it to her sides. When I grip her waist, she leans back and rolls her upper body in my hold like we're doing a dance.

I'm mesmerized as I watch the action. The way her hair sways with the motion, how she's trusting me to hold on to her and the sexy way she bites her lip as if she's totally enjoying herself on my cock. When she comes back upright, I lean in and take her lips.

Carleen

I need to get this dress off, but I don't want to get up. He's stretching me in the best way possible. I get into the kiss and lose myself as I continue to ride him.

It feels amazing, not just him inside me, but this connection between us. I've never had it with anyone else. The dress forgotten, I place my hands on his shoulders as he breaks the kiss. Placing my forehead to his, I look him in the eyes as I start to ride him harder.

"Dario, please," I plea even as I'm full of him.

He growls and crosses his arms behind my back as he moves with me. His fingers bite into my skin. My mouth falls open but no words come out. I breathe him in as my orgasm builds. He reaches for one of my oily mounds and pulls my nipple into his mouth. My pussy clenches around him as he sucks and feasts on my breast.

I love the feeling of his tongue flicking against my nipple as he sucks it in his mouth. Allowing my flesh to pop free from his lips, he looks up at me and groans, palming my ass as he thrusts into me. He tugs me closer and my oil-slick chest presses against his. His strong muscles flex around me and I can't help crying out his name.

I want to tell him I love him, but I'm too afraid, even if it felt like he was spelling the words into my pussy. Once he starts to thrust up into me harder, I'm completely done for. I cradle his head in my arms and hold him to me.

My heart feels like it's going to come through my chest. He grunts and licks at my chest as I start to quiver against him. He moves his lips to my ear.

"That's my girl. Come all over me, baby. Just like that."

It doesn't take long for him to growl my name and begin to release into the condom.

We're both slick and sweaty. I kiss his lips and smile at him. I look over my shoulder at the mess he made when he cleared the table.

"You know I could have taken the dishes to the kitchen," I pant.

"I didn't have patience for that. I've wanted you from the time you walked in the door."

"Well, my friend. This was the best first date I've ever had."

He laughs and it vibrates through me as he's still semihard inside me.

He kisses my lips. "I promise to do better."

"You're not doing so bad. I don't think I was much help."

"Um, if I were any other guy, I would have to hear about this in the morning. The guy who couldn't keep his hands off you and fucked you on the first date instead of watching the movie and feeding you a real dessert."

We both laugh. "Okay, I get your point, but still, I'm not complaining."

He pulls me in for a kiss. "Which is why I'll always overdeliver. I don't want to become complacent because of who we are to each other. I really wish you would have talked to me about how you were feeling back then."

I think back to five years ago. I knew something was changing in his life. I didn't want to burden him with my drama. Little does he know. He saved the day regardless.

CHAPTER FIFTEEN

Power Plays

Frances

"Can I get you anything else to eat, honey?" Sylvia asks as she places a plate of lunch before me.

I look up at her and those red locks that enticed me to her all those years ago. She's still a stunning woman. Gorgeous enough to make a man stupid.

"No, I need to get back to the house. Dario's coming by and Giuseppe is in town."

"Humph, why does that man have to stay with you whenever he's here?"

"Sylvia," I snap.

She throws her hands up in the air. I understand how she feels in all of this. My sins have fallen on my sons tenfold, and still I know the worst has yet to come.

The stress and guilt have eaten through my stomach for years. However, I'm not about to argue about the matter. We were all wrong.

"Why the fuck won't Dario answer my calls?" My father bellows as he strolls into the dining room of Sylvia's home as if it were his.

I bite back a groan. I don't need this shit. I come here for peace. My father is going to get me killed someday with his bullshit. I've been doing damage control for over twenty-six years. Make that more like forty-three.

I'm tired and at my wits' end. Honestly, I think it's all in vain. Somehow, I get the feeling my father has outmatched me and I've missed key things that could cause this all to come down on my head.

I grunt. "How am I supposed to know? He's your pet. You said you had things under control. He listens to you, no?"

"Don't get smart with me, you little son of a bitch. I wouldn't be in this position if it weren't for you."

"Right, because you had nothing to do with all of this in the first place."

He places a hand over his heart. "Me? You're pointing the finger at me."

I stand and slam my hands on the table. I've had enough of this.

"Yes, you, you are the one who—"

My phone rings, cutting my words off. I look down at it and see it's Bethany. Yet, another issue my father has made for me. I roll my eyes and answer, readying myself to empty my pockets to make my father's mess go away.

"Hello," I grunt into the phone.

"Dad, you won't believe what Dante has done to me. I'm so embarrassed."

"What has he done?"

"I'm at the dealership and I ran my card for the new truck I'm trying to purchase, but he told the bank to deny the purchase and closed my card. This is humiliating."

"Listen, calm down and relax. Is the truck really necessary?"

"It is if you and my parents want me to keep my mouth shut."

Her entire demeanor has changed. Gone is the frantic, innocent act and the real Bethany has appeared. I look to my father and scowl. I'm disgusted by what I'm being forced into. I wish the entire Kumar family would disappear. No, I wish I never listened in the first place and introduced them to Dante. That one is one of my biggest regrets.

"Fine, put me on the phone with finance. I'll pay for the truck, but I don't know how much longer you're going to get away with this. Dante is going to start to ask why I'm the one you always run to."

"No, he won't. He thinks you do it for Bella. A doting grandfather who understands the importance of his grandchild's mother."

I snort. "You keep underestimating that boy—"

"Mr. Esposito, this is Brian from the Mercedes Finance office. I understand you will be providing the funding for Mrs. Di Lorenzo's vehicle."

I grit my teeth. It's a wonder Dante hasn't snapped and strangled her by now. It's not like the boy doesn't have it in him.

I make arrangements to purchase the car while fuming. My father has been glaring at me the entire time. I snare at him as I hang up.

"That is a problem," I seethe.

"Which you've handled nicely."

"Are you not seeing that family's greed and how they're taking a mile for every inch you give?" I run a hand through my hair. "How did I even get involved in all of this?"

"Because you couldn't do what I asked like a man. That's how. You could have kept your goomar on the side and saved me all this bullshit."

"You need me more than I need you, Dad. Don't burn your last bridge."

"Are you threatening me? One word to Giuseppe and this all goes away like that." He snaps his fingers.

"I'm the only reason you still have any access to the Di Lorenzo name and family. You have no more chips on the table. That's why you're here.

"Dario is shutting you out and it's all falling apart. That little crew of yours is shit and you know it. Get outta here and stay away from what's mine. We're not sinking with this ship. I'm done."

He snorts. "You're done when I say you're done. I still have a full stack of chips and I'm running this table. You should follow your own advice and not underestimate me."

With that, he storms out. I crack my knuckles as I question my loyalty. I once was loyal to a fault, but I had to be. I created this and I was trusted to make it right. Now, I've betrayed everyone and it's coming back for me.

What takes Riccardo Esposito's head will take mine too. However, it's my boys I'm most worried about. My father has no regard for his grandsons. They are just pawns in his play for power.

CHAPTER SIXTEEN

How'd this Happen

Carleen

Things have been going so well with me and Dario, until now. I can't believe my luck. My stomach roils as I prep this seafood line for service. My head hurts and I haven't been able to keep my thoughts together all day.

"You okay?" Dario asks as he comes over and places a hand on my hip as he kisses the side of my head.

Coos and cheers fill the kitchen. They've been doing that since Dario started openly showing me affection. Our staff seems to be happier about our relationship than we are.

"Yes, I'm fine," I reply even as my mouth waters and my stomach turns.

Dario talks about our future all the time, but something has been holding him back, causing a distance I can feel. I haven't pressed him about it, but it's nagging at me now. I don't know if this new news will bring us together or pull us apart. Which is why I'm struggling with whether I should keep it to myself, at least for now.

He's leaving in six weeks, no matter what. I only confirmed my suspicions this morning. Maybe it's not the best idea to place this on his shoulders before he goes. He seems to be getting more stressed the closer the trip gets.

"You sure?" He cups the side of my face and rubs his thumb back and forth over my lower lip.

"Yeah, it's been a long day."

"I told you I would handle going to your place. You should have let me take care of it."

"You had things of your own to handle. *Nonno* wanted to go shopping with you for Bella's Christmas and it's your week for inventory."

"And? I could have fit in a ride to your place."

With a frown, he tugs me in with a hand on the back of my head and places his cheek against my forehead before pulling away and pressing his lips to the same spot. It's such a sweet gesture, tears almost come to my eyes. I have to fight them back with a cleansing breath.

"You're a little warm," he murmurs. "Anthony, come cover for Carleen. Get this prep done. Apollo, can you work her station for the night?"

"I got you, boss."

"*Dario*," I drag out. "I'm fine. Apollo, stay where you are. I've got it."

"Apollo, if you don't take over her station, you're fired."

I gasp. "No, you're not."

When I look in Apollo's direction, he's headed my way behind Anthony, who takes over my prep wordlessly. I groan and wipe my hands on a towel.

This man, I don't know why I bother. I look up into his eyes and for the millionth time today I get ready to tell him the truth. I'm pregnant by my best friend. It wasn't a part of my wish, but it has happened.

Dario reaches for the buttons of my coat and removes it from my body before he starts to unfasten the buttons of his own. I frown. Dinner service starts in ten minutes.

"What are you doing? You have to start service if I'm leaving." He places a hand on Apollo's shoulder and leans into his ear. My frustration rises. I don't want to call attention to this. If I'm going to leave, I want to do so quietly.

"I got it, boss," Apollo croons.

"But don't you need to be here to make the sides and breakfast for the turkey drive tomorrow?"

"Apollo has it covered. He and Anthony will have it all prepped and ready for me by morning. I'll work from the kitchen there. The new restaurant is handling most of the sides. I'm only doing the signature dishes. I can head in early and handle all of that tomorrow."

I sigh. "That's a lot. I'll help."

"Not if you're still not feeling well."

Dario pats Apollo on his shoulder, then turns to wrap an arm around my waist. He leans in to kiss my temple and I swear I nearly burst into tears.

Maybe I'll tell him tonight.

He leads me to the back room to retrieve my backpack and our coats before he takes me out to his car. We both drove today so I try to break away to get into mine. He tightens his hold on me and leads me to the passenger side of his car.

"Apollo will get your car to the apartment later."

"I'm fine, really. I don't need to leave, and you shouldn't be going with me. We have a business to run."

He purses his lips. "None of this comes before you."

A sour look comes to his face as the words come out. I can see the wheels turning in his head. He drags a hand down his face and works his jaw.

"Come on, let me get you home and in bed. I'll make you some soup."

I smile. How can I not love him? My heart pangs. I do love him and now I'm having his baby.

Yet, neither of us have proclaimed our love since we've been in this relationship, if that's what we're calling it. If this were anyone else, I'd say we're fucking. Nothing more, nothing less.

Sadly, it's starting to feel like I'm a live-in fuck buddy. We try to do couple things, but our schedules are so busy. When we're not working, Dario has been with his grandfather.

I haven't asked for more because I don't want to sound like a whiny brat. Heck, this was only supposed to be one night. Does a real couple really look much different than who we've been to each other?

"Car, talk to me. What's going on in your head?"

"Maybe we're rushing things. The timing couldn't be more off. You're going away and we don't know for how long." Tears fill my eyes. Ugh, I don't know if I can do this emotional shit for nine months. "I don't want to ruin our friendship."

He stops at a light and looks over at me and narrows that sharp gaze on me. I reach to run a hand over my hair and twirl the end of my ponytail nervously.

"I'm uncertain about a lot of things going on in my life at the moment, but you're not one of them. You're bringing me peace in all of this."

All of what? I want to scream. However, I don't because this is Dario and we never fight. I don't want to start now. Fighting would only be the beginning of the end. An end I can't afford for us to have now.

"I'm tired. That's all. Can we talk about this later?"

He blows out a breath of frustration and moves forward with traffic. Guilt settles in my chest. I don't even know how this happened. We've used condoms every time we've had sex.

My stupid pill failed me. Thank God it was with Dario and not one of the few others I've slept with. I think of Lou and groan. This is some shit he would have hoped for.

It was his talk of children and moving across the country to be a stay-at-home mom that turned me off. All things I never wanted with him. I wanted them with Dario, but now something doesn't feel right about it. I just don't know what it is.

It's nothing but your pregnant brain telling you this is going to fall apart.

I certainly hope that's the case.

Dario

I work my jaw as Carleen's little snores fill the car. She passed out. She's doubting us.

I haven't gotten anything from my *nonno* so far. He keeps saying I need to have this meeting in Italy before he can tell me anything else.

I'm so fucking frustrated. It's becoming clearer with each day that something else is happening right under my nose. I regret getting Carleen involved in my life. She's right, the timing is complete shit.

I shouldn't have read her diary. If I hadn't, I wouldn't have gone to her bed and claimed her. I would have gone to the other side, done my duty to my family and then, maybe then...Who am I fooling?

I would have lost her, like I feel like I'm doing now. The strain of this transition is taking a toll on us. My mind is always occupied. I want to talk to her about it, but that's not an option.

My phone rings, causing Carleen to stir in her seat. I tighten my jaw and grip the steering wheel. It's Apollo, so I pick up right away.

"I'm in the car and you're on speaker," I bite out.

"Call me as soon as you can, boss. You have my number." His accent is thicker than usual, telling me this is business. I need to get to my burner.

I hang up without a word and glance over at Car. My heart squeezes. I fucked up. In my heart I want to put her first, but my oath says I can't. If I keep going like this, I'm going to hurt her and not intentionally.

Carleen is a civilian and I want to keep it that way. I love her so much, but I know I'm going to fuck this up. Her words from earlier come back to me.

Maybe we're rushing things. The timing couldn't be more off. You're going away and we don't know for how long…I don't want to ruin our friendship.

So what do I do? I can't put these feelings back in the box they were in. I punch the steering wheel and bite out a curse. She's already pulling away from me. Maybe I should allow her to.

She whimpers in her sleep, pulling my attention as I park in the parking garage of my building. "I'm sorry, Rio. Don't leave. I love you."

I lean in and kiss her forehead. "I love you too. I just need time to figure this out."

I pull away and stare at her for a few beats. I furrow my brows as her words set in. *What's she sorry for?*

This was on me. I read her diary. I pushed us into this new relationship. I'm leaving and placing everything in such a state of uncertainty.

I run a hand through my hair. "*Fuck.*"

I swallow all of my thoughts and get out to grab her backpack and carry her upstairs. Once in the apartment, I carry her to my bedroom and remove her coat and shoes before tucking her under the sheets.

I kiss her nose then her soft lips. My anger with myself rises. There are people out there who don't want Nonno to pass the family to me. Carleen is in more danger than ever and it's all because of me.

I've become a selfish bastard and now the most precious thing to me in the world stands in harm's way. I shake my raging thoughts away and head to my office to call Apollo. He picks up on the second ring as I take a seat at my desk.

"The uncle is here to see you."

"Which one?"

"The fed."

I groan and rub my temple. This is the last thing I need. Talon Thompson has been connected to my family for as long as I can remember. Nonno has made friends in a lot of places that have had my curiosity for years. My grandfather has only been a presence in the States since my mother disappeared and Dante started to lose his shit.

Yet, he has an amazing reach that I'm inheriting. If only Carleen knew how deep her family is in the life. It used to give me hope that she would accept all of me. I shake my thoughts clear.

"Is he looking for Car?" I ask.

"No, he asked for you."

"Fuck, what now?"

"What do you want me to do?"

"I'm not leaving her tonight. Find out what he wants. See if he'll talk to Gio."

"Are you sure it's good to ignore a fed, boss?"

"I'm not ignoring him. I just told you what to do. If he can't talk to Gio let him know where to find me tomorrow."

"Sorry, boss. Got it."

I grunt and hang up. Suddenly, I'm bone tired. I wish I could have a look in Gio's crystal ball right about now. Something is coming for me. Something I can't stop, and I get the feeling it's well in motion.

I drag my exhausted body to my bedroom and kick my shoes off then climb in bed next to Carleen and wrap my arm around her. She snuggles into my embrace, and I blow out a breath.

"Is everything okay?"

"Yeah, go back to sleep."

CHAPTER SEVENTEEN

Thanksgiving Drive

Dario

"Hey, Dario, we got any more trays in the back?" Anthony calls from the tables where they're serving dinners.

I shrug. This isn't my place. I don't know the inventory here. "Give me a minute to check."

I start for the back storeroom. Normally I would have stopped over yesterday to get everything in order and to figure out what would need to come over from our place in New York. However, I stayed by Car's side the entire night.

We never did get to address her concerns in the car. I made her soup and ran her a bath to relax. I thought it best to *show* her we belong together. A coward move, I know, but I don't have the words to explain what's going on in my life and how I need to keep her far from it all.

"Hey Dario, this is a great spread this year."

"Thanks."

"It's always good to see you guys work so hard for the community."

I grunt and pick up my pace. I hear the request coming before it leaves his lips. We do the charities we want to do. Not the showboating these motherfuckers are always trying to rope us into because they don't want to cough up cash to run the bogus events they throw.

I duck into the supply room and sigh in frustration. This day has been total shit. Carleen has been more distant, but I haven't had the time to press her to see what's going on.

We decided not to go public with our relationship in front of my brothers today, but I'm regretting that decision with every second. It's one thing not to show public displays of affection but our friendship is missing as well. It's the main reason I've been trying to corner her to talk. I may not want Gio learning about us to start his prying, but I need Carleen near enough to keep a lid on my shit.

Silvio's son got whacked. It wasn't one of my guys, but it sure looks as if it could have been. We've been up his ass for the last few weeks. No telling how that's going to blow back on me. It was messy.

Talon is only willing to talk to me and I have no clue what about. He's supposed to show up here tonight. I just don't know when.

It's all bubbling up and I wish I could bury my head in Carleen's neck to inhale her for a moment to clear my head. I haven't been able to steal a single second all day. First, I had to leave out to get breakfast started for the drive and finish the side dishes for the evening. Then as a Di Lorenzo, I needed to mingle and host along with my brothers.

We have such a great turnout this year. Which would be awesome if not for the gap I feel building between me and Carleen. I grumble to myself as I look around for the trays.

I find them and grab two boxes. At least Dante was on top of placing these orders. This restaurant doesn't have much need for them. I have them in stock at my place because we cater more events like this at *Anima Mias*. If he had dropped the ball we'd be screwed. I know my ass wasn't driving to New York and back.

"I need to get my shit together," I mutter as I head back out of the storeroom.

I step out and lift my head to see Dante walking away from the door of the office across from me. This is one of our bigger restaurants. The place has way more offices and storerooms. My curiosity is piqued as I see Gio in a heated discussion with Lizzy's sister, Nyla.

As usual, I should mind my damn business and head up front with these trays. However, I don't. I turn and find Anthony in the hall and wave him over to take the boxes from me. Once he's out of sight, I move closer to the office Gio and Nyla are standing in.

I take in everything about them. The look on Gio's face, how close he is to her. I've never seen him like this with anyone.

Nyla looks up at him with moist eyes and what looks a lot like longing in them as he hovers over her. Gio cups her face and runs his finger across her lips. His posture is possessive and protective, raising my curiosity even more.

She shakes her head at whatever he says to her and Gio moves closer to crowd her space. I can't help myself. I creep a little closer to hear them.

"You come first. You always come first," Gio rumbles.

"That's a lie, Gio, and you know it's a lie."

"No, it's not. That's what you don't seem to understand. It's all for you."

He leans in to whisper something in her ear that I can't overhear. When he pulls away tears slip down her cheeks and my brother shocks the hell out of me as he leans in and captures her lips.

I'm so shocked I don't notice Jace until he's standing in front of me with his arms folded over his chest. I look into his gray eyes and take a step back. Jace nods and closes the door, cutting me off from the sight of my brother and a woman I didn't know he knew.

I pull a hand down my face. Gio sounds like he's going through the same thing I'm going through. Can the women in our lives ever truly come first?

I rub at my chest. Gio has always made sacrifices for me and my twin. I feel guilty for not wanting to make this one for him. Maybe I should allow this distance Carleen has created. At least until after I go to Italy and gain a full understanding of what is required of me.

I blow out a breath as my thoughts turn to Gio and Nyla. How do they know each other? Since when has Gio been interested in anyone other than his dolls and—?

Fuck. What does this all mean?

Again, I have a million questions and no answers.

"Well, fuck me."

Carleen

I sit on a crate off to myself as I watch Dario and his brothers horse around. I bounce my leg and lift my thumb to my lips to chew on my nail. I should tell him.

I've wanted to all day, but something else has grabbed my attention and caused me to pause. It happens again right as I have the thought.

Apollo moves to Dario's side and whispers something in his ear. It's like the millionth time tonight. Sure Apollo is our sous-chef. However, there's something else about the interactions that pull my focus, I've noticed it a few times.

My stomach turns as reality sets in. I don't think I know my best friend as much as I thought I did. Dario turns from Apollo to murmur into Gio's ear, and I know I've been ignoring some huge things about the Di Lorenzo family all these years.

"What have I done?" I whisper and cover my stomach with my hand.

Suddenly, Dario's words from a few weeks back come flooding to mind and I feel so stupid.

It's a blood thing. Our children wouldn't be considered for a lot because you're not Italian. Your family can't be traced back to the other side.

"Holy shit. He *is* a made man."

The words are whispered but as if hearing me, Jace appears at my side. I look up at him and stand. "Hey," I say as I come out of my thoughts.

"You all right?"

I shake my head to clear it. "Have you ever felt like you've been intentionally ignorant?"

Jace scoffs. "Story of my life." He winks at me. I note his eyes are gray tonight. "We all play fools for love every once in a while."

"Yeah, but when's the right time to stop being the fool?"

"When it hurts or threatens to strip us of what we deserve. Never sacrifice more than you're willing to lose, Carleen."

I suck in a deep breath as his words punch through my heart. Have I been sacrificing me for my love for Dario? Even now, I'm avoiding this conversation I know we need to have because I don't want to add pressure to his already loaded plate.

I look up at Jace with tears in my eyes. "I...I didn't realize what I was doing. He's always been there to take the lead and make sure I'm okay. The least I could do is make sure he's happy."

"But at what cost? I've known you a long time, Carleen. You're right, he's always been there for you. However, I've watched something change in you every time things change for him. For each of his promotions, you seem to lose a part of you. It's like you compensate for his...something, I can't explain it."

Promotions?

He holds up his hands as a commotion starts behind him. "It's none of my business but maybe you need to start looking deeper. Find out what you're a part of. That goes for diving into everything around you. I'm always here if you need me."

With that, he turns and heads for the small crowd that has gathered around Dante and Lizzy. I push his words to the back of my mind as Bethany starts one of her scenes. I watch Dario as he looks like he's going to lunge at her. My hackles go up and I want to slap her for him and Dante. However, when Lizzy's sister grabs Bethany by the back of her hair, I can do nothing but smile.

One of these days that woman is going to get what she deserves. If she keeps playing with my man, it may come from me.

CHAPTER EIGHTEEN

Distractions

Carleen

I watch Dario from my seat at the kitchen island. He's full of tension. That scene Bethany pulled changed the entire night.

He's been on the phone since we arrived home from the turkey drive. I narrow my gaze as if I can see through him. I feel like I'm dissecting a body. Jace's words are playing in my head on repeat as I pull them apart as well.

But at what cost...I've watched something change in you every time things change for him. For each of his promotions, you seem to lose a part of you.

Every time Dario has become distant and tense like this, I've made excuses and I've never pried. Always thinking, if he wants me to know, he'll tell me.

What am I really missing? Clearly there's a whole lot.

Maybe you need to start looking deeper. Find out what you're a part of.

What could I possibly be a part of? I know nothing. My ignorance is the problem here though, isn't it?

That goes for diving into everything around you.

My own family comes to mind. Uncle Rick may be my favorite but I've always questioned how clean he has kept his nose. If I'm honest, when Uncle Kington is around, he reminds me of the way the Di Lorenzo family moves. I used to think it was because he's the oldest, but my uncles all treat him like some Don or something.

"Baby...baby, did you hear what I said?"

I come out of my thoughts and look up at Dario. He's standing before the island, watching me closely. I clear my throat and push my shoulders back.

"Sorry, what was that?"

"I asked if you were hungry? I can cook something up real quick."

"It's late and you've been cooking all day. Let's order Chinese. You okay with that?"

He shrugs. "Chinese it is."

I smile as he doesn't ask what I want. He knows. How can you know someone so well and not know them at all? I frown as I think of how little I know myself.

What I do know is that if I tell Dario about this baby, he's going to take charge the way he always does, and I may never find what I've lost. I toughen my resolve to keep this to myself for now.

Realizing I've lost myself in Dario changes a lot for me. While I'm not sure how I feel about him being a part of the Mafia, I know for sure I have some soul searching to do. I can't do that when Dario goes all alpha. It's always his way.

I can't love any man more than I love me. If I have a little girl, I don't want my daughter to think that's normal.

I smile to myself. This baby may not have been planned but now that it's on its way, I want to do what's best for it and me.

Dario comes up behind me and plants his hands on the counter on either side of me. His sharp inhale pulls me from my thoughts.

"You've been distant all day. Listen, about what you said yesterday. Yeah, we have bad timing. I wish like hell I wasn't leaving.

"If it were up to me, you'd be with me. I want this to work. I just need some time and your trust."

I turn in my seat to look him in his eyes. Blind trust. That's something I've given this man all my life. However, I don't think I can anymore. Not at the cost of me or this baby.

"If our timing is wrong, maybe we should pause. You go to Italy and do whatever you need to, and I'll focus on all that needs to be done here."

His face clouds over and his jaw tics. He bounces his gaze over my face. I hold my breath as I await his response. He moves between my legs and cups my face.

Before I can catch on to what he's about to do, he takes my lips in a heated, passionate kiss. I moan into his mouth and wrap my arms around his neck. When he breaks the kiss, he places his forehead to mine.

"You are mine no matter where I am. Don't get this fucked up, Carleen. This space"—he narrows his eyes and points between us—"you're trying to put between us isn't going to change that. What would we need to pause for? A pause means being free to fuck other people and neither one of us has that freedom.

"If I'm gone for an entire year or two, this cock will be leaking for you and you alone. Just like your pussy better be so tight I have to pry that shit open with a toolbox to get back in it."

I open my mouth to speak but the intercom buzzes, announcing the arrival of our food. Dario kisses me hard before he saunters off to get our dinner. I tighten my lips as I watch him walk and remember Toni's words about the way he walks—as if he owns the world. All that BDE is real. I'm wet from his words as it is, despite my anger.

And this is my problem. For all my intelligence, I'm a fool for Dario.

I look at the clock. It's eleven twenty. I should probably call it a night. However, I didn't have much to eat today. I was wound too tight.

Dario places the food on the counter and my mouth starts to water. I tear into the wings first. I think I'm hungrier than I thought.

"You want some of this rice?" Dario asks, holding the box in my direction.

"No, thank you."

My stomach turns and I jump up to rush to the nearby powder room. Dario is right on my heels. He pulls my hair from my face and holds it back as I empty my stomach.

"Motherfucker. If you have food poisoning from that place, they're never opening their doors again."

I grunt and keep heaving. If only he knew.

"*Marone.* Baby, I'm so sorry."

I groan and fall back onto my butt. He pushes my hair from my face and kisses my forehead.

"I'm going next door to get Dr. Brown. You good for about five minutes?"

"You don't need to disturb that man. I'm fine."

He twists his lips at me and stands. "I've catered enough shit for him over the years. Every time he smells food coming from this place, he's at my door. He can get his ass up and see to you for me."

I groan and roll my eyes. This is why I can't tell him. I'd be locked in this apartment with a babysitter until he returns from Italy. Nope.

Dario

I just put Carleen in the bed and came out here to clear this food away. I pick up one of the cartons and sniff at it. It doesn't smell off, but Carleen was fine before eating this shit.

I'm pissed at myself. It wouldn't have taken me long to make her something to eat. I should have followed my first mind. I trash it all and wipe the island down. I'll have an inspector in that place by morning.

Grumbling to myself, I pour a drink of whiskey. This has been one long fucking day. I snort as I think of Carleen with that pause bullshit. I may need time to figure things out, but I am going to figure them out.

My caution doesn't mean I'm claiming defeat. When this is all over, I'm claiming my woman for good. All thoughts of distance are bullshit. I know I can't walk away now, and I've only been lying to myself when I think about trying.

My phone rings, pulling me from my rambling thoughts. This thing hasn't stopped ringing all day. I expect it to be Apollo with an update on Talon, but it's Dante's number. I furrow my brows and pick up the call.

"What's up?"

"Bethany's gone."

"She took off? Why am I not surprised?"

"No, Dario. She's dead. Someone killed her."

"What?"

"I'm leaving the precinct now, they're still collecting evidence and figuring out the details. I heard her screaming…Bella heard me tell her to go somewhere and die. What the fuck is wrong with me?"

I haven't heard my brother sound like this in so long. His voice is so detached. Talk about bad timing.

I freeze and think of Gio. I would never outright ask him, but I have to wonder if he's involved. I need more information before I can confirm the fact, but after Bethany's performance earlier, I wouldn't put it past him.

"Don't do this to yourself. We all know she's pushed you to do worse. You've shown more restraint than I thought you were capable of."

"Yeah, I guess you're right. I'm so fucking numb right now."

I look down at my watch. "Listen, get some sleep. Take a day or two to process and pull yourself together. Call me whenever you need. I'm here for you."

"Thanks, Dario."

Hanging up, I groan. Dragging my tired body into the bedroom, I strip and head into the shower. My thoughts are riding me hard as I move through a quick shower.

I climb out and crawl into bed with Carleen. I spoon her and wrap her in my arms. She snuggles into me. Exhausted, I kiss the top of her head.

My need to keep her safe and protected rears up. What if that wasn't Gio who had Bethany killed? Could Carleen be in danger? I make a mental note to change Apollo's instructions for while I'm gone.

"No one will ever take you from me," I murmur into her hair.

Everything is changing. I think of my niece. She's probably better off without her mother. Bethany only cared about herself. However, Bella will now know what it's like to lose a mother.

But did you really lose yours? There are answers, Dario, you just need to find them. Italy has them all.

I close my eyes and allow my mind to settle. Things will fall into place. They always do.

CHAPTER NINETEEN

I Run This Board

Dario

The weight of the world is on my shoulders as I stand in my twin's home gym, feeling the bitter sting of the lie I spoke only moments ago.

I didn't say we're together. I leave for Italy after the New Year. Nothing has changed.

However, everything has changed, but Gio doesn't need to know the truth. I have enough going on in my life without him meddling. Hell, I do believe Bethany's blood is on my hands. I snort and toss a thumb toward an exiting Gio and Jace.

"And *Nonno* wants me," I say and turn to leave.

The conversation we've just had nags at my brain. My curiosity burns to know if Gio was indeed involved. I pick up the pace and jog after Gio and Jace to catch them before they leave.

I find them outside in the courtyard. Gio has Jace pinned to the side of their SUV. My brother is all up in Jace's face, snarling like an angry lion.

"You need to calm down," Jace says calmly.

"I knew I smelled her all over you. You said nothing happened."

"No, she told you nothing happened."

"Are you crazy? This doesn't work if I can't trust you."

"Gio," I call out.

"Fuck," he growls and releases Jace with a shove before taking a step back and turning to me slowly.

"You don't have to tell me details…but was this…," I whisper the last part.

Gio licks his bottom lip. "What do you think? And if you don't wise up"—he moves to get in my face—"I'm going to stick my nose in your shit too."

I whip my head back. "I don't need you in my business."

Jace snorts behind Gio.

Gio grins and pats my cheek. "You keep telling yourself that. See you later, Rio."

I glare after him as he climbs into the SUV.

Gio

I'm still pissed. I take a calming breath and remember the task at hand. Jace has an airtight alibi, that's all that matters. I turn to look at him as he pulls out of Dante's front gate.

"They behave just like twins. So fucking stubborn."

"It's a family thing," Jace grunts.

"Shut up."

He snorts. I run a hand through my hair and run my tongue over my teeth. I run this fucking board, it's my game and I'll win every time.

"Bring Holly back. Ny will need her."

"But Carleen's pregnant."

"I fucking know that," I roar before I catch myself. I crack my knuckles and work my jaw as I reel it in. I shift in my seat. "Change of plans. If we can't trigger her through training, maybe we can by proximity. I'm counting on Car being Car. When I asked Dario what he wanted, it was her. Only her.

"I've opened the gates of hell, Jace. I can't leave her vulnerable. Not now, not after putting things in motion. Bring Holly back. She and Ny belong with Carleen. That's an order."

CHAPTER TWENTY

Training Day

Dario

"I'm about to walk into this meeting, baby. Tell Toni and Blake I said hi. I'll call you on my way home," I say into the phone as I cross the street to get to the new restaurant.

This will be my first training session with Jacob and the new line. I met him briefly at the turkey drive, but we didn't get to talk much. He's not our usual clean-cut chef, but Dante and Gio said he can cook. I'll be the judge of that.

"Don't forget to pick up your tux."

"I'm on it, gorgeous. I have it in the car."

"Okay," she sighs. "Look at us sounding like an old married couple."

"Nothing wrong with that. After all, we had an epic playground wedding almost twenty-seven years ago." I chuckle.

"And you are my work husband, remember?"

"How can I forget? Maybe I need to remind *you* when I get home."

"Ugh, that is if we're not interrupted again."

"*Marone*, you have that right. I guess it's good practice for when we have kids. They'll always need attention—"

Carleen starts to choke on the other end. I pause on the sidewalk, ready to turn and go back home. "Baby, you okay?"

"I'm fine. Water went down the wrong pipe. Listen, Blake and Toni will have a fit if I'm late. I'll talk to you later. Have a good day."

"You too, baby."

I hang up as I walk into the restaurant. The first thing I notice is Jacob pacing the dining room while on the phone. Not usual but his expression grabs my attention as does his posture. Last I heard, he's been trying to get into Lizzy's pants.

She's the sweetest person ever, I can't see him being frustrated to this point with her. He sees me approaching and rushes to end his call.

"Hey, man," he says and holds out his hand for me to shake. I return the handshake. "Dario, nice to meet you."

He shakes his head. "Damn, you and your brother look just alike. It's unreal."

"Twins." I shrug.

He rubs the back of his neck. "Sorry, I'm sort of nervous. This is a huge move and all."

"Speaking of moves. This is a long way from Boston, what brings you to New York?"

"One of my brothers has a real estate firm here in New York. My parents are in Jersey, that's where I'm from originally. That's why I was at the other restaurant you guys poached me from. I planned to settle there," he replies.

"Oh yeah? Well, based on your performance after a year you could request to transfer to a Jersey house."

He looks around the new place. "I'm sort of digging this place. Nicest restaurant I've worked in a long time."

I take a look around and grin. We do know how to build them. Dante and Gio are masters at scoping out locations and opening premium restaurants. Our kitchens are always the finest. A long way from where our family started.

I, for one, am proud of the workspaces we design for our chefs. Even the hidden back room at *Anima Mias* is state of the art despite not being used for restaurant purposes.

I shrug and gesture for him to take a seat at the table we're closest to. "They're all like this."

He nods. "The Di Lorenzo brand. You guys have built some empire."

"Your last name is Kelley, right? Is your family Irish?"

"My mother is. Kelley is actually her maiden name."

I narrow my eyes. Jacob has blue eyes and dark hair that's pulled up in a topknot. Nothing about him reads Irish to me. However, I do note the Celtic tat peeking from beneath his short-sleeved chef's coat.

"Can you bring anything from your background to the kitchen? Colcannon and champ, soda bread, boxty, black and white pudding."

He reaches to rub the back of his neck and frowns. "No, I don't know much about her side of the family or the culture. We grew up knowing more about our father's side."

"Oh, where's he from?"

"He's Italian. I can relate to your family more than my mother's."

Now this, I can see. The Rome features are strong on him. I would have pegged him for Italian first.

I pull a face and nod. "This can work. We usually ask our head chefs to come up with a signature dish that speaks to their background."

"No problem. I'll come up with something. I could always ask Ma if she has any recipes I can make my own, but I have the Italian side covered."

"Great, can you have a dish ready for me by next time I drop in?"

"You'll be in all next week, right?"

"Yeah, to get you started. Is that a problem?"

"Not at all. I'll head to Ma's today after work and I'll work on the other dish I have in mind."

"How are you doing with learning our point-of-sale system?"

"I think I have a handle on it. You guys use nothing but the best, but I'm getting the hang of it."

I tap my knuckles against the top of the table. "Let's go talk with your line and front-of-the-house staff. We'll talk menus after."

"Sounds good."

Carleen

"What's going on with you two?" Toni says as she glares at me and Blake. She turns to me. "How you going to invite us here to have lunch and you've had a long face from the time we come? Not to mention you refuse to drink with us."

I chew on my lip as I look between the two. I'm debating on if I should tell my cousin and friend what's going on with me. I invited them here to the restaurant for a sense of comfort.

However, I've been in my head since we sat down. Some things have occurred to me in the last few days. Jace may be right, whenever I sense Dario has or needs change, I react as if it's my own anxiety in my life. I blink a few times and look to Toni.

"Can I ask you something?"

"Ut-oh."

"No, seriously. When I called you about opening this place, did it sound like my decision?"

Toni gives me a stern look. She rolls her eyes and sits back in her seat, folding her arms over her chest. I hold my breath as I wait for her to speak.

"I see you're finally waking up. Girl, as always, Dario told you what you were going to do and then it was done. I'm not going to lie and say you didn't seem happier, but that man knew you wanted change, and this"—she waves a hand around—"was his solution."

I slump my shoulders and purses my lips. She's right, he didn't really ask me if I wanted to do this. He suggested it when I said I was looking for a job and then it happened.

It's occurring to me that Dario has stepped in to fix things for me a lot over the years. What seems like decisions I've made are all things Dario decided were best for me.

When I started to show interest in cooking, he handed me the brochures for schools. When I wanted to buy a home, Dario handed me a list of neighborhoods and had a realtor call me.

"At least he has your best interest in mind," Blake says, seeming to come out of her own head.

"Well, what's going on with you?" Toni says to Blake.

Blake frowns, it's so out of place on her pretty face. Blake is honey colored and has the most striking gray eyes. They are slanted and large, but perfect for her face. Her full lips stand out.

Since we were kids, she's had the fullest wavy hair. At this moment she has it pulled back in a natural ponytail, with artfully done baby hair.

Blake has always been pretty. However, she does look a bit tired. No doubt because of Fred, her high school sweetheart, husband, and the bane of her existence.

"Same old, same old. How did I marry such a bum?"

Toni snorts and pushes her glass away. "I should probably keep my mouth shut but there must be some epiphany juice in this cocktail."

"Yeah, you should shut up," Blake says.

"Don't be mad at me because you married the first dick to turn you out. His bum ass got so lucky. Even he still can't believe it."

Thankfully, our food arrives, cutting off Blake's reply. I push my plate away as my appetite disappears. Toni narrows her eyes at me as she chews.

I can feel in my bones she's about to dig into me. I'm saved by the three people who walk into the restaurant. Gio saunters in with all his swag as Jace and Nyla, Lizzy's sister, follow behind him. I wasn't expecting them, but they head straight for our table.

"*Gio,*" Toni sings.

"How you doing, gorgeous?"

I watch closely as Gio moves to kiss each of Toni's cheeks. He smoothly places something into her palm and Toni drops her hands into her lap.

As if nothing happened, Gio moves to kiss my forehead and then my cheeks. "Hey, Car."

"Hi, Gio." I give him a warm smile as he takes one of the chairs Jace has brought over to our table. I move my seat over a bit to make more room for them. Gio sits beside me, and Nyla takes the seat between him and Jace.

I'm a little surprised to see her with them, but I don't pry. I'm still wondering what the exchange between Gio and Toni was about.

I lean forward. "Good to see you again, Nyla. This is my cousin Antonia and my friend Blake. You guys know Dante's assistant Lizzy, this is her sister."

"How have you been, Blake?" Gio says while looking down at his tie he's smoothing his hand down, seeming not to be paying attention to anyone in particular.

I know Gio, he's aware of everyone and everything. The nonchalant act doesn't fool me.

Toni perks up. "Actually, Gio. Maybe you can help Blake."

"*Toni,*" Blake drags out in warning.

Toni continues as if she hasn't heard a thing. "She's married to a bum-ass dude that won't get off his ass to provide and has the nerve to be so jealous, Blake can't keep a job either. She's been through four in just the last month and a half."

"Toni," Blake hisses low.

Gio lifts his gaze to Blake and allows his eyes to roll over her. Blake will look anywhere but at Gio. Gio turns to Jace, and I notice the ever-so-slight nod Jace gives before Gio turns to Nyla. The two have a silent conversation.

Nyla stands and rounds the table to lean in and whisper in Blake's ear as she hands her a card.

"How's the house coming?" Gio asks, grabbing my attention. I frown and roll my eyes. "I'm so mad at you. I swear you hooked me up with the opposite of what I asked for. I'm about to say fuck it and tell Dario to take over."

Gio chuckles. "We both know you don't want to do that. Forget about it. I'll have a talk with Ralphie. I'll set him straight."

I sigh in relief and smile. "Thanks, Gio."

"Anytime." He winks at me then stands and Jace follows. Gio buttons his suit jacket and leans to kiss my cheek.

Just as smoothly as the three walked in, they walk out. I'm left staring after them with a ton of questions. I look to Blake, and she has a dazed look on her face.

"What did she say to you?" I ask.

Blake looks down at the card in her hand. "She offered me options."

CHAPTER TWENTY-ONE

Thompsons and Mitchells

Carleen

I place my hand on my stomach for the millionth time. My belly is still flat, but I swear someone is going to jump out and reveal my secret. It would happen here at my uncle's event.

"You look lovely, Carleen," one of the surgeons from my old hospital compliments as she walks by.

I smooth a hand over the one-shoulder, sleeveless high-low hem silk gown I'm wearing and grin as I think of my six-inch heels. It's amazing to date someone who still towers over you when you're in heels like mine at my height. It doesn't happen often for me.

I swallow hard and look around the room. So many important people mingling together without a care in the world. Now this is a power party—doctors, actors, politicians, investment bankers, and so many other big high-powered world influencers.

I take a deep breath. "I can do this."

Dario and I finished up the catering and went to change to join the party. The staff can handle the service. My uncle made it clear he wanted me and Dario to attend as guests. No doubt my father didn't want me seen as the help.

"You look like you've never been to one of these before," Dario says into my ear as he walks up behind me and covers my hand with his.

Tears come to my eyes. He's covering our baby and doesn't even know it. I break down and turn to tell him.

"What's wrong?" he asks as his face clouds over. "If one of these assholes said something out of line, I swear to God."

I swallow my words, reminding myself this is why I need to wait. Maybe his trip will only take a month or two and he'll return before the baby comes.

"I'm fine," I say and fix the collar of his tux.

He fingers one of the curls that has slipped free from my updo. "You're simply gorgeous," he murmurs.

I give him a smile. Before I can protest, he leans in and takes my lips. I moan into his mouth as he tugs me in close. A throat clears behind us and I jump away from the kiss.

Turning, I find Uncle Ernesto and Uncle Talon watching us. My father stands with them with a huge frown on his face. Why do I suddenly feel like a little girl with her hand in the cookie jar?

"It's good to see you, Dario," Uncle Ernesto croons.

"Good to see you too, Senator Thompson."

"Hey, Uncle Ernie." I give my uncle a big smile.

"Oopies, I'm so glad to see your face. Not sure how I feel about the boy sucking it, but glad to see it."

I groan and roll my eyes. Maybe we should have decided to keep things from my family as well. I've seen Gio meddle in Dario's life, so I understood the need to keep things from his brothers. The last thing I need is for the all-knowing Gio to get up in my business.

"You're a hard one to catch up to," Uncle Talon says to Dario.

"It seems we've been missing each other a lot," he replies.

Uncle Talon nods. "I'll need your ear before the night is over."

My father sucks his teeth so hard, I look to see if any have fallen out. He scowls at the two of us before he turns to walk off.

I sag into Dario's side, too tired to entertain whatever is up my father's butt.

Dario possessively places his hand on my hip and moves me in front of him. I close my eyes as he kisses the back of my head, then nuzzles the side of my neck.

"Oopies, you a big gyal now, eh? Running with bad men." Dario stiffens behind me. I open my eyes to look at my uncle, Kurt. He's the youngest of my uncles. Now this is my uncle you go to for all the things your parents tell you not to do. While I always see him in some powerful people's ear. I still don't know his official title. His words trigger my thoughts to race for those dots I know I need to connect.

"Carleen has been a friend of mine all my life. Nothing about me has changed. I am who I am. Only difference now is she's my woman."

Uncle Kurt sucks his teeth and narrows his eyes. "Remember who you're talking to. I know all about your new upcoming promotion. Word of advice, don't shit where you eat."

"Kurt," Uncle Talon and Uncle Ernie hiss in unison.

Uncle Kurt kisses his teeth again and waves them off. "Come gyal, your auntie wants to see you."

I look up at Dario and he drops a kiss on my lips. I don't take my eyes off him as my uncle drags me away, not until someone bumps me and I have to look forward.

"That family, boy. They always get what they want. Your grandfadda rolling in his grave, you know. Your uncle too."

I lean into my uncle. "Uncle Kurt, what am I missing?"

"This not the place, Oopies," he says and clamps his mouth shut.

Of all the times for him to shut up. He never bites his tongue. I tighten my fists at my sides. Someone needs to give me some answers.

Dario

"I only have one thing to say. She's a big girl and she's been in love with you all her life. You know who we are as we know you. We'll bring all of hell down on your head if something happens to her or if our sister sheds one tear for that gyal," the senator says.

"I hear you," I reply.

"Do you?" Talon says. He moves in closer and turns so no one can read his lips. "You have a problem. Maybe you should take your trip sooner. I've heard your name one too many times in the office. You don't have much time before they're on your doorstep."

My head almost explodes. The last thing I need is for the feds to show up on my doorstep. They wouldn't find anything, which means they have a rat who can nail me. I've kept my nose the cleanest, but it's stupid shit like Silvio Jr. that threatens to link me to bullshit.

"Do I have until after the New Year?"

"No, maybe Christmas, but some of those assholes would love to ruin that for you and your family. So be mindful."

I nod and rub my fingers over my lips. That only gives me a week at most. I lift my gaze and find Carleen. She's with her aunt and uncle laughing. My world is squeezing me and she's about to pop right out of my grasp.

When her father moves to their little group, I groan. I don't know why the man hates me so much. It wasn't always this way. Mr. Mitchell and I used to have a mutual respect.

"I don't want her involved. I'll leave."

CHAPTER TWENTY-TWO

Change of Plans

Carleen

"You look stunning. You have a glow about you," my mother coos as she walks over to me.

I'm trying to make an escape. Dario looks like something is wrong, but I haven't been able to make my way over to him because my auntie was chewing my ear off.

I stifle my groan and give my mother a smile. She reaches to pinch my hip. "You want to be careful you don't start to spread too much."

And just like that, my mother displays my family's ability to boost your ego and shoot it back down in the same breath. There's always something, no matter how hard you try to be perfect.

Mind you, my mother is as tall as I am, and you can see her booty from the front and her hips match. She's a doctor, she understands how genes work. Lord forgive me if my ass and hips are wide and curvy.

I wasn't going to remain rail thin my entire life. That went out the window at sixteen.

"Ugh, finally," Toni says as she comes over with two champagne glasses. She hands me one. "Two people I'm willing to talk to. I wasn't coming near you while you were talking to Uncle Kurt and Auntie Judie."

My mother tries to hold in her laughter. I shake my head at my cousin. Toni rolls her eyes, sucks her teeth, and places a hand on her hip.

"What? Where's the lie? All these people here are looking for the next favor and Auntie Judie doesn't know how to shut the fuck up."

"*Toni,*" my mother groans.

Toni smirks and holds up her glass. "To intelligent women who make things happen," she says.

"I'll drink to that," my mother says.

I pretend to lift the glass to my lips and turn away. Damn it. I've lost sight of Dario again.

"Oh, you girls excuse me, I see someone I need to talk to. Carleen, you and Dario should stop by the house soon, as the couple you've become."

"Yes, Mommy," I reply, hearing her words for the command they are.

I turn to Toni and she has her eyes narrowed on me.

"What?"

She moves closer. "Your ass is pregnant. Pushing away your lunch, not drinking with us. Now that fake ass sip you took of that champagne."

"Shh," I hiss.

"What? You don't want Uncle Percy to know."

"No, and the father doesn't need to know either. I'll tell him when he comes back from his trip."

A look comes over Toni's face. I'm surprised when she moves on to a new subject. It's out of character for her. I think back to our lunch and the exchange between her and Gio.

Umm.

Dario

I'm stopped for the millionth time as I try to make my way back to Carleen. Everyone wants something—reservations, a private table for an anniversary, catering for some event.

Normally I would work the room for the business and connections, but I need to be near Carleen. So much is going on in my head. What could the feds have that they would come for me? Other than my brothers, Apollo, Jace, Mitch, and Anthony are the only ones who could point a real finger.

Anthony is our little cousin. Apollo's father was a good friend of ours and they've always been loyal. Apollo's father stepped up in Papa Esposito's place.

Mitch is another cousin of ours and Jace is as good as Gio's twin. I know I can trust them all.

Bethany. Son of a bitch.

"You okay?" Gio asks as he plants a hand on my shoulder from behind. I turn to find him and Jace.

I frown and shake my head. "No, I need to talk to *Nonno*."

Gio searches my eyes. "He's here. Let's find him and a private place to talk."

I nod and follow him. We find Nonno talking with the senator. Nonno has a big smile on his face until he sees me. He excuses himself and we all exit the party to find the SUV they came in. Climbing inside we settle in the back seats.

"What's this face? It's a nice party, no? I've eaten the food. My father and his father would be proud, Dario."

I shake my head. "It's not that. Uncle T says I have a problem. The feds have been talking about me and he believes they're coming for me soon."

"Ah, I see. What do we do? You Americans and the law. Don't they see the good we do for our community?"

"I think we should leave as soon as possible."

"Not before Christmas. Bella needs her family."

"I may not have that much time."

Nonno's eyes turn hard. "We will make time. Nothing comes before family."

I rub my fingers across my lips and look to Gio. He nods his head at me.

"I'll take care of this. You and *Nonno* can leave the morning after. Trust me, I'll have things held off until then."

I grunt and nod, needing Carleen in my arms more than ever. This is the storm I've been feeling coming for me. Even with Gio's connections, I don't know how safe I'll be. I don't even know what they want me for.

"Go, find your pretty partner and celebrate your success. The guests are talking about the food. This is good for Di Lorenzo business."

I open the door and step out, leaving them behind. My mind turns over so many things from over the past few months.

What the fuck am I missing?

Gio

"That went better than I thought," I say as the door closes behind Dario.

"Yes, but will he remain in Italy while you make these moves?" my grandfather asks.

"As long as he doesn't find out about the baby and she's safe, I think he will."

"But why hasn't she told him about the *bambino*?"

"I don't know. I'm counting it as luck so I'm not going to pry."

"You don't think she's thinking of…getting rid of it?"

The amount of sadness in Nonno's eyes tugs at my heart. The thought never crossed my mind. Carleen loves my brother too much for that.

"No, she would never."

Nonno turns to Jace. "To be safe, you will enter her life. Make sure my great-grandchild is safe."

I smile to myself. I already have this covered, but just like I made it so Dario thinks he's made this decision to leave ahead of schedule, I'll allow Nonno to think he's given Jace this command.

CHAPTER TWENTY-THREE

My All

Carleen

It's been a few days since my uncle's party and Dario has been distracted, distant, and grumpy. He's never been this way with me.

I'm trying to give him his space. I've been in the guest room all day even though he's been at work and it's my day off. I used to hate when we didn't have the same day together. However, I've been happy to have time to think.

My phone rings, pulling me out of my thoughts. I see it's Blake and smile as I answer. We haven't talked since our lunch.

"Hello."

"Hey, Car, you have a minute?"

"You know I do for you. What's up?"

"I'm tired, Car. You're the only one who understands why I married Fred in the first place. I thought I'd be safe and loved.

Now…I feel trapped. He wants nothing from life and thinks I'm supposed to be content with that."

"Oh, honey. You deserve so much better. You can't let your past haunt you forever. Especially not for some dusty-ass white boy who lucked up and caught you at a really vulnerable point in your life."

"Car, he's gotten us into so much debt with some really bad people. I'm going to have to leave him and hide somewhere until his shit blows over…I'm not coming back to him. I just need to make sure his BS doesn't reach me."

I think of Gio and get ready to tell her to call him. I pause as I think over what that would say about me. How that would involve me.

I'm going to be honest and say to myself that I haven't been asking questions because I don't know how that could tip the scales. My cousin is a federal prosecutor. One whiff of what I think I know, and Toni could be after my man and his family.

"Blake, you do what you need to do. I'll be here anytime you need. My money is your money."

"Thanks, Car. I just wanted to let someone know before I disappear. I'm done. I can't do this anymore. My soul is tired. I love you, Carleen."

"I love you too."

"Car?"

"Yeah?"

"I didn't get to answer you the other day, but I just want you to know. Yes, you've changed, and Dario has always been behind those changes, but it's not all bad.

"You seem happier now. Dig for that spark, that's all that's missing. I think you've become consumed by your man without realizing it. You know how you get lost in taking care of the people you love? How you do so much for them, you lose yourself in the process? Even becoming them to compensate for them?"

"Yeah," I reply softly. I know exactly what she's talking about.

Mommy calls it a transference of spirit. I become the better version of someone to bridge the gap to their success. Filling in the holes they leave in their process of growth.

Mommy says I care too much, I do things for people they won't do for themselves. I don't see it that way. If I can make things better for someone else, I'll do all I can to see them happy. I don't want to see them be denied happiness if I can help it.

I get things faster than most, so I try to be there to right things before they fall apart. It's my thing. I love to restore things for others. However, sometimes I can go too far and lose myself to the point I'm taken advantage of by those who don't care as much for me.

It's something I hate and love. When you mix that with my need to excel at everything I touch, I can get lost. It's frustrating at times. I always realize what I'm doing too late.

"I know you can't help it, but you've never checked it with Dario, not like with the rest of us. I think that's what's pissing your family off. Anyway, I've got to go. I'll call you as soon as I can. Bye, best."

"Bye, Blake. I love you, best."

We hang up and I sit staring off into space. Being a sponge as my mother calls it is a gift and a curse. However, not once have I ever noticed that I've done so with my best friend. Blake's words make a lot more make sense for me.

"But what do I do from here? I'm not cutting my best friend from my life," I yawn to myself.

Dario

I walk into my home wound tight with a headache trying to form. I still have more questions than answers. Not to mention, I'm acting like a pussy because I've yet to tell Carleen I'm leaving the morning after Christmas.

I rub the back of my neck and drag my tired body into my bedroom. The first thing I note is that Carleen isn't in my bed. My anger rises because this is what I've been looking forward to all night. Coming home to my woman and wrapping her in my arms.

The last time we texted she said she was going to call it a night. I grumble to myself and hop in the shower. She must be in the guest room.

"This is on me. Get your shit together before you lose her," I murmur to myself as I stand in the shower. I push my hair out of my face and throw my head back as I stare up at the ceiling.

None of this is her fault. I'm just so fucking stressed. I went to pick up Car's Christmas gift and saw an engagement ring that's meant to be on her finger. The impulse to place it there was so strong I bought it.

However, I'm not a total douchebag. With everything I have going on, it would be fucked up to propose before I leave. I think that's weighing on me most.

I blow out a breath. At least she didn't get pregnant that first night. I should have told her we had unprotected sex, but it sort of slipped my mind at first and then I didn't think it was such a big deal as the weeks went by and we became a couple.

Needing to shut my brain down, I finish up and step out to towel off. It's been a few weeks since the last time we had sex.

Not for lack of trying. Every time we get ready to, something comes up. My phone rings, we have to work, the list goes on and on.

What I need in this moment is to be buried so deep inside her, nothing else matters. One of her stellar blow jobs wouldn't hurt either. I'd be more than happy to return the favor.

I stroll my naked ass out of my bedroom, headed to find my woman so we can do all of the above. Hearing movement in the kitchen when I get to the end of the hall, I switch directions from the guest room and head toward the noise.

When I enter the kitchen, I find Carleen in a hot-pink teddy with a glass of water in her hand. She lifts her gaze from the countertop and starts to choke as I saunter toward her with a grin on my lips.

I round the counter and she turns to face me, causing me to miss the review from the back. I stop and fold my arms over my chest. Carleen lifts a brow as a smile lifts her lips behind her glass. She empties the glass, keeping her eyes locked on me.

"Thirsty?"

She shrugs. "I was. You just get in?"

"Not that long ago. Why aren't you in our bed?"

"It's your bed and I wanted to give you your space."

She turns to place her glass on the counter and her dark-chocolate ass comes into view. The way the pink fabric is swallowed between her plump round cheeks has me so hard my vision blurs for a moment.

I close the gap between us and plant my palms on the counter. Not able to help myself, I nip her shoulder. She gasps and sinks back into my body with her soft one.

"Did I ask for space?"

"No, but as you said before, I don't want to make assumptions based on our friendship."

I suck the flesh on her neck into my mouth. She pushes her ass back into my erection. I groan and palm her waist in my hands, fingering the satin fabric.

Slowly, I lick the shell of her ear. "Bullshit, but I'll allow you to tell yourself that," I breathe. "You're not dressed as if you want to keep space between us. As a matter of fact, you're dressed as if you want me to fuck the shit out of you."

She palms my hands, now digging tightly into her flesh. "I sent my boyfriend a few pics to tide him over since I planned to be asleep when he arrived. Did you get my text?"

I grind my hips into her. "No, I haven't checked my phone since I've been home. I've been looking for my girl so I can give her this hard cock."

"*Dario.*"

"I think I can get you to a few higher octaves. Come on, baby, it's been too long. Let me show you how to sing my name. Don't you miss me?"

I nip her ear as I slip my fingers beneath the fabric of her teddy and into her waiting, slick, hot sex. I pump them into her soaked pussy and pin her to the counter with my hips.

"Dario," she pants as she leans forward with her top flat against the countertop.

I groan and kick her legs farther apart, watching as her ass jiggles. Finding the snaps of the now soaked fabric between her legs, I release them with my free hand.

"That's it, come for me." Her walls ripple around my fingers as I coax her juices to flow.

"Yes," she whimpers.

Carleen lifts on her toes and keens as her legs start to shake. She's so wet for me. I drop to my knees to come face-to-face with her weeping core. It glistens at me as I lick my lips and spread her open.

My girl reaches back and spreads her cheeks for me, and I almost lose my shit. She's so perfect for me. I was just thinking how hot it would look if she made this exact move.

I dive in and feast on her until her legs give and she spills down to the floor, landing her ass on her heels as she twists to face me. I stand and my cock brushes her lips as I come to my full height.

My precum glistens from her lips as they catch the moisture. Carleen licks her lips and lifts her eyes to mine. I stare down at this woman, knowing as soon as I return home, I'm going to make her my wife.

She opens her mouth and covers me whole. I cup her jaw in one hand and wrap her ponytail around my other. My hips thrust forward as if having a mind of their own. I drop my head back and bare my teeth in a growl.

All stress from the last few days melts away. I'm breathless as she works me with her hands and mouth. My nostrils flare and I pant her name. Needing to brace myself, I reach for the counter behind her and ground myself.

"Baby," I groan. "That's so fucking good."

"Mm," she hums.

"I want you in my bed. I need you in my bed now."

"What if I can't wait that long?"

I push off the counter and look down into her eyes. The fire I see there matches what I feel inside. I don't think I can wait that long either. Reaching under her arms, I lift her up and place her on the counter before me. Wrapping my arms around her thighs, I pull her to the edge until her ass is almost hanging off.

With my palms behind her knees, I push into her hot, wet sex. She clenches around me, and I nearly blow on the spot. I grit my teeth and slowly work my hips.

"*Dario*," she cries.

"Yeah, baby? Tell me what you need. Pleasing you is my only goal in life. I'm yours. Own me, make me yours. Tell me what you need from me, how you need me to fuck you. How you like me fucking you."

I rub her clit as I continue to pump my hips. "You're so wet. Look how you cream for me. I could fuck this tight pussy all day. Is that what you want, what you need? Don't be shy, tell me, baby."

I grab the back of her neck and drag her to me. Crushing her lips, I kiss her like I'm trying to eat her face. I love this woman so fucking much. Every time I'm inside her, something inside me roars to life.

"Dario, I...I...I," she pants against my lips.

I cut her words off with a kiss. I'm not ready for us to go there yet. Once we do, there's no turning back. She'll be mine forever and where I go, she goes. I can't take her to Italy yet, so these words are impossible to be spoken.

"*Fuck*," I roar as I pull out and spill into my hand.

I don't think either of us thought about a condom. I chide myself for not thinking. It felt so good it wasn't a thought until I felt the first rope jet free.

Carleen runs a hand through the front of my hair and ducks her head to look me in the eyes. I lock eyes with her and peck her lips before moving to grab a paper towel and then washing my hands.

When I'm done and I find my legs, I move back to my woman and scoop her into my arms. I kiss her forehead as she wraps her long legs around my waist.

"Let's get you into my bed," I breathe against her skin.

"Only because you're carrying me," she says sleepily.

I chuckle and kiss her temple.

Carleen

"Rio?"

"Yeah, baby, what's up?" he replies and turns his head to plant kisses on my stomach.

I close my eyes and try not to burst into tears. I almost told him about the baby while he was making love to me in the kitchen. It was right on the tip of my tongue. All my love for him had come to the surface and the words wanted to burst free.

I calm myself as he settles his head back on my thigh, holding my hand in the air as he plays with my ring finger.

"Can I ask you something?"

"Yeah."

"Do you think I've done my thing with you? You know, losing myself in you, becoming a clone of you?"

He's silent for a moment. When he turns his hazel gaze on me, I realize I've been holding my breath. He furrows his brows.

"I never thought about it, but maybe a little. The way you took to cooking, I guess I can see where you might have sponged on me. I'm mean, you're damn good so…"

"Shut the hell up, Rio. I'm serious."

He chuckles and lifts to shift and lie beside me. He cups my face and runs his thumb across my lips. I stare up into his eyes as he searches my face.

"I think what you do is amazing. Yeah, you may have watched and picked up a ton of things while in the kitchen before you went to school, but you can't imitate a palate for flavors or intuitions for the most elevated and composed dishes."

I sigh. "I'm not just talking about in the kitchen though."

He snorts. "Outside the kitchen, you're nothing like me. You are everything I'm not. No, you haven't taken on who I am. You could never."

I reach to cup his face and search his eyes this time. I go to bite back my words, but something forces me to push forward.

"Why? Because I don't know who you really are?"

He stiffens and the shutters come down in his eyes. I think he's about to retreat from me altogether, but he purses his lips and shakes his head.

"There are parts of me you should never get to know or see. I've spent my entire life shielding you from so much. It's why I need you to trust me. Some things are better unknown."

"Is that realistic, Rio? Can we do this without me knowing who you truly are?"

He looks up at the ceiling and blows out a breath. I chide myself for pushing and ruining the moment. He reaches for my hand and brings it to his lips.

"I know we can. We have to. Losing you isn't an option in any of this. There's a lot going on, but I'm going to make it all go away one way or another. We'll be together. I promise."

I smile and snuggle closer to him. His heat is so welcoming. He wraps my legs with his and pins me beneath him. I look up into his eyes with my next words.

"And you've never broken a promise to me."

"I'll give my all to have you. My life, my title, everything I am. So be sure it's a promise I plan to keep."

The words are on the tip of my tongue, but I don't get them out as he shifts his body and slides into me and rocks my entire world, leaving me speechless.

CHAPTER TWENTY-FOUR

Who Are You?

Dario

It's Christmas Eve and I still haven't told Carleen about the change in my plans. Things have been too good the last few days. It's been like the calm before the storm.

I want to keep this feeling. I don't know how long I'll have to be without my woman and I'm already going through withdrawal. I haven't been able to stay away from her all service. I've abandoned my station and thrown the line off all night. Thank God for Apollo.

"Fire two rib eyes medium rare, an order of crab ravioli and an order of chicken francese," Anthony calls.

"Firing chicken francese," Carleen calls back.

"You're sexy when you cook."

"Dario," Car whines and wiggles in my hold as I cover her hand while she cuts the salmon in front of her. "What's going on with you? It's a short night. If you get your head in this, we can all finish and get out of here sooner."

"Time is ticking. I'm going to miss you," I breathe in her ear.

"Dude, this is not how we're going to run our business. This is a kitchen. Get it together, bro. You keep it up and you'll burn off that thing you keep poking me with."

I roar with laughter. God, I'm going to miss her and her humor.

"All right, all right. I know." I throw my hands in the air and back up to give her some space.

"You two are adorable," Daisy, one of our line cooks, coos.

"He's okay," Carleen says with a smile.

"I wish I had someone to love me so much," Daisy says.

I frown and work my jaw. I've come so close to telling Carleen I love her. Honestly, I've almost proposed a few times. I'm still going back and forth with whether I should give her the ring for Christmas. In my gut I know I should wait.

I go to save the moment as I realize it's been silent too long, but the day is saved by one of the waiters.

"Yo, Chef Car. There's some guy up front asking to see you."

Carleen looks up at me with confusion written all over her face. I chuckle when she frowns and points a finger at me.

"Wipe that smug look off your face. You made me fuck something up. If there's someone important out there tonight, I'm going to choke you."

I move behind her as she goes to walk away and lean into her ear while splaying a hand over her belly. "I'll let you choke me tonight while you ride me. We can take turns. I know how wet that shit makes you." I nip her ear and let her go.

I laugh as she trips a little over her feet. I remember when she used to have so much trouble walking in a straight line. I adore when she gets tripped up because I've turned her on.

However, I frown as I remember her accident after my mother disappeared. Carleen was in the hospital for about a week or two. At first, I had no idea, it was once she returned home Uncle Lucas took me to see her. Her memory was a little fucked up for a bit.

We haven't ever talked much about it. I think she was embarrassed.

"Fire two garlic butter salmon," is called, drawing my attention.

Shaking the memory off, I turn to wash my hands and fire the next ticket, knowing Car's absence will slow the line. After plating the two salmon dishes, I wash my hands again and get ready to head out front as my curiosity gets the best of me.

"Hey, boss," Salvatore calls as I get to the door that leads out to the dining room.

I turn to find him giving me that look. The look that says he needs to talk to me. I nod and go to meet him in the hallway to my office. We slip inside and I close the door behind us.

"What now?"

"I got a call from Gio. He said to let you know time is up. You have to leave tomorrow. Your grandfather is ready to make the trip tomorrow evening."

"Fuck, still no word on what this is all about?"

"*Stugots.*"

I work my jaw. He has dick and I feel like I'm being dicked at this point. Not even our lawyer could get me any straight answers.

"Okay, I'll be ready, I'll take my bags with me to Dante's. We can head straight out after Bella opens gifts."

Salvatore nods. I blow out a breath. I need to tell Carleen. I can't put this off any longer.

Carleen

Something is up with Dario, he's been super clingy the last few days. I don't mind, but it's been a bit much in the kitchen, especially tonight.

I can't wait to close this place for the night to get home and relax while I wrap the last of my gifts. I'll be going to my parents' after spending Christmas morning with Dario's family. I'll have to ask if we're still keeping our relationship from his brothers.

"Everyone's going to have questions when your belly pops," I murmur to myself.

When the time comes, the time comes.

I'm looking forward to Christmas tomorrow. I have the perfect gift for Bella. I think she's going to love the doll I got her. They'll both have matching outfits. The little doll resembles Bella and all, with hazel eyes, dark hair, and a brown complexion.

I stop our hostess, Shabel. "Hey, which table is asking for me?"

She turns and points to the exclusive tables where all our VIP guests make reservations to sit. My mouth falls open as soon as I see who's sitting at the table.

I groan, I'm not in the mood for this. I almost turn and head back into the kitchen. However, Lou stands the moment he sees me and waves me over.

"Carleen, you look lovely," he says as I stop at his table. He leans in to kiss my cheek. "Mom, I want you to meet Carleen. The friend I was telling you about."

"Hello," I say and hold my hand out.

She takes it limply as she rolls her eyes over me appraisingly. I stiffen and take my hand back. I don't need this woman's approval.

I'm not even interested in her son. I frown at her and her red hair and blue eyes. She looks nothing like Lou. It's time for her to get a touch-up on her hair color.

"Nice to meet you," she says.

I dismiss her and turn to Lou. "What are you doing here?"

"I was telling my mother how good the food is here and I had to bring her in. I was hoping you were working tonight so I could say hello. I hope things aren't too busy and that I'm not keeping you."

"Well, we are pretty busy tonight."

He frowns. "That's unfortunate. We'll have to come by some other time so you can sit and eat with us. Maybe my brothers can join us next time."

"Yeah, sure," I say to be polite.

Lou leans to kiss my cheek again, but before he can complete the gesture, I'm tugged out of the way. I know it's Dario instantly. My body hums from his nearness.

"Has everything on the menu been to your liking?" Dario says, his voice deep and his words firm.

"Actually, we haven't eaten yet," Lou replies.

"Um, that's strange. People usually call for the chef after they've eaten, not before. Unless they are special friends of ours."

"I am a special friend of Carleen's. My name is Lo—"

"Is that supposed to mean something to me?" Dario cuts him off.

I groan. This is not how I wanted these two to meet, not that they ever needed to meet after the level Dario and I have taken our relationship to.

"Not everyone can be a Di Lorenzo," Lou's mother huffs. She looks Dario over and turns up her nose.

I can't slap this man's mother. I can't slap this man's mother.

"Ma."

"What? She works for one of the largest names in the industry, what's the big deal? I'm not impressed."

"Nor do you need to be," I snarl. "And for your information, I'm co-owner of this establishment. I work with Chef Di Lorenzo, not for him."

She waves a dismissive hand at me. "Well, excuse me. Your father must be very proud of you," she says to Dario with a smug smile on her lips.

"Ma," Lou grinds out. He then sticks his hand out to Dario. "I've heard so much about you."

"And yet, I still can't recall who you are or why it matters."

"I'm Carleen's boyfriend."

I choke. "Excuse me, what?"

"I mean, we're taking a little break, but—"

"No, I told you I didn't think we should see each other anymore. You were the one who tried to bogart me into taking a break."

"Carleen," Lou hisses. "Can we not make a scene and talk about this later?"

"No," Dario and I say in unison.

"Lou, I'm in a relationship. I have no intention of seeing you again, not in a romantic sense."

"Or any other." Dario places a possessive hand on the back of my neck.

"Is he who you're seeing?"

I roll my eyes and suck my teeth. "If you must know, yes."

Lou narrows his eyes at Dario. Then looks to me. Something crosses his face before I can get a read on it.

"You said he was only a friend."

"Okay, *Biz*. Well, now he's not and we have a kitchen to get back to, so can you go somewhere else and sing about this?"

Dario snorts. I didn't mean to become all sarcastic, but I'm annoyed, tired, and becoming frustrated. Lou's face has turned several shades of red by now. Just when I think I'm going to have to kick his ass or restrain my man from doing so, Jace appears.

"Is there a problem here?" he asks.

"It's fine. I'm done here."

"Not a moment too soon. You were wasting your time anyway," Lou's mother mutters.

I suck my teeth and turn to head back into the kitchen. I leave Jace and Dario to their conversation as I calm my temper. I don't need this type of stress in my life.

Dario comes up behind me as I wash my hands, once I'm back inside. He wraps his arms around me and tightens his embrace.

"Biz Markie? You said she's just a friend?" He chuckles in my ear. "I might have been wrong. You are more like me than I thought. I've definitely rubbed off on you."

I turn in his arms and look up at him. "Yeah, whatever."

He pecks my lips. "That cocksucker isn't going to be a problem, is he?"

"No. I'll handle it if he tries to be. Come on, let's finish this service and go home. It's Christmas Eve, don't let him ruin our night."

He nods, but I can see he's still seething beneath the surface. He looks away from me, then back into my eyes.

"Listen, we need to talk."

My heart begins to race. There's no way he could have found out about the baby. Toni is the only person who knows. I haven't told anyone else.

"Things got pushed up and I'll be leaving for Italy tomorrow night."

"But it's Christmas." I pout.

"I know, baby. I'm so sorry. I'll make it up to you when I get back."

I push my hands into his hair, knowing I'll have to wash them again. I don't want him to leave. My heart feels like it's breaking.

"I wish we could leave. I don't want to be here knowing you're leaving tomorrow night."

"Your wish is my command. Apollo, you're in charge for the rest of the night. Merry Christmas all. Have a good one."

"Dario."

"You ask, I give. Let's go."

Gio

"Hello," I answer my phone as I sip at my cognac.

"All the players are on the board. Everyone is in place and where you need them to be," Jace's voice comes through the line.

"Good, we can finish this."

I hang up and toss back the rest of my drink. He's wrong though. A few players have moved to grab my attention. They need to find their way center stage. When the dust clears, there will only be so many left standing and they all belong to me.

CHAPTER TWENTY-FIVE

What Happened?

Dario

I have my legs straddled over Carleen's as I thrust inside her from behind. Taking my time, I pour more oil onto her ass and rub it into her skin. She moans and lifts her hips.

Swiftly, I slap one ass cheek and then the other. The way she creams on my cock causes me to bite my lip. Looking down, I marvel at the way her brown skin gives way to reveal the pink ring that's sucking me in.

"The most gorgeous pussy I've ever seen in my life," I groan.

I pull out and lift her hips in the air. When I drive back in, she collapses face-first into the pillow and screams my name. How the fuck am I supposed to leave her behind, even for half a second?

"Dario, please."

"I love it when you call my name."

I lean over her body and plant my hands beside her head, then ride her ass until I explode.

"Always so fucking good. I'm going to miss you so much."

"I'm going to miss you too."

She turns onto her back as I climb off her. Her breasts come into view, and I can't help but lean in and capture one peaked tip in my mouth.

"Dario, we have to get out of bed. Your family is expecting us."

"If this is the last time I get to have you for months, I want to enjoy it. Besides, I need to give you your present," I say against her skin, causing goose bumps to rise.

"Present?"

I release her nipple and look up at her with a smile. "Yeah, I wanted to give it to you in private this year."

"Oh, this sounds good," she says and rubs her hands together.

I chuckle and peck her lips. She's right, we do need to get moving. "Stay here until I come for you." I kiss her again and groan.

Reluctantly, I get up and head into the bathroom to draw her a bath. I move over to the cabinet I hid her gift in and pull out the bags. I start with pouring the bubble bath first. The aroma fills the room and brings the calm I need.

Next, I empty the rose petals into the bathtub. In the center, I place the floating tray the clerk suggested I get. Now for my decision, which gift box to place on the tray?

My heart screams for me to go with the engagement ring, but my mind tells me I need to wait. I open both boxes and stare. Everything in my nature says go with the ring.

"Rio, I have to pee, babe."

Making a choice, I quickly place the other box back in the bag and rush to place it back in my hiding spot. I move swiftly to place the box on the tray and give it a once-over.

"Come in," I call out.

Carleen pops her head into the bathroom with an adorable smile on her lips. The little minx. Her ass could have gone to any of the bathrooms in the apartment.

"Whatcha doing?"

I laugh. "Come here and see."

Carleen

I tiptoe into the bathroom like I'm about to rob the place. Rio starts to laugh more. It looks good on him. He's been so stressed out lately. I'm glad I decided not to add more to his plate. The news can wait, I keep telling myself. I move over to where he's standing.

"What are you up to?" I purr.

He wraps me in his arms and turns me around to face the tub. My breath catches as I see the small jewelry box floating in bubbles and roses. The box is open but not facing me.

Guilt has me frozen. Here I am keeping a huge secret from him and…my stomach drops when the box spins in the water to face me.

I release the breath I'm holding and burst into tears. It's not what I thought it was. I feel like such a fool.

"They're gorgeous," I choke out.

"They're three carats. The screw-back kind you wanted. Come, let me put them in for you."

"No, you don't have to."

"Baby, what's the matter? If you don't like them, I can get you something else. I thought they would look pretty on you."

My emotions are all over the place. I feel like I'm suffocating. Why am I so upset?

Because nothing in your life is certain. Everything is up in the air. Your restaurant, your career, your home, this relationship and now a baby. Nothing is stable.

"Car, talk to me."

Everything from the last few months comes crashing down on me. Then it hits me that I still don't have answers and he's leaving. My future has never been more uncertain.

"This is stupid. You're leaving, I'll be here. This isn't going to work. We ruined our friendship and for what?"

"What?" He looks at me incredulously. "Babe, is that time of month coming or something?"

"Wow, really? I never pegged you for toxic masculinity. I'm expressing my feelings so it must be that time of the month."

I know I'm losing it. I just can't shut my mouth. The hurt on his face should do the trick, but I keep going.

"Maybe I should go stay with my parents or at Toni's. This was such a bad idea."

I turn to leave the bathroom. He halts my retreat with a hand on my wrist. He places his face against the side of mine.

"Don't do this. I'm leaving tonight. These are the last hours we have for…don't do this."

"You don't even know for how long. I don't know what you're going for. For all I know, you could be going to marry someone your family has had picked out since before you were born."

He snorts. "Baby, what's really going on? What just happened?"

"I need some space. I'll be with my family. You go be with yours."

I tug away and storm out of the bathroom, feeling like a crazy woman and ready to fall completely apart. I sob as I run to the guest room. Once there, I fling my naked body on the bed and really cry.

What the hell is wrong with me?

CHAPTER TWENTY-SIX

Merry Christmas

Carleen

I sit in my old bedroom with my knees in my chest. This is not how I wanted to spend Christmas, but I'm too embarrassed to go to Dante's after what I did this morning.

The worst part is, I don't think Dario is even mad at me. He left the earrings on the kitchen counter with a note. I sniffle and wipe at my nose as I think of the words.

"Hey, what are you doing here? I didn't expect to see you until later. Where's Dario, everything all right?"

I burst into tears all over again. Toni moves into the room and closes the door behind her. I have my face in the pillow between my knees as I sob.

"Is it Dario, the baby? What's going on?" Toni whispers as she sits on the bed.

"It's me. This baby has turned me into a madwoman. I went off on Dario for no reason and now he's leaving, and I don't know for how long."

"Aw, Oopies. Calm down, honey. Tell me what happened."

"I…I…he bought me these." I finger one of my earrings.

Toni releases a long whistle. I roll my eyes at her and pout. She folds her arms over her chest.

"Okay, explain the problem. Please."

I blow out a breath. "I feel so stupid. I thought it was a ring at first. When I saw it wasn't, I sort of freaked out. I mean, look at my life right now."

"You're doing great. You have a fine-ass man, you have a business that's doing amazing. Again, what's the damn problem, Car? You're pissing me off and I'm not the one dating you."

I huff and ball my fists. "From the outside you would say all that. But see it from where I live."

"Explain."

"I spent all that money on that brownstone and I'm not even living in it. It's been problem after problem for weeks."

"Okay, construction shit. You knew the risks."

I glare at her. "I love the restaurant. I'm happy I made the decisions I did, but now I'm questioning it all. Did I follow my dream or Dario's? Can I keep the place going while he's gone? Will I ever master savory cooking?"

"*A*, I watched you torture yourself over being unhappy in the operating room. Do I think you could have looked at other options before entering the kitchen? Yeah, but I also think what you did was wise. You relied on that weird shit your brain does and girl, you're badass in the kitchen.

"Honestly, I think that would have been the case with Dario or not. Stop putting so much pressure on yourself and enjoy what you're accomplishing as a chef. Car, if only you knew how they lick my ass at work because they know I'm related to you, and they all want reservations to your restaurant.

"*B*, you run that place like a tight ship. You'll be fine. You're a brilliant woman. You have Thompson blood, eh. We don't fail.

You will keep that place going and probably earn some damn award or something while doing so.

"C, your pastries are to die for, but so are your salmon, steak, and those pasta dishes you make. Again, take some of that pressure to be perfect off yourself."

"And this baby? How could I be so stupid to get pregnant? I don't even know how it happened. We've used condoms every time."

"Boo, that man is so fine, I'm sure his swimmers said fuck this condom, we're coming through, she needs to carry our fine-ass babies."

I cover my face with my hands. "Where the hell do you come up with this shit?"

She laughs and falls back onto the bed. I shove her thigh and laugh with her. I feel a little better.

"So what's the problem again? Because none of that's working for me."

I bite my lip. I can't tell her I have concerns about his family's business dealings. Or that I think I'm having the baby of a mobster.

"I have your gift downstairs. It's a Birkin."

"So why are we still in here? Say less, Oopies, run me my gift."

We get up and start to head out of the room. Toni stops and turns to me. She folds her arms over her chest.

"Call him and say sorry. He's your best friend. The earrings were a nice gift."

"I know."

I think back to his words in his note. *This is just the beginning of me spoiling you for the rest of our lives. Trust me. Wait for me.*

Dario

I'm still confused as fuck about what happened this morning. I'm trying to put on a happy face for Bella and the rest of my family.

I feel like such an ass for reading Carleen's diary. I brought this all on myself.

If I had never read it, I would have kept my feelings to myself, and I'd be off to Italy without all this on my head. Now, I don't even know where we stand, and because she's still my best friend, I'm not going to press her.

This is so unlike Carleen. She's never been like this. Our morning had been going great. Great sex, we talked a bit about me leaving, everything was fine.

"What's on your mind?" Gio asks as he finds me in Dante's theater room by myself.

I came in here to take a break from all the false smiling I've been doing. I should have known someone would find me. I run a hand through my hair.

"I fucked up," I admit.

"How so?"

"I read Carleen's diary. She had some things written in there about me. I acted on the feelings I've had for her, but the timing is so fucked up and I feel like I'm losing her and our friendship."

Gio grunts and moves into the room to take a seat beside me. I look to my older brother and feel like a little kid all over again. After Ma, Gio spent most of his time in Italy with Nonno, but whenever he was around, he was the best big brother one could ask for.

Nonno made us all closer. He closed the gap between us. Age, distance, you name it. Nonno made sure none of that mattered. We're brothers and we do what we have to for each other. Which is why guilt sets in for not telling him about Carleen sooner.

"You know what I love about you?"

"What's that?"

"Your curiosity. When we were younger, that shit used to get on my fucking nerves. I couldn't do anything without you asking questions or trying to figure shit out."

I snort a laugh. "Yeah, I bet."

"Now as a man, I respect it. It's taught me something. If you don't ask questions, you don't have understanding. You read her diary and learned something you didn't fully understand. I've known for years that Carleen is in love with you.

"There is nothing you can do to ruin the way she loves you, short of cheating on her. Have you cheated?"

"Fuck outta here. I'd never cheat on her. I…" I take a pause. "I'd give everything up for her. This indictment is the only reason I'm leaving. If the feds didn't have a hard-on for me, I wouldn't be going. All I want is her, Gio. Nothing else in this life matters. Only her."

He places a hand on my shoulder and gives a gentle squeeze. His eyes soften for the briefest moment. "I know the feeling. Listen to me. Good things are coming your way, Dario, more than you know. In time it will all work out and make sense. Breathe. I promise, little brother. If it takes my last breath, this I promise you. You will have Carleen and the life you've always wanted."

"How? It's all so fucked up."

"Trust me."

I nod, feeling his words in my bones. I do trust Gio. I don't know how he can fix this, but I trust him.

"Now, *Nonno* sent me looking for you. He wants to give you something."

I nod and stand to follow him. When we get up to the first floor, I have to bite back a growl when I hear Papa Esposito's voice. I knew there was a chance he'd be here today, but I was hoping his ass wouldn't show his face.

"Dario, there you are," he croons as I come into view.

"Grandfather."

"What is this? First you ignore my calls, now you're greeting me coldly. What have I done?"

"How about telling an eight-year-old girl she should stick to her own kind? Have you always been out of your fucking mind?" I growl and storm for him.

Gio and Jace jump between us, placing a hand on each of my shoulders. I go to shove by them both, but my phone goes off. I rush to pull it from my pocket and read the text from Carleen.

I sag in relief. I wasn't leaving with this shit between us like this. One more hour and I was heading to her parents' to work this out.

Car: *I'm sorry. I trust you. Have a safe trip. Let me know when you get there safely. I'll be waiting.*

I point to my grandfather. "Keep your ass away from me."

I turn and storm from the room while returning a quick reply to the text. When I lift my head, to my surprise, I find Nyla and Nonno huddled together in the hall. Nyla has her back to me. Her hair has been pinned up since earlier, now revealing the back of her neck and shoulders.

The tight sweater dress she has on is off the shoulder and reveals the figure my brother seems to be so drawn to. It's nice, but nothing like Carleen's. However, that's not what has my attention.

She has a bold tattoo in the center of her shoulder blades. The dark letters read *Doll Master*. Jace comes out of the great room from the other entrance and places a hand over the tat, causing Nyla to look up at him.

He gives her a warm smile before leaning to whisper into her ear. Nyla laughs and places a hand on his chest. My curiosity goes through the roof.

"Ah, Dario," Nonno croons. "Come, I have something for you."

Nyla hands him a gift bag and Nonno turns and starts for Dante's study. I follow, turning only once to find Jace and Nyla laughing as Jace pulls the stick from her hair, causing it to fall and cover the tat once again. His eyes lock on mine and he winks.

What the fuck?

I enter the study and close the door behind me. "You are still curious about so much. I can't give you all the answers now, but I feel it only right to clear up these lies you've been told. You are still curious about Gio's lifestyle, no?"

Hell yeah, especially after what I just saw. Nyla touched Jace in a familiar way. Jace hardly ever allows anyone to get close to him, nor does he get close to you if he doesn't know you.

"Tell me, what is it you think you know that I don't?" Nonno asks as I get lost in my musing.

"I was told Gio is bi, a *finook*. His dolls aren't just for him, they're for him and Jace and the two have been together for years." Nonno snorts in what seems to be disgust. "I should have him killed for the lies he has spread," he says heatedly. "*Stupido figlio di puttana*. Riccardo was once a dear friend. Greed and disloyalty plague his heart. It has made him blind and stupid. You…do you believe this about my Michelangelo?"

"I don't know what I believe. He's my brother so I don't care either way. If he's happy, I'm happy. However, I've never seen Jace and Gio apart and I've never seen Jace in a relationship. I've only seen him with Gio and those dolls once or twice. To be honest, even then I couldn't make any assumptions about them." I stop and laugh.

"What? What do you find so funny?"

"Have you seen them? The dolls Gio has. I was too busy being in awe of my big brother to think of much else. They're gorgeous women. I mean, the type of women you'd sell your balls for."

Nonno scoffs and waves me off. "And this is what makes your brother special. Come, take this." He holds out the gift bag Nyla gave to him.

I go to sit and look inside. As I remove the box inside, a knock comes at the door. Papa Esposito pushes into the room and the air around us shifts.

"Dario, I'm ready to take my leave. I think we are done here."

I push the box back into the bag. I hear what's not said. We're leaving.

"Dario, can we talk?"

I snap my head up, but I'm no longer in the here and now. I'm thrown back in time. His voice…it's the trigger.

Dante had been sad all day. Ever since I found him in his room playing alone earlier. I don't know what happened and he won't tell me what's wrong. I think he got in trouble with Mama.

Gio and Jace went out with their skinny friend, the one with the dark makeup, who's always around. I think she's related to Gwen, but then again Gwen treats everyone like family. Beth, Mama's personal guard is close to Skinny Girl too.

However, after some thought about it, Mama was always nice to Gio's friend as well. Although this one is the only one Mama really talked to. I wondered why that was?

Maybe I should ask. I headed for Mama's study to do just that. I had nothing else to do. I'd already taken my bath and put on my pajamas like I was told.

Yes, I want to know if Skinny Girl is related to Gwen or Beth and why Mama seems to like her more than the others. I get close to the study and that's when I hear the voices.

"Why do you hate my son so much? Why can't you leave him alone?"

"I've warned you repeatedly about the friends he keeps. If this gets back home, you're going to ruin your family's name."

"You speak of things you know nothing about," Mama says in her angry voice.

I don't know who the man is. He sounds familiar but I can't be sure it's who I think it is. The anger in his voice makes me question who he could be.

"This isn't what we agreed to. My son was meant to be head of the family. You've given more respect to those mulignons in New York. You won't even take his name and now this. The insult."

"Is that your real problem? I won't bow to your son, and he will never have the title of head of my family."

"Ava, please." That's Papa.

Why is he allowing this man to talk to my mother like this? He tells us all the time to protect our women. Why isn't he protecting Mama?

"You shut the fuck up. You...you're the reason things are the way they are. You're a pussy and she treats you like one."

"I think it's time for you to leave." Mama sounds so angry. She doesn't even get this mad at me and Dante when we're bad.

"No problem, but know that I won't stand for this. This isn't over."

It sounds like Mama clears her throat. "You should respect who I am and what my papa has decided. If I have to make myself clear, I'll erase your entire bloodline. I'm a Di Lorenzo by blood, don't make me prove it."

"You're a whore, your son is a finook, and that other little one is a psychopath waiting to happen."

"Enough." I know that growl, it's Uncle Lucas.

"You," the man roars and scoffs. "You're lucky to be who you are."

"And you will be wise to remember who I am. We're not too far from the other side for your actions to have repercussions. Now leave as Ava asked you to."

Footsteps moved in my direction. I took off for the stairs to hide. I bit my lip as I flattened against the wall. My eyes were squeezed shut as I held my breath.

"That's a huge problem. I think it's time we send word to your father," Gwen's voice fills the hall.

"I can no longer trust anyone. I need to go to my father myself."

"I'll go with you," Uncle Lucas says.

"No, I need you here to watch over my boys. Gio, Jace, Dario and Dante are my world. None of this matters if something happens to them. That man has a hard-on for Gio and Jace. They're not safe around him."

"I'll go." That's Mrs. Beth.

"Dario, *Dario Giancarlo Luca Di Lorenzo.*"

I shake my head and focus on Nonno growling my name. He gives me a nod to follow him. I stand, trying to find my bearings.

That memory. It's so much clearer now. I remember more details. The voice of the angry man, that was Papa Esposito. He was in that room.

I snarl as I brush by him in the doorway. This motherfucker. When I find out the truth, I have a feeling I'm going to need to flay his ass.

"Dario."

"I told you to stay away from me," I bark at him without stopping.

CHAPTER TWENTY-SEVEN

Viewing The Past

Dario

I sit on the plane, awaiting takeoff. The memory from earlier clinging to my brain. Why have I never put one and one together before?

I don't remember much about Papa Esposito before Mama disappeared. He became a presence in my life, even more so after the fact. One of the reasons I was surprised and a bit shocked he approached Carleen after our playground wedding.

"You should open my gift. We have a long flight. I can explain it while we're in the air," Nonno says.

I bob my head and reach for the bag in the seat next to me. Nonno sits across from me, watching me closely. I take the box out and place it in front of me. Removing the lid, I reveal what looks to be a picture album.

I remove it from the box and push the box out of the way. When I flip to the first page, I smile. At first, I think it's a picture of me and Dante. However, one of the babies has blond hair. I look at the hospital bands beneath the photo and lift a brow.

"Gio and Jace?"

"Yes," Nonno says with a smile in his voice.

"My first extended stay to the States was for their birth. Your mother was so happy for her friend and his son. You would have thought Jace was her own boy. From that day, the two have done everything together."

I flip the page. It's like a few years have passed by. Gio stands between Jace and a little brown girl with knobby knees. Gio has an arm around each of their necks.

"He's always been a protector. Those two were his to protect. You messed with them, and he'd declare war on everything you hold dear.

"I'll never forget their first summer in Italy. The three were so adorable. Jace has always been the quiet one. His life started hard and only got harder. Well, some of the kids in town were picking on Jace.

"That little one there"—he taps another photo of Gio, Jace and the girl—"she's as protective as Gio. She beat up a few of the boys, but one made the mistake of placing a hand on her.

"Gio was already angry about Jace, but when he saw Ny's lip. I learned my grandson was an entirely different person from the sweet boy we thought him to be. We had to send them all back to the States while I smoothed things over—"

I froze and look down at the picture more closely. Then cut him off. "Wait, Ny as in Nyla?"

Nonno nods and his eyes twinkle as he looks back at me. "Yes, this is the same girl. Do you not remember her?"

"No, I…Oh shit. The skinny girl with the Goth makeup. That was Nyla?"

"Yes, my boy. Beth's oldest daughter."

I lick my lips as my curiosity burns. A million more questions fill my head.

"I remember Beth. How does she fit into all of this? What happened to her?"

"Not yet, first you have to understand the lies, then I can unwrap the rest of what you seek."

I keep flipping through and find page after page of pictures of Gio, Jace, and Nyla. With each picture, they seem to grow closer. However, once I get to the back of the book, something has changed. Nyla is missing and the happiness is gone.

Gio and Jace look to be about sixteen. I note this must be around the time my ma disappeared. The anger in Gio's face is palpable. I remember that time. He was so full of rage, it's why he left to begin with.

I look up from the album into Nonno's eyes. "I never asked before because I've only known him to be like a brother and a part of our family, but what happened to Jace's family? How did he end up with us?"

Nonno nods and thins his lips. He gives a nod before he speaks. "Emil, the Dane. He, your mother, and Beth were as tight as those three." He nods at the album. "The year you were born. I received a call one night. I thought your mother was calling with news about you boys. The way my daughter screamed over the phone.

"It broke my heart. Ava was so strong. To hear her sob that way wasn't right. She loved Emil and Jace..."

"This one is hard. The memories are still fresh as if not from thirty-five years ago. Jace watched the murder of his father and mother. He then walked over ten miles barefoot in the rain to your home. Not one of them would allow Jace to be raised by anyone else. So he became ours. That night sealed all our fates."

"Wow, I didn't know any of that."

"Yes, well, there is a lot you don't know. Riccardo told you all the things he wanted you to know, but none of the truth."

"But why allow him to feed me such poison?"

"Have I not taught you boys that every move has a counter and should always have a purpose? When we ring this bell, it will sound around the world and you, my boy, needed to have a taste of the blood in the water, you needed to see the man for who he is, and I needed him to get comfortable. You, make him comfortable."

I run my hand through my hair. It's clear there's an enormous picture here I'm not getting a full view of.

Marone.

CHAPTER TWENTY-EIGHT

Welcomes & Realities

Dario

Two weeks later...

"You did well, my boy," Nonno croons as we enter his study in his Catania home.

"You think it went well?"

"It all went as planned."

I take in the room, remembering this place from when I was a small boy. Not much has changed, it still smells of cigars and Nonno's cologne.

However, I do notice the frames on the bookshelves. I don't know if it's because I'm taller or because they were recently placed there. For some reason, I don't recall ever seeing them before. I glance at a few of the pictures. A smile comes to my lips as I notice one of me and my brothers.

"The meeting was shorter than I was expecting."

Nonno laughs. "They had to go for their naps."

"I wasn't expecting them all to be so old."

"Ha," Nonno gives a full belly laugh. "You speak as if I'm not an old man. You boys are the ones who keep me young."

"I didn't mean it like that. It's just you've always been so vibrant. I don't see you as old. Those guys are one breath from meeting Jesus. You still chase after Bella, and I hope someday soon you'll be able to chase after a little one of my own."

"I can't wait for it. Carleen will make an excellent mother."

"Carleen?"

He gives me a pointed look. "You have been in love with her since you were a little boy. I saw it the first time I saw you two together. Your mother loved her. She had hoped you two would grow to be more."

"Really? With this thing of ours? How would that be possible?"

"You confuse me with that room of old men we just left behind. I didn't always see things the way I do now, but things change, people change."

"How so?"

"Come, come, sit with me and have a drink and a cigar." He waves me to get the drinks and smokes while he moves for the wingback chairs in front of the fireplace and takes a seat.

Someone from the staff must have started the fire that was going before our arrival. This big place can have a chill to it at night. I move to the bar and pour us both a drink. Handing Nonno a glass, I grab two cigars from his cigar box.

"Thanks. You're a good boy, Dario. You know that?"

"I try."

"You've always been a good boy. When you were little, you were observant and smart. A lot like your mother."

"Ma was the best." I nod and light my cigar.

"My little girl. The reason I am the man I am. You know, I was a hard man once. Ruthless, they called me. Then I met your *nonna*. I fell in love at first sight, she made me a better man. She was a beautiful woman. *La mia bellezza.* I married her right away, after a year, she was expecting with your mama. We planned to have a houseful of children, but we were older and your *nonna* didn't make it through the childbirth.

"I couldn't bring myself to marry another. It was me and my Ava, my little *bambina*. I raised your mother on my own. Taught her everything I knew."

"How did she end up in America?"

"Your mother, she was strong willed. When she became a teenager, it was America this and America that. I was growing older and wanted her to see the world, gain some knowledge, prepare her a bit more for this thing of ours.

"Wait, hold on. What are you trying to say, *Nonno*?"

"I named your mother my successor. She was the Donna of the Di Lorenzo family. This...it's an acceptable thing here, especially in Naples—rare, but acceptable, there have been others.

"Ava was a strong one. She surrounded herself with all the right people. However, someone wanted her out of the way, with my failing health at the time, they saw an opening and started to remove her circle."

"Why do I feel like I'm missing a big piece here?"

"Ah, because you are. The real reason you are here has yet to be revealed. Just know when the time is right, I will be at your wedding to our little friend, Carleen. Things are changing all around us, *nipote*. The old ways of thinking and doing things are turning on their heads. Your mama changed a lot of the things I thought. It's a good thing she did because the storm that's coming will eat the weak minded and unyielding."

"Where does Gio fit into all of this?"

"That's my boy. Always asking questions. This one is good. You are here to be a fresh face, I am old, they don't respect me the same. They have their young people in their ears. America has changed so much. You, you are young and have years before you. Proof the Di Lorenzo bloodline lives in strength. That room you settled today with your presence was our first goal.

"Even if I didn't come out and name you my successor, they assumed as much and that's what we wanted. In that room were half friends, half foes. You, *mio nipote* brought us more friends.

"Gio is a...what do they call it in America? Ah, yes, a carbon copy of your mother. You, *mio nipote,* are the rabbit your brother is about to pull from the hat. Your job is to sit in the hat and hold everyone's attention."

"What?"

"You are a chef, Dario. This is who we've always wanted you to be. Take this time with me to plan what you will do when you return home, the family you will build. Everyone has a part, yours is to distract from what your brother is doing."

"Why not tell me this before now?"

Nonno empties his glass. Then looks me in the eyes. "Today, I watched you walk into a room like a true Di Lorenzo boss. That is what we needed them to see. If you knew the truth, there was no guarantee you would have walked into that meeting and certainly not with the energy that was necessary. *Capire?*"

"Yes, I'm starting to understand a lot."

Nonno stands and pats my cheek. I look up at him and smile. "I'll leave you to think. There is more to learn of the past. We will share it all with you in the right time.

"You will return home as soon as this business is finished. For now, enjoy. My home is your home. This other business back in the States will work out. It's being made sure of. You can relax."

With that, my grandfather leaves the room. I take a long drag from my cigar as my mind reels. This changes everything. I'm finally going to marry my best friend, there's nothing to stop me.

I need to call my woman. We have much to discuss. I want her here with me, but we both can't be MIA from the restaurant at the same time for so long. Maybe she can come join me closer to when I plan to return.

I'm not going to be the Don. Wow, what the fuck just happened?

I look down at my watch. Fuck, she should be in the middle of the dinner service. I'll have to wait a few hours for her to get home before I try to call.

I dial Gio instead. I need a favor.

"Dario, how you doing?"

"I'm great now that I understand what's going on. Listen, I need to talk to Car. Her phone, the connections ain't so good. Can you get her a line that's clear?"

"Not a problem. You need anything else?"

"No, I just want to talk to her. Make that happen for me."

"You got it."

He hangs up without another word.

Carleen

My thoughts have been preoccupied with the little sonogram pictures in my backpack. I had my first glimpse of our baby today. Talk about a dose of reality.

I've had a little baby growing inside me for ten weeks now. This peanut is real, I'm going to be a mother. A part of me wishes I had told Dario, so I'd have someone to gush about this with. I miss him already.

"Wow, what's the smile about? I thought for sure you were going to be miserable for the entire time the boss is away. I was willing to bet on it. You're costing me money here," Daisy teases.

I turn to her and wrinkle my nose. "First, when do I give you guys time to bet on my happiness? I think I'm slacking. Second, it's been two weeks. Can't I be happy? I didn't burn the place down or cause us to have an empty dining room. I'm proud of myself."

It's only half of the truth. I don't plan to tell anyone about the baby until I have to. If I'm not showing, no one will be knowing.

"Did you seriously doubt that would happen? You run one of the best kitchens I've ever worked in. Your work ethic has been A1 since day one. I admire that. I think Dario does too. I see him watching you with that proud grin, even before you two became a couple."

I smile as I sauce the plate in front of me. "Balsamic salmon, table fifty-six in the window," I call as I think about Daisy's words.

I'll admit I've been doing a lot better than I thought I would. Apollo informed me on our first day without Dario that my man had added my dish to the menu.

I was so nervous the first few nights. However, it's become a favorite. I had to double the seafood order for the scallops.

I can't wait to talk to Dario and tell him about its success. Maybe I can hide my excitement about the baby with news about the restaurant.

I run an arm across my brow and look up at the clock, it's almost closing time. I can't wait to get home and take a nice bath. Hopefully, I'll get a call tonight.

"Okay, guys, that was the final ticket. That's a wrap for the night," Apollo calls out.

I give a clap. "Great job, guys. Another awesome night."

"Yo, chef, Jace is out front looking for you."

I wipe my hand on a towel and start out of the kitchen. As soon as I step into the dining room, I find Jace at the back table near the kitchen.

"Hey, Jace."

He nods and stands. Without a word, he hands me a phone. I look up at him in confusion.

"Dario will call you on this line. I'll see you home tonight too. Take your time, I'll wait here."

"O…*kay*. Can I get you something to eat?"

He gives a small smile. "A couple out front raved about a new dish as I walked in."

"Ah, the scallops and pasta with herbs. I got you."

"Thanks."

He shrugs out of his black leather and retakes his seat. Not for the first time I note how handsome he is. His eyes are a light green tonight. He has his hair in a topknot and his black jeans and green thermal speak volumes to the broad and chiseled body he carries so well.

I head back in the kitchen and go to make Jace something to eat. Starving myself, I make two servings. Thankfully, Apollo and Anthony are handling cleanup tonight. I'll check everything after I get some food into my system.

"Here you go," I say to Jace as I place a plate in front of him.

"Do you mind if I join you?"

He stands and nods for the seat next to him in the booth. I smile and take it, not expecting him to say much. Once I'm seated, he retakes his seat and we both tuck in.

"This is amazing," he says, surprising me.

I swallow and smile at him. "You know, I've never heard you say much for as long as I've known you. I used to think you didn't talk at all."

"Remember when I told you about my parents?" I nod. "Well, I had a heavy accent as a child, my mother didn't speak English well and my father spoke it when it suited him. I was teased a lot in school, so I refrained from talking. I would only speak to Gio."

"That makes sense. It's a shame though. You have such a soothing voice."

"So I've been told."

The phone he gave me rings in my pocket. I pull it out and answer.

"Hello."

"Hey, baby," Dario replies cheerfully.

My face hurts from smiling so hard. "Excuse me," I say to Jace and get up to pace the restaurant while the staff cleans the dining room. "I was hoping I'd get to talk to you. How are things?"

"They are much better than I thought they would be. I miss you like crazy though. How's the restaurant?"

"Things are great. My dish is a hit."

"I saw the sales from last week. You're doing amazing. I told you, you would."

"I must say, I'm proud of myself."

"I'm proud of you too, baby. How you doing? This isn't too much for you, is it? I mean, with the renovations and all."

"I'm fine. A little tired tonight, but I'm great."

"Are the guys still closing the kitchen? Do you need to go?"

"You hang up and I'll be on the first flight to Italy to slap box you," I tease.

He groans. "I wish. Just hearing your voice has me hard."

I stumble to a stop and look around as if someone has overheard him. I cross my legs to squeeze my thighs together. Bath time will definitely involve a little flicking the bean tonight.

"I wish I could do something about that for you."

"Soon."

"Does that mean you're coming back?"

"Not yet, but I was thinking... You should come join me. This is a beautiful place to talk about and plan a future."

My heart races. I would love to join him. However, I know it's not possible. I have to be here for the restaurant and to oversee my place.

"I can't. I want to so bad, but I can't."

"I know. I'm coming off a high from a great day. It's wishful thinking. Carleen?"

"Yes?"

"Nothing. Go finish up so Apollo can get you home."

"Oh, Jace is here. He mentioned seeing me home. You know, you don't have to have someone escort me every night."

"But I will. Keep this phone. I have some things I want to talk to you about."

"Oh, yeah, like what?"

"Not tonight, you sound exhausted. We'll talk soon. Good night."

"Good night, Dario."

CHAPTER TWENTY-NINE

Reacquainted

Gio

"Ladies, this is it. We only need to trigger her memory. I'm hoping she'll do the rest," I say to Nyla and Holly.

"You think it will work?" Holly replies.

"Yeah, I think it will."

I've been sitting on a sleeper for years, waiting for the right time to wake her. All of my dolls have a purpose. Now is when I need them. My collection is almost complete. However, this one isn't for me. I have my very own.

I remember seeing what Carleen is capable of. She was all but five. Her accident was unfortunate, but we all thought it best to leave the truth asleep, so to speak.

"Holly, I want you to work your way into the hostess position at *Anima Mias*. You can watch over her while there. She'll become aware of the vacancy within the hour," I say as I finish my text and put my phone away.

"Got it. Thanks for the opportunity."

I nod and glance back at Nyla. She's still trying not to make eye contact with me. I'm prepared to do this dance for as long as she wants. Patience has become my strong suit.

The ladies exit the SUV and I turn to Jace. I've felt his eyes on me this entire time. "What?" I snap.

"She's annoyed."

"When isn't she? Let's go, I have shit to do. We're going to see that friend of ours."

He grunts and starts the car, pulling off without another word. I'll always be the villain, no matter how much I work to protect everyone.

I'm fine with that. I accepted the fact a long time ago. So be it.

Carleen

I sit catching my breath and calming my nerves. I'm a little pissed off. Fraya was a bit more aggressive than usual. I beat her ass after that one kick near my ribs.

I think it's time I find a different type of workout until after the baby is born. I read that I could continue for at least the first trimester, but since I don't plan to tell Fraya my business, this will be my last day.

"Hey, you."

I look up, wiping my forearm across my forehead. Nyla and, to my shock, the woman from the coffee shop five years ago is standing in front of me. I gasp and jump up to hug the woman who changed my life and listened to me make a huge decision in my career.

"Hey, Doc," she says.

I release her and hold her at arm's length. She's about my height, maybe an inch taller. She's still as pretty as I remember. Her hair is pulled back away from her face in a messy bun.

Nyla looks between the two of us. "You two know each other?"

"Yeah, remember a while back I told you about that resident I met? She was totally cool, and we talked for all that time."

"Oh, yeah. This was her? What a small world. This is my sister's bosses' brother's business partner and best friend."

"No shit, Doc. Is she serious?"

"It's actually Chef now and the best friend is kind of my boyfriend these days."

Nyla lifts a brow. "Oh really? I thought I picked up on something there."

"Oh, that's awesome. You took the leap with your career. How are things? Are you happy?"

A face-splitting smile covers my face. I'm more than happy. Much happier than I was five years ago.

"Yes, things are wonderful."

"We have to catch up. You want to join us for this mixed martial arts class?"

"I just finished my kickboxing training. I was actually on my way out."

"Oh, come on. Please, I've often thought about you and wondered how things went. Stick around, we can grab a bite after."

I look to Nyla and smile. I'm in some pretty damn gorgeous company. I'm not insecure, I know how to give a woman her props and these two are a testament to the beauty of tall dark-brown women. Going out to lunch with them is sure to turn heads. I chew on my lip, it's been so long since I've had time for new friends, I miss Blake and Toni has been busy.

"Okay, why not? I've always been curious about that class. I'd love to sit in."

"It's an awesome class, but I honestly love the range more. Quick and to the point."

"You mean the gun range?"

"Yes, Ny and I go twice a week. You should join us sometime."

I think back to Dario and his words that day we were here together. *I'm leaving. This is the one thing I know you have to protect yourself while I'm gone.*

"You know what, I might take you up on that too."

"Cool, we'll exchange information this time. Hopefully, we can stay in touch."

"Yeah, I've wondered how things worked out for you too. I'm so happy to see you."

"Shit, he's always right," Nyla says, almost to herself.

I look to her and wrinkle my brows. She has a frustrated look on her face.

"Holly," my old coffee mate says, grabbing my attention as she holds out a hand.

"Oh, I'm Carleen. I can't believe I told you so much about me and I never got so much as your name."

We both laugh. "Truth be told, I probably wouldn't have told you. Not back then."

***

"Ugh," I groan as I check my phone I've just taken from my locker.

"Problem?" Nyla asks.

"My hostess at the restaurant has quit. She didn't even give me notice. What am I supposed to do?"

And so it begins. This is the type of thing I was afraid of. How am I supposed to fix this by tonight?

"I've done some hostess work and I'm sort of in between gigs. That is if you need someone," Holly says and shrugs.

I chew on my lip. Our old hostess was very attractive and charismatic. Holly fits the same description. "Really? You'd be saving me."

"Hon, tell me the time and place and I'm there."

I sag down onto the bench and exhale. "Thank you."

"No problem. Like I said, I needed to find work as it is. You're actually doing me a favor."

She drops her towel to her side and saunters her way into the shower. I take notice of the bold two-line tat in the center of her shoulder blades. It says *Doll House* on top, and underneath in smaller lettering, I think it says, *Master NY.*

I try to remember if she told me she was from New York. I talked so much back then, I don't know if I allowed her to tell me much. I frown at myself.

"You decide where you want to go for lunch?" Nyla asks, drawing my attention.

"I was thinking I'd take you guys to the restaurant and cook for you both."

"You don't have to do that. I think Holly wanted time to catch up with you."

"My sous-chef should be there by the time we arrive. He'll help so I can spend more time with you guys. It's not a big deal."

"Okay, if you say so. Thanks."

With that, she tosses her towel around her neck and holds the ends as she walks into the shower.

CHAPTER THIRTY

Get it from Nonno

Dario

Four weeks later...

I stand in the great room of Nonno's home, staring out of the window. There's a beautiful view of the sea from here. I've found myself in front of these windows a lot since I've been here.

"What is with the long face? Did you not make your phone call to America?"

"I got through, but she's always tired. We never get to talk much."

I'm worried I placed too much on her shoulders. Running that place is a lot of work for the two of us together. I can't imagine what must be going on without me there.

"You do something romantic for her, yes? Remind her how much you're thinking of her and want to be there."

"I hadn't really thought about that. I've been trying to figure out how to get her here with me."

Nonno sighs. "You young people. She's still at your place, no?"
"She is."

"Send flowers. Lavish her with gifts. You are my grandson,
show your Di Lorenzo charm. We Italians are suave, debonair, we
are the masters of romancing women."

I chuckle. "You're right. Thanks, *Nonno*."

"Ah, to be in love. It's a wonderful thing. I will never regret
losing my heart to your *nonna*."

I move to take a seat next to Nonno on the sofa. Other than
missing Carleen, I have been enjoying my time here with him. He
loves to tell stories and only wants someone to listen.

"What about my parents, were they in love?"

Nonno gives me a strained smile. I study his face and take in
his posture. The tension I see there is new.

"Well, yes, between your parents, there was love. Gio is so
much like your mother. She had a big heart and loved those close
to her.

"If you were hers, you were hers. There was a time I wasn't so
sure I'd have grandchildren from Ava. Gio changed everything."

"Yeah, how so? What do you mean?"

"I don't like to talk of things that aren't my own to tell if it
can be told by someone who understands it better than I do. Your
father should be the one to explain what happened back then. I
think those still alive should give you those answers. Only they
can explain what really happened."

"*Nonno*," I say in frustration. "You said I would have answers
once I arrived here. All due respect, but the things I really want to
know, you're talking in circles about them. What happened to my
ma?"

There, it's out there. I want the truth. I'm not going to dance
around this as he seems to be doing. I want the whole truth.

"Circles are never ending. Go order Carleen some flowers. I'll
see you at dinner."

I grit my teeth and ball my fists. This is driving me crazy. I
know he has the answers I need. The more time I spend here, the
more I know there was more to my mother's disappearance.

However, I bite my tongue and flop back on the couch. My mind turns to Papa Esposito. Maybe I should go back to the States and step on his neck for the truth.

And end up in cuffs?

I growl and toss an arm over my face. If I were Dante that's exactly what I would do. However, I'm not my twin. I need answers. I'm not going to ignore that I'm missing something.

***

I can't sleep. I've been walking the halls thinking about my talks with my grandfather. He wouldn't say any more during dinner.

My phone rings as I enter the great room, headed for the window with the view, hoping to settle my mind. When I pull it from my pocket, I see it's Carleen.

"Hey, baby," I answer.

"Hey, you. It's so good to hear your voice. What are you doing?"

"I can't sleep. I'm walking the halls of the house. How are you?"

"I'm fine. It's my day off. I thought I'd call while I have some energy. I miss you."

"I miss you more."

"Thanks for the flowers. I was so surprised when they arrived."

"Did they bring a smile to your face?"

"Yes, they did, as did the bracelet."

I sent her a diamond tennis bracelet to match her earrings. I know it will look amazing on her. Jewelry always stands out against her skin.

"I wish I were there to see your face. Listen, you have perfect timing. I need to get something off my chest."

I open the French doors and step outside to inhale the sea air. Between Carleen and the salty air, my nerves calm a bit. I run a hand through my hair.

"I'm all ears. What's up?"

"I've never told anyone this, but I overheard a conversation the night my mother disappeared that has always led me to believe my mother didn't just leave."

"Seriously? What did you hear?"

"It was an argument. Back then I didn't know with who. Christmas at Dante's, it came back to me. I remembered the voice."

"Who was it?"

"Papa Esposito," I bite out. "I'd never heard him in a rage like that. He was always so nice to me. I didn't put two and two together."

"Babe, you were eight."

"I know, but I should have known. I feel like he's been using me all this time. For what? I don't know, I'm still trying to figure that part out, but *Nonno* shuts down when I dig there.

"I'm here looking for answers. I have this gut feeling my *nonno* has them, but for some reason he's not giving me what I want to know."

"I've known *Nonno* since I was a little girl. He has always done things with purpose. I don't think he's holding this back to hurt you. After all this time, he has to have a reason."

My son was meant to be head of the family. You've given more respect to those mulignons in New York...The insult.

The words float into my head so fast I have to plant my feet to ground myself as pieces start to stand out.

"Carleen."

"Yes?"

"Your family—" I pause. She doesn't know how connected they are. I chew on the inside of my cheek. "Never mind. Forget I said anything."

Movement on the grounds catches my attention. "Babe, I need to call you back," I say quickly into the phone.

I hang up right as the first bullet whizzes by my head and shatters the glass behind me. I move for cover as the lights in the house come on. More shots are fired and hit the pillar I'm crouched behind.

A commotion comes from within the house. I turn as the doors I came out of burst open. I expect to see one of my grandfather's men, but it's Nonno himself.

He comes out guns blazing. I haven't been carrying since I've been here. Clearly, I've become too comfortable. My shock wears off when the gunfire ceases and Nonno stands with his chest heaving.

"Dario, are you hit?" he demands as he ambles over to me in his pajamas.

"I'm fine, *Nonno*."

"Don Giuseppe, what were you thinking?" Nonno's head of security says.

"My grandson was in danger. I wasn't thinking. Something I should be able to say about those protecting us. What the fuck were you all doing?" he roars. "Find out who dares pull this shit at my home. We've had peace for years. Who has lost their fucking mind?"

"Maybe we should head to Naples. We can have more security there."

"I've bent as much as I will. This is it. I will not be run from my home."

One of his men comes over after checking the bodies out in the yard. He leans in and whispers to Nonno. I watch in awe and still in somewhat shock.

Nonno nods. "I see. Get Michelangelo on the phone."

"Gio? Is he in danger? Should I go back?"

"What you need to do is start carrying a gun," he replies and places one of his still-smoking guns in my palm. "Vacation is over."

I swear, in this moment, I see Gio, Dante, and me in my grandfather. We get it from Nonno without question.

CHAPTER THIRTY-ONE

Blind Sacrifices

Carleen

I sit in my car and take a deep breath. I'm almost fifteen weeks and there's no hiding this bump any longer. Nyla and Holly were the first to notice about a week ago.

I cover my face and groan. I have so much on my mind. It's been a week since that call with Dario.

I freaked out when he rushed off the phone. However, after he called back to tell me he was okay, my mind turned to the question he almost asked.

He was going to ask me something about my family, but what? What does my family have to do with his mom or what he overheard that night all those years ago?

"Don't rush me, baby. I'm thinking. We don't want to go in there anyway," I say to my little bump as my blander feels like it's going to push the pee right out.

Ugh, I don't want to go into this house. My dad is going to lose his shit.

A tap comes at my window, causing me to jump. My nerves have been shot. I swear, I feel like someone is always watching me. I'm grateful for the firearm Holly and Nyla talked me into getting. It's made me feel a little safer.

"When did you turn into a punk, Oopies?" Toni says as I roll down the window.

"Shut up, big mouth," I say as I wave her off.

"You need to start packing if you're going to be out here scared. I get it, sis, your bodyguard is gone."

"My boyfriend is away for a bit, but I'm not helpless. And, for your information, I am packing."

"Oh shit, you might just be a Thompson after all. Bad gyal pull up. Dem Brooklyn streets live in the blood." She snickers and opens my door. "Come on, get out. I want to see this belly you were crying about."

"I should have ignored your call. I wouldn't be here."

"You can't hide this from your dad forever. Your mother seems like she might already be onto you." She pauses to squeal when I step out of Dario's truck. My jacket is too tight to close, so my bump is pushing it open.

Gio came by with Jace to check in on me and he insisted I start driving Dario's truck once he noticed my baby bump. He had a point. I was starting to struggle to get in and out of my smaller car.

"You look so adorable. I'd touch it, but I'm not sure I'm ready for that luck."

I laugh and tug her into a hug. I don't know why I'm ready to burst into tears as I embrace her. I swallow them down and release her.

"Let's get this over with."

She pitches my butt. "This baby looks good on you. When do you plan to tell him?"

I shrug. "He's not coming back yet, and I don't think he knows when he will. I was thinking of telling him for Valentine's Day though."

"*Ohhhh*, that's only a few days away. Not a bad idea. You're almost five months. He should know soon."

I don't respond, but I don't disagree with her. I want to tell Dario. Especially if it continues to look like he's not going to return soon.

"Toni, do you know if our family had some type of connection with the Di Lorenzos?"

She looks to me with wide eyes as we walk up the steps to my parents' front door. She rolls her gaze over me and bursts into laughter. My lips part and I narrow my eyes on her.

"Why are you laughing at me?"

"You're the smartest dummy in the family. It's your father's fault." She shakes her head. "This is not a question for me, Oopies. Talk to your parents."

I start to get pissed off. I'm tired of feeling like I'm out in the dark about so much in my life. It seems Jace knows more about me than I do. As those thoughts catch, I realize I haven't resolved much in Dario's absence.

I'm still stewing as my father answers the door. His gaze falls on my belly and his face hardens. I still myself for his reaction.

"Pat," he roars. "Patricia, come get your daughter. I told you. I told you."

My mother comes running to the door with confusion all over her face. My father rarely raises his voice unless he's super pissed and right now, I think we should call an ambulance for the stroke he's about to give himself.

"Carleen, you are pregnant," Mommy sings as she tugs me in for a hug. "I knew it. I had a dream about a fish months ago."

I roll my eyes. She could have warned me about this, it would have been nice to know before I hopped in bed with Dario.

But did you hop in bed with him?

I shrug off my thoughts as my mother ushers me in the house while asking a ton of questions. I make my excuses to release my bladder, but she's waiting right outside the powder room when I'm done.

Mommy leads me into the family room where the rest of my family is. All eyes are on my bump, making it feel bigger than it is.

"Oopies, what's that?" Uncle Kurt asks.

"A baby, Uncle Kurt. You know about those."

"Toni," Uncle Rick warns.

It's no secret that Uncle Kurt has a busload of kids and not all by Auntie Judie. However, we also know Toni will make that blatantly clear in the worst possible way if she keeps talking.

"But who baby dat?" Uncle Kurt continues.

"Humph," my father huffs. "As if we don't know."

"You let the white boy put a pickney in you? The bad man, that woman's—"

"Kurt, for once in your damn life, keep your mouth shut," Uncle Ernesto barks.

"Thank you because if I had to say it, I wasn't going to be so nice," my mother says to my surprise.

Uncle Kurt throws his hands up. "I didn't think we were getting this close to them. That's all. Some favor this has become. And she still don't remember nothing, eh?"

"Shut the fuck up, Kurt. I'm not going to say it again. Your mouth runs too much. Respect my home or get out."

"Hold on, Mommy. Is that called for? What's everyone's problem with my baby's father? Why has Dario suddenly become an issue around here?"

"It's not the boy," Uncle Talon says.

"Humph," my father grunts again.

"*Humph*," I mock. "Is that all you have to say? What's your problem, Daddy? I love Dario, always have, but I didn't leave my residency because of him. I was unhappy. I wanted to find my own thing—"

"Then find your own thing and stop sacrificing yourself for people who wouldn't do the same for you," he says with pain in his voice.

"What?" I choke.

"You're gifted, baby. You can do anything you set your mind to. You've never allowed being a Black woman to hold you out of doors your mother and I had to tear our way through. That's the woman I know deserves better than this. Where is he? Why isn't he here with you and that child?"

"He had to go tend to his grandfather. He doesn't even know yet."

"Why? The Carleen I raised would have made sure he knew and that at least a ring was on her finger. That's my daughter, that's the woman I raised you to be."

I stand, staring at my father, not having a reply for him. I allow his words to sink in. Hurt slices through me.

It hits me in that moment. I didn't lose myself. I found who I want to be. I've made choices and was given help to make them happen. Yeah, I may take on Dario's feelings when he's frustrated. As a result, I start to get antsy in my own life, but I can't help that. It's how I react to those I'm close to. It's time I speak up for me.

"You're wrong, I haven't sacrificed myself for him. I want to be the best at something I love, and I bust my behind to do so.

"But you know what? I've been too scared to own up to my accomplishments because it's never enough. I've been chasing your approval and impossible standards because I want you to be proud of me. Enough."

I punch at my chest. "I'm an award-winning chef. I co-own one of the top restaurants in New York City. Three stars, count them. Three. Michelin. Stars—" I punch my chest with each word. "It don't get no better than that. I have a James Beard Award under my belt." I hit my chest again. "Me. Not Dario, *me*. He wasn't in the kitchen when I cooked my damn heart out and gained those accomplishments. I've sold over a million copies of my cookbook.

"Did I do it all with my best friend by my side? Yes, I did because he's been my support system in finding myself, but for the first time, I'm admitting to myself it wasn't him. It was *me*. I'm not his clone, I'm his partner.

"I did all that. Just like Mommy had your back as you made your way to chief of staff, I've been by Dario's side as we've built a powerhouse of our own. You can't take that away from me. I earned it. *Me.*" I punch my chest again.

"Carleen, the baby. Calm down," my mother pleads.

"No." I turn back to my father. "Do you even know why I started acquiring the skills of others? Toni learned to play the piano and Justin had the violin. You seemed so disappointed in me for not picking an instrument, when I asked them to show me, they didn't want to. *You should have gotten your own*, they told me.

"I watched how proud you were of them, so I sat with them as they practiced and learned. I watched and listened and learned. I became better at it than they were because I wanted to please *you*.

"From there it became my thing. People didn't want to teach me things, they didn't want me to know something. I wouldn't ask them to teach me, I became them to the point of mastering whatever it was to show you all I could do anything. I can be anything. It's just this time I learned something I love."

"But at what cost? Of all the people you had to attach your star to, why him?"

"Why not him? What aren't you guys telling me?"

My father looks at me with tears in his eyes. I look to my mother as I blink back my own tears. Her lips are trembling.

"You're my only daughter. I only want the best for you. Everyone who gets attached to that family, I lose. We've given them so much. Not my daughter."

I stumble to an accent chair and collapse into it. "What?" I ask in confusion.

"It's time, Pat. The girl should know."

I look at Uncle Talon and wrinkle my brows.

"Listen, I need to go. I shouldn't hear any of this. My relationship with the Di Lorenzo family works because I don't know the details. I want to keep it that way. We're only useful to each other because I don't understand the connection," Toni says.

"I'm going to leave too," Justin says as he walks over to kiss my mother's cheek. "Congratulation, Oopies."

"I can't do this," my father says and storms from the room.

"I think we should all go," Uncle Ernesto says and moves to kiss my mother's cheek. "We'll get together to celebrate the baby soon. Congratulations, Oopies."

Uncle Ernesto leans in to kiss my forehead and Uncle Rick and Uncle Talon follow suit, giving their congratulations as well. I try to smile but I'm confused and crumbling inside.

Something tells me whatever my mother is about to say is going to change my life forever.

CHAPTER THIRTY-TWO

Connections

Carleen

Once everyone is gone, my mother goes to get me something to eat. I don't even know if I can stomach it through this bundle of nerves. I just want answers.

She takes a seat after handing me a plate, then cups my face. "I have always only wanted the best for you. Make no mistake."

I blink back my tears. "But?"

"Ava Di Lorenzo was a charismatic person. She made you think everything that happened around you was fate or coincidence, not her moving your life around like God.

"The Di Lorenzos were entwined in my life way before my first encounter with Ava. I just didn't know that at the time." She pauses and takes a deep breath. "Do you remember the story of how I met your father?"

"You guys met in college or something, right?"

"Actually, I was in college, but I met your father through my little brother, your uncle Steven."

"The painter?"

Mommy scoffs. "I wish he would have stuck to painting. Steven wanted to be just like Kington. He thought he could build a big name and earn the respect of his big brother.

"From what I heard, he was doing it. He was building a name and reputation. Making all the friends he was told to and anchoring relationships that would benefit the future. Your father and I included."

"He set you guys up?"

"I don't know if you can say that. Steven was smart but he got caught up with some women who may have been smarter. You see, Steven met your father through your daddy's sister, Gwendolyn."

"Right, Daddy had an older sister. The one he never seems to want to talk about. I've never seen any pictures of her, but that one he keeps in his office."

"That was some woman there. I think your father fears you're too much like her. She adored you, you were her little shadow.

"Anyway, Gwen pushed Steven to get me and your father together." Tears fill my mother's eyes. "We were already engaged when your uncle was killed, murdered in the streets by a corrupt police officer.

"It was a hit. I knew nothing of these things and just thought he was in the wrong place at the wrong time. I didn't understand why my brothers were so angry and I wouldn't know for years.

"Your auntie Gwen was a part of the Di Lorenzo inner circle. She's the one who brought Steven in, he was an asset to them. Once he was gone, access to what they really wanted was gone. They needed my marriage to obtain what they lost through Steven."

"So how did your family get involved if Uncle Steven was gone?" My stomach is tightening into knots. I have a bad feeling about this story.

Mom wipes a hand across her forehead and starts to look nervous. Her eyes grow distant.

"I never met Ava before that night, I didn't know who she was. I was so tired and just wanted to go home. I was coming off a seventeen-hour shift. Your father wanted me to come stay the weekend with him so I was driving into New Jersey.

"It was raining, the thunder shook my little Volvo with each boom. I barely heard the shot. I remember seeing the taillights of the other car speed away.

"At first, the Brooklyn in me saw that woman on the side of the road and said, *nope, Pat, mind your damn business.* But I took an oath, I was a surgeon, so I pulled over to see if I could help.

"Ava was shot in the shoulder. I wanted to get her to the hospital, but she told me it was too dangerous, and they would come back to finish her. She gave me an address that wasn't that far away, and I took her there.

"I patched her up and was on my way, never thinking I'd see her again."

"But you did, she's the mother of my best friend."

"Oh, Ava was much more than that. I was shocked when she and her father arrived at my wedding as friends of Gwen's. Her gift, I was so naive I thought she was being generous because I saved her life and she wanted to thank me." Mommy stops to look around the house. I gasp and my eyes grow wide.

"No," I breathe.

"Yup, she purchased this house for us and along with it my loyalty. I thought I had gained a real friend. I didn't question it. Your father, on the other hand, was skeptical. Ava made sure never to reveal herself to him. It didn't dawn on me she was avoiding me introducing them.

"She knew I wanted into this neighborhood and the schools. I'd mentioned it as I patched her up. She kept me talking that night and I thought it was to distract herself from the pain.

"She and her charming father worked my wedding like pros. My family took right to them. I thought nothing of her father talking to Kington. If you can get my brother to talk to you, you're someone special.

"Within weeks, promotions started to happen for your uncles. They worked hard, I thought it was due to that, so I didn't question the timing. A year passed and Ava and I were both pregnant at the same time. Her with the twins and me with you.

"When you were born, she insisted on being your godmother. The way she spoiled you, I didn't see why not. Ava weaved her way into our lives—playdates, birthday parties, getting you into the top school when I wasn't light enough for them."

I make a sound in the back of my throat. I hadn't been light enough either. Elementary through high school, it was made clear I was well past the brown-paper-bag complexion they accepted. My father, being lighter, didn't have that problem when he entered a room.

Mom starts to sob. "I didn't know. Not until your aunt revealed it to me. A friend of theirs was hurt. He'd been shot in the stomach. Ava sent Gwen for me. I just barely saved his life.

"Ava told me he was a friend of her family's and doing this favor would go a long way to help her. Your father had ranted about who your aunt worked for once she left the military, but I didn't get it until that night.

"That's when the playground visits started. My brothers used me as a go-between to deliver messages to Ava and she to them. I quickly learned they were who Ava wanted to begin with. She tied herself to me and my family in every way she could. She placed the world at your feet to gain my brothers' trust."

"But that still doesn't explain why Daddy is so upset," I huff.

The tears really start to flow. "Gwen was murdered. Your father lost everything. First his best friend, my brother and then his sister, Gwen. He has hated the Di Lorenzo family since.

"It's gutted him for years that you've remained friends with Dario, but he tolerated it. He felt bad for the boys. And, after your accident. Dario was the first person you called for, the first person you remembered."

I blink back tears. I tripped over my feet. I was trying to get to Dario. I overheard my mother talking about Ava's disappearance and the boys being upset. I tripped going up the stone steps and cracked my head.

It took a while, but I got my memories back. Or so I thought. My head hurts as I try to remember my auntie Gwen. Suddenly, I feel like something else is missing.

However, one thought does click as my mother's words sink in. "Daddy tolerated Dario until I left my residency and opened a business with their family. Shit," I breathe.

My mind starts to race. One by one, the pieces come together. I look at my mother and my mouth falls open.

"His mother," I gasp. "She was connected to the mob."

"She was the mob, baby. Donna Ava Di Lorenzo. Your aunt was her consigliere for years. She offered your uncle Kington the cop who murdered my brother and granted your other uncle's elections and promotions to whatever they wanted, we've been tied to them since. The promotions, the Senate seat, the Di Lorenzos have had a hand in it all."

"I loved my sister. I never understood her choices or how she fell in with those people." I turn to look at my father as his choked voice fills the room.

"I didn't know who the Thompsons were. I'd only fallen in love with my best friend's sister. I met Steven in high school and in college he introduced me to your mother. If I'd known his intentions or my sister's…I never approved of any of it, but to lose my sister, it was all too much. I fear every day that you're going to fall into that life or have the same fate."

"My brothers would never allow that to happen," Mommy says.

"You can't promise that. My sister was one of the best-trained soldiers, she started a security business to protect others from what happened to her, but she and her partner both fell at the hands of the monsters those people brought into their lives. How can you promise me my daughter and grandchild will be safe?"

"Because I will fight to the death before anything happens to this baby and I would never leave my child to live without me, so you don't have to worry, Daddy. I know for a fact Dario would never allow anything to happen to us. I know this in my heart."

"Humph," my father grunts and shakes his head. "You don't even remember what my sister gave you. You can't make that promise. God, now I wish like hell you could, but you can't."

I sit staring at my dad in confusion. *You don't even remember what my sister gave you.* I have no idea what he's talking about, but my phone rings as I go to ask.

Seeing it's Dario, I excuse myself to take the call. The six-hour time difference throws everything off. I try not to miss his calls when I can help it.

CHAPTER THIRTY-THREE

You Did This

Frances

"Have you heard from your cousin?" I ask Peter as he walks into Sylvia's living room.

Her nephews aren't the brightest, but they are all eager to find themselves. This is what annoys me. My father is well aware of this fact and it's dangerous.

"No, I've been busy watching the boards like your father asked me to do."

"And I've told you to stop doing things my father tells you to. You're going to get yourself hurt following him."

"I like the girl." He shrugs. "He's getting me close to her with this job. It's a win-win," he says like a goof.

"What ever happened to just asking a girl out if you're interested? Peter, you're a good kid, I'm warning you not to get mixed up in whatever my father has going on."

"I don't see you warning the others. Franky is up to something too. That's probably why you can't find him. There's a payday coming. Why should I be the only one to miss out?"

I jump up from my seat and grab him by the collar. "What money can you spend if you're dead?" I growl into his face.

"If I were one of your sons, you wouldn't treat me like this."

I shove him out of my hold. "He's feeding you that bullshit. I've looked out for you boys like my own flesh and blood. I'm looking out for you now. You don't mean more than shit on the bottom of my father's shoe. Leave him and his scheming ass alone. I'm not going to warn you again."

"Does this have anything to do with his guys that are going missing?"

I look at Peter and narrow my eyes. "What? What guys?"

He shrugs. "I don't know. I heard him yelling that guys were missing. They've been disappearing. No-shows, no calls, no one knows where they are."

I bare my teeth. There's no telling what my father has gotten those boys into.

"He's pretty pissed about it. Some other job got fucked up or something to—"

"Peter, honey, is that you?" Sylvia calls through the house.

"Yeah, Aunt Sylvia. I'm talking to Uncle Frances."

"Come to the kitchen when you're done. I have something for you."

"All right."

"I mean it, Peter. Stay away from my father."

"Yeah, yeah."

I grind my teeth as he waves me off. Pulling my phone from my pocket, I dial my father. It rings a few times before he picks up. However, I'm not expecting him to sound so distraught when he does.

"Hello."

"What's the matter with you?"

"It's Franky."

"What about him?" I snarl.

"He was supposed to lie low for a while as I figured some things out. He's been checking in twice a day. It's been two days since I last heard from him. A few of my guys have been coming up missing but Franky—"

I hang up, not able to hear anything more. I bury my face in my hands and my shoulders shake. I knew he would bring this down on us. All I ever wanted was to save my boys from this. Now…now, I can't even breathe.

Gio

I light a cigar and blow out the smoke as I sit back in my chair and listen to the voice on the other end of the phone. I have the call on speaker for Jace to listen in as he sits across from me with his head bent, blocking my view of his expression.

"It had to be done. No one I care about was hurt. Dario was too comfortable. I want him relieved of the pressure of Don, but he can't be lax yet."

"Yes, I get it, but your grandfather got involved. He's getting older. I need you to be more careful with him."

I grunt and nod as if she can see me. She's right, I should have considered Nonno's protectiveness. We're all just like him.

However, I was shocked to hear he went all Nicky Santoro at his age. Although Giuseppe Di Lorenzo is the stuff the mob movies are made of. My nonno is the Don for a reason. This wouldn't be the first time they've tried to wipe out my family and my grandfather earned his respect then. Only, he lost his brothers, I don't intend to lose mine.

"I'll keep this in mind. You don't have to worry about him."

"How's Carleen? Has she remembered yet?"

"No, nothing yet. Ny and Holly are still working. They have to be cautious because of the baby."

"She was so small. How can we be sure she will remember? Maybe we shouldn't trigger this."

"We've all talked about this. She wants her to remember. Let me worry about it. I have everything under control."

"As always." She laughs softly. "Your brother still doesn't know he's going to be a father. I don't like it. Maybe jogging her memory can wait. She belongs with Dario."

"I can make that happen. I was actually thinking the same thing. As Jace said, we'll need to set that in motion soon. She's already showing. Maybe I can kill two birds."

"*Gio*," she says in warning. "Nothing to harm the baby."

"I would never. Jace will control everything."

She sighs. "Do what you must. I could use Ny with me for a while."

At this, Jace lifts his head, he looks how I feel. I work my jaw. I'm not ready for Ny to take off again, but I already knew this was coming. Another sacrifice.

"I think it's time you let Dante loose on his own problem. He doesn't need to know the whole truth," she continues as I remain silent.

I shake off my annoyance. I need to bring this all to an end. When I do, everyone will be where they belong. All my sacrifices will be worth it.

"No problem, I'll give him a reason to address Kumar. As a matter of fact, I can connect it to Dario, ease his mind about the shooting. Make it all fall in line with everything else," I say.

"Perfect. I like that idea."

"And the wife?"

"Mine. I know where she is. I will be in and out."

The call ends and I smile. I know exactly how I plan to handle this all. The Kumars were hired to, as the Italians say, taint the bloodline. Riccardo believes himself to be a crafty son of a bitch. He's not.

A Black wife will never be the end of the Di Lorenzos no matter which brother marries one, but I get what he thought he was doing.

"No male heir who can be traced back to the other side, no Di Lorenzos," Jace says as if reading my thoughts.

"Or so they thought. Make sure Ny is there when she lands, get her whatever she needs.

"Also have Ny uncover the paper trail, I want Anderson to find it when I send his team digging." I pause to think. "As a matter of fact, make it look like payments were going to a third party. Keep the third party hidden for now. Make sure it can be linked to that guy's shell company in the end."

Jace stands and nods before he leaves the room. I sit puffing a few rings before I put the cigar out and make a few calls of my own.

CHAPTER THIRTY-FOUR

Your Problem

Dario

I don't like feeling like a sitting duck. After the shooting, I'm not willing to bring Carleen here anymore. She's safer where she is.

It's tearing me apart to be so far away from her, but her safety always comes first. My biggest problem is feeling like Apollo is hiding something from me. Whenever I ask about Carleen, he starts to act strange on me.

Last time he changed the subject to the indictment. That's the last thing I wanted to talk about. I'm growing more frustrated by the day. I have no answers from Nonno and I'm not entirely sure my woman is okay.

"Enough," I mutter to myself. I may not be able to get what I came here for, but I can find out what's going on with Car.

I pull my phone from my pocket. At first, I go to call Dante, but I remember he's not in Jersey and hasn't been for weeks. He wouldn't know what's going on with Carleen any more than I would.

I close out of his contact and go to call Gio instead. He will know what's going on. Carleen has mentioned more than once that Jace has been the one to make sure she gets home safely.

I'm grateful to my brother for that. It has gone a long way to put my mind at ease.

"I was just about to call you," Gio says in greeting.

"Oh yeah? What's the matter?"

It's clear in his voice he's frustrated. My mind goes straight to Carleen. I'll never forgive myself if something happens to her.

"I'll call you back in two."

He hangs up and I get really worried. I don't think I breathe fully until my phone rings. I answer and try to remain calm.

"I have news on the shooting. Our brother's problem is raising its head. The hit at Nonno's came from rumors of Dante not handling business with that family. They say we're showing weakness.

"It's falling on you. They don't think you're ready. That's not good. I need them focused on your strength. The New York and Jersey mess can't touch Italy. Not now."

"Am I clear to come home?"

"No. You need to stay where you are."

I start to think it over. Dante should be the one to handle this. However, knowing what happened to Bethany was partially my fault, I want to be the one to handle it.

"Have Dante clean up his own shit. This motherfucker has been skimming from us like we're his personal bank. It stops now," Gio says as if reading my mind.

I groan. "Gio, do we really want to send him back there? He's been so much happier since Bella was born, and he hasn't had to become that other guy."

"Dario, they made an attempt on your life. On *Nonno's* property at that. If our allies are questioning us enough to allow this. It needs to be handled and Dante should be the one to do it. Talk to him, maybe he'll send Mitch."

"You and I both know he won't. I'll take care of it."

"Good."

"Have you seen Carleen? Is everything okay with her?"

"Jace says she's fine. I can go check on her this week if you want me to."

"Apollo sounds off, like he's keeping something from me. If you can just look in on her for me. Thanks, man."

"I'll talk to Apollo and look in on her. The numbers look great over there. She's been earning better without you."

"Fuck you, Gio." I give a dry laugh.

"I'll have to talk to her and give her some options. She can totally run a place on her own."

"I'd choke the shit out of you."

He laughs on his end, and it makes me smile. Gio doesn't laugh the way he used to. A lot changed after Ma.

"Gio, I've been meaning to ask you something."

"Yeah?"

"What's up with you and Papa Esposito?"

He scoffs. "That cocksucker tried to take everything from me. I'm just returning the favor. I'm going to make him eat the shit he created. Call Dante, I need to go."

I sigh as the call ends. That's more than I thought I'd get from him. I rub my temples and think over all he said about Dante's situation. I know what I need to do. I read between the lines.

I take a deep breath and resolve myself to the fact that although I won't be promoted to Don, I'm still an underboss with responsibilities.

Someone made an attempt on my life, so someone is comfortable with targeting the heads of my family, that's unacceptable. They have no respect for the rules or for my family. I fume as the phone rings and the seriousness of all this sets in.

Dante's line picks up and I release a breath through my nose. "Hello, can I call you back?"

"No, I need to talk to you now," I say tightly, the more I think about the shooting and Nonno having to come to my rescue the hotter I get.

"Excuse me." I hear him say away from the phone.

"Who are you with?"

"Lizzy, we were watching TV. What's going on?"

"Did you hear about the shooting?"

"What the fuck? No. I've been traveling. Mitch didn't say anything."

"I was fired on here at Nonno's. Your old friend has been digging in our pockets and it's making me look like a chump."

"Wait, old friend? The father? So it was confirmed?"

"Yes. We look weak and our friends here are responding to what they think is a weakness. I can't have that. I can't come back Stateside yet, but this needs to be handled."

"It's my problem. I'll deal with it," Dante seethes. "I'll leave in the morning. It will be handled. I'll call Mitch to make sure he has a package waiting for me when I land."

CHAPTER THIRTY-FIVE

Ducks in a Row

Gio

I sit in my car with Ny at my side, watching the back entrance of *Anima Mias* right as Dante pulls up.

"Why are we here?" Ny asks with that attitude of hers.

"I have a few balls I'll be tossing in the air tonight. Kaling has to go. Dante's temper will take care of that.

"Next, I need Dario to know what's going on here in his absence."

"Don't you think this is her secret to tell?"

I shrug. "Maybe, but this move has its purpose. I know he's going to be pissed at me and Jace, but I'll deal with that later. For now, I need him to know Carleen is pregnant. With that information, I can guarantee his next move."

I know the twins better than they know themselves. Dante won't leave without telling his brother what he sees, and Dario isn't going to allow his woman or his child to remain outside of his reach, not when their well-being is threatened. Which leads me to the third ball.

"Ever the puppet master," Ny scoffs.

I chuckle, despite knowing it's an insult. She's still salty because she wasn't able to run off. I need her here. My final selections have been made. My collection will soon be complete, and I need her to make that happen.

I continue, going back to my original train of thought. I'm not doing this to hurt Carleen or Dario. Every move I make has a purpose.

"Dario is to be named in an indictment, but it's truly meant for his twin. I need to make this right for both twins. I could clear Dario easily, but that would put Dante in the hot seat.

"The mistaken identity was done on purpose if you ask me. Dario is the bigger fish, but I'm not allowing either of my brothers to go to jail."

Ny turns to look at me with wide eyes. "How do you plan to pull this one off?"

"How do you blow a hole in a federal case? You remove all their evidence, witnesses, and any informants who are comfortably trying to nail you to the wall." I wink.

You're not going to rat on my brothers and think you're going to live to tell the tale. The Thompsons have done their job well. I'll handle the rest.

Maybe, just maybe, I'll finally trigger Carleen to remember who she is while I'm at it. All the ducks are lining up. I can see them in the row I need them in.

Focusing back on the restaurant, I dial Jace as Dante disappears into the back door. He picks up on the second ring and grunts into the line.

"He just arrived. You know how he works. Give him time to do his thing. I'll give you the call when he's done. Just keep her in the kitchen. I need him to see her, not the other way around," I say into the phone.

"This, I can do."

I hang up, knowing he can't say more because Carleen is right in front of him. My mind turns back to why I needed Nyla to remain here in the States.

My phone rings and I grin as the name of one of my new treasures appears. Yes, this one is ready.

"Hello," I croon into the phone. Ny turns and narrows her eyes at me.

"Okay, I'll do it."

"I'll send a car for you in an hour. Take nothing but the clothes on your back. I'll provide everything else. Make sure you're not seen when you leave."

"You don't have to worry about that. I'm dead if he sees me."

"No, he is. You now belong to me. If he touches one hair on your head before you're in my possession, he'll pay with his life. One hour, the same place we met last."

I hang up. Nyla shifts in her seat as her hot glare remains on me. I lick my lips as I drop my gaze to her long, sexy legs in the miniskirt she's wearing.

Carleen

"This is so sweet of you," I say to Jace as I get out the ingredients to make the cake he asked me to teach him to make for his Valentine.

However, I'd be lying if I said I'm not wondering who his Valentine is after watching him, Ny, and Gio in the gym the last time we were there sparring. I watched the three in the ring together in what I can only explain as a sensual dance.

Jace gives me a little smile. I was totally surprised when he asked me to do this. When he stopped by the apartment to check on me, I'd already been debating on coming back to the restaurant anyway. I have some ideas I want to hash out.

"Thanks for your help."

"I'm a little hungry. Do you mind if I make us something to eat before we start on the cake?"

"I could eat. Take your time. Feed the baby. I can wait."

"Do you mind if I put on my headphones? It calms me while I'm cooking."

"It's not like I'll talk much. Why not?" He shrugs.

I laugh and go to get out something to cook up. I'm craving chicken egg rolls. I know we have some meat marinating in curry and coconut milk that will go perfect in them. They'll be quick and tasty.

"You like chicken egg rolls?"

"I like food," Jace says and pats his flat belly.

I place my headphones on and get busy making us egg rolls. My mind turns to Dario. I'm going to tell him about the baby tomorrow. It's my Valentine's Day gift.

I'm nervous, but excited. The worse that could happen, he'll have me booked on the first flight to Italy. I wouldn't mind. I miss him. I actually want to be with him through the rest of this pregnancy.

I get lost in cooking and the kitchen. This is my haven. I find a peace here like none other. I've never had this type of peace in the operating room. This is what I want my father to understand about me.

I find myself humming as I turn to place a plate in front of Jace. I push one of my headphones back away from my ear and watch him closely. His hair is down, softening his hard edges but not taking away from that silent-killer vibe he gives.

He gives me one of those nods before he picks up an egg roll and tucks in. "Mm," he hums and nods some more.

"You like?"

He wipes his mouth. "This is great. So much flavor."

"Thanks." I turn and grab my plate as my own mouth waters.

I take a seat beside Jace and devour my food. I'm stuffed by the time my plate is empty. I look at the clock and see it's getting really late and Jace still needs to drop me home and get home himself. I clean our dishes and get started on the cake.

As I'm measuring out dry ingredients, I look up to find Jace with his attention on his phone. I hope whoever this Valentine of his is appreciates him. He's such a nice guy.

"Is that your Valentine?"

He looks up at me and smiles. "Let me help with that," he says, as I go to pour the wet ingredients into the dry.

As he reaches out, he knocks over the metal mixing bowl with the flour in it. It tumbles to the floor, making a mess. I go to pick up the bowl, but he stops me.

"I'm sorry. I got it. I'll clean this up. Don't worry about it. You have a broom?"

"Yeah, over in that closet, right there."

"Cool, I got this."

He saunters over to the utility closet. I put my headphones back in place and go back to measuring and mixing. A caramel cake will be nice. He didn't say what kind he wanted.

My thoughts turn to Dario. I wish we could be together for tomorrow. As the thought crosses my mind, my phone lights up with a text.

Rio: *Hey, baby. You awake?*

I smile, clean off my hands, and pick up the phone to reply.

Me: *Yes. In the kitchen. Making a cake.*

I put my phone down and place my hands on my back. It's starting to hurt. I can't help but wonder how hard being on my feet will be as I grow near the end of this pregnancy.

"Hey, you know what, you look tired. I don't have to have this cake. It was a good idea in theory. Maybe next time. I'll get this cleaned up and we can go," Jace says.

"You sure?" Honestly, I'm pretty tired. I feel bad, but I'm also ready to face-plant.

"Yeah, I could always bring her here for dinner. That might be nicer."

"I'll hold a reservation for you two."

"Thanks."

CHAPTER THIRTY-SIX

Dante

I'm lying in bed, about to send Carleen another text before I hop into the shower, when a text comes through from Dante. I open it and find a picture of Carleen. At first, I smile, thinking Gio told him to check in on her for me.

However, I narrow my eyes and enlarge the picture. Like her text said, she's in the kitchen at *Anima Mias*. What stands out about the picture is her little protruding belly.

I sit up bolt straight with my head bent over my phone, trying to process what I'm looking at. I go from elated to ready to explode.

"Why wouldn't you tell me this?" I breathe to myself.

My first thought is because it isn't mine. However, I stop that train of thought because that's not my Carleen. She's always honest with me. If she were pregnant by someone else, she'd tell me.

I can't see her cheating on me, and she said she wasn't sleeping with that cocksucker she was seeing. Not wanting to jump to conclusions, I dial her phone to get the truth from her mouth.

"Hey, babe," she answers, sounding so tired.

Now it all makes sense. Apollo, her always being so tired. She's been pregnant all this time. I try not to lose my shit. She has to have a reason for keeping this secret from me.

"Hey. Carleen, is there something I should know?"

"Uh, like what? I emailed you the numbers for *Anima Mias* and added all the vacation requests."

"I'm not talking about the restaurant. I don't give a shit about that right now."

She's silent for a moment. I tell myself I can't be angry with her. I was the one who didn't use a condom.

"Carleen."

"Yes?"

"We don't have secrets."

She scoffs. "The hell we don't."

"What's that supposed to mean?"

"We're not friends by accident, Dario. My family has been tied to yours from day one. I know who you people are. Your mother bought my family. Oh, there's so much more," she seethes.

"Car. Not now. Baby, calm down. The baby," I say quickly.

She gasps. "How do you know?"

"I got a text— Never mind that. I know. We need to talk. How do you know all of that stuff? I don't even know what you're talking about."

"My mom and dad. Rio, it's a lot. I was related to Ms. Gwen."

"What?"

"She was my father's sister."

"Fuck me. I don't remember that. Listen, I want to know everything you know but not on this line. How are you doing? How's my baby?"

"We're fine," she says with a smile in her voice. "I planned to tell you for Valentine's. I still don't know how it happened. We always used protection. That one time you pulled out couldn't have been it. I was already pregnant by then."

"Actually, Carleen. I'm so sorry. That first night I was so drunk. All I could think about was making love to you. I didn't use a condom. This is my fault."

"Your fault," she whispers. "You don't want it?"

"Fuck outta here. I'm so fucking happy. I need to get back home. I want to see you in person. My baby needs to hear my voice. Do you know what we're having?"

"No, I was hoping you'd return soon. I wanted you there when I find out."

I smile like an idiot. "I'm going to be a father. Carleen?"

"Yes?"

"I love you." I close my eyes as I wait to hear the words from her lips.

"I love you too. I love you so much, Dario."

My chest swells. This is a day I've only dreamed of. My mind starts to work on how I'm going to make it so she can come be with me. Nonno can double security, or we can go to Naples. Now that Dante has handled his father-in-law, maybe things are safer here.

"I need to figure a few things out, but I want you here."

She releases a heavy breath. "I knew that was coming. You know that's why I didn't tell you before you left. I have a life here, Rio."

"And you're now carrying one of the most important lives to me. I need you and my baby with me. I want my wife in my arms when I wake."

"We're not married. Rio, slow down. Let me think."

"Think about what? I've loved you all my life. I spent so much time denying myself the love I needed. I can't spend another day denying myself that or you. I want you as my wife. I'm going to make that happen as soon as I can."

"Wait, hold on. Give me a sec." She moves away from the phone. "Hey, you don't have to go. It's late. Stay in one of the guest rooms. I'll feel bad if something happens to you. You look tired."

I start to see red. Who the fuck is she talking to? Is that why she wants to slow things down? There's someone else.

I don't share. And who the fuck does she have in my place? All rational thought leaves me.

"I just need to use the bathroom." I reel my shit in as I recognize the voice as Jace's.

"Okay," she says, away from the phone. "Rio. Listen, babe, I'm super tired. We should talk later.

"I'm fifteen weeks pregnant and have been on my feet all day. My brain is mush. I hear what you want, and I want it too. It just has to make sense. You can't lock me up and hold me in Italy until you plan to return. Let me think."

The fuck I can't.

Instead of saying what I think, I say, "Get some rest. We'll talk—"

A loud crashing sound comes from her end and then she screams. My blood runs cold and my heart feels like it's going to come out of my chest.

"*Carleen, Carleen,*" I bellow into the phone. "Baby, answer me."

A shot is fired and my world spins. I can't breathe.

Carleen

I watch Jace walk to the bathroom and sigh. I'm so tired. I know Dario and I have a lot to talk about, especially concerning his family, but my eyes are ready to close.

As I tell Rio this, a tap comes at the front door. The doorman downstairs would have rung if someone were here for me. It must be one of the neighbors. Maybe Dr. Brown, he's been checking in since he noticed my belly.

I turn and head for the front door, still talking to Rio.

"Get some rest. We'll talk—"

I scream as the door is pushed in on me, dropping the phone to the floor. I'm in shock at first. It takes me a moment to realize three men have stormed the apartment on me.

Time slows and I'm no longer in the here and now. I'm about five years old. The memory is so clear.

"Focus, Carleen," the woman in front of me says.

"You never let them get the drop on you. It's like a dance, Car. They come for you, you take their heads off. I don't care how big they are. Your body is a weapon, use it."

I come back to the present with a gasp. Without thinking, I reach for the gun in the hand of the guy in front of me. I disarm him and disable the gun in seconds, dropping it to the ground.

Using my elbow, I rock his head back then headbutt him. Spinning out of his reach, I then grab the hair of the next guy and flip him onto his back. I surprise myself as this all comes so naturally and it's not my usual kickboxing style. This comes from somewhere else.

I grab the gun from the third guy and put it to his chin before I blow his brains out. Not taking a chance, I turn the gun on the first guy to pump two in his chest and then turn to the second guy to blow his brains out and stop his groans.

"It's done." Jace's voice draws my attention and I turn to find him on his phone. "Yes, she's awake."

Confused, I bend to pick up my phone. "Hello," I breathe as my chest heaves.

"Baby, what the fuck just happened? Are you okay, the baby?"

"We're fine. I think I know what my auntie gave me."

"What?"

"I'll explain."

"Good, you can do it in person. You're coming to stay with me. That's final."

CHAPTER THIRTY-SEVEN

Get Things Settled

Carleen

I have so much to do before I board the plane to Italy. There are my clothes I need to pack, stopping by the house. Getting the staff prepared to be without me and Dario.

Apollo will be taking over. Gah, my head is spinning with all I have to do in just three days. Dario wouldn't give me a single day more.

He has called almost every waking hour on the hour since the break-in. I need to get to him before he loses his mind. Our Valentine's Day wasn't what I thought it would be.

He's been too high strung, trying to find out who was behind the break-in. Jace has been here since. I feel like a child with a babysitter. I mean, I proved I can handle myself. I don't need to be guarded.

But where the hell did all that come from?

"Hey, cuz. What's up?"

I turn for the bedroom door to find Toni with two frappés in her hands. I can't help but smile, I've been craving one all day. I walk over and take the one she's holding out.

"You didn't tell me this fine-ass man was here with you. Got me in here looking basic."

I laugh as I look over her sweat suit and sleek ponytail. There isn't a single day where Antonia Thompson looks basic. We share the same color eyes, dark complexion, and thick, dark hair. Toni is a little thicker than I am, but it works on her frame.

I take a look behind her to see Jace with a suitcase at his side and his phone in his hand. He's always on that thing. He's shirtless. He was working out doing sit-ups the last time I was in the living room.

My gaze drops to his chest that's exposed. The words *Doll Curator* are tatted across his skin in bold lettering. I've never seen the tat before. I blink a few times. Something about the tat is familiar and distracting.

"I have all the things you asked for. The place is coming along. Although, I don't think you should go there. It's still an active construction site," Toni says, causing me to pull my gaze away from Jace's chest.

Jace pops his head up. "Is she talking about your place?"

"Yes. I was going to head over to check on things one last time."

He shakes his head. "I'll take care of that. Gio says he'll make sure the place is finished by the time you return. We're already on it."

"Oh my God, the entire family has taken over my life."

Jace laughs and winks. I'm stunned for a second. He's become more open with me in the last day. I guess after you watch a woman drop three bodies and then proceed to dispose of them for her, you build a bond.

"Where do you want this?" Jace asks, pointing to the suitcase Toni brought over.

"Set it next to the door. It's coming with me."

Without a word, he turns and heads to the living room. I'm left with Toni sipping at her straw with a smile on her lips. I don't even want to know what she's thinking.

"I hope you've packed a lot of lingerie. After being under the same roof as that and not getting any in months, you better be ready."

"Shut up, Toni."

"What? Like you haven't been daydreaming about riding that dick as soon as you land. I'm just making sure you plan ahead, you have that little bump, you need to make sure you take stuff that fits."

"I've packed everything I'll need."

"That's my girl. What was it you wanted to talk to me about?"

"Do you remember my auntie Gwen? Was there another woman she hung out with, a Black woman?"

Toni scrunches up her face. I can see the wheels turning. She moves farther into the room and sits on the ottoman at the foot of the bed.

"I can't remember fully, but I think there was. A pretty lady. She was only around when the white lady was." She pauses and gasps. "Yeah, I remember she carried a gun. Tall and pretty."

I hold the dress in my hands to my chest and take a seat on the bed. The memory from the other night clinging to my mind and taunting me.

"I think I remembered something about Auntie Gwen and that woman. I had to be so young."

"From what I remember, you were always with her. Like a little shadow. If you weren't with your mom, you were with Gwen. That's how you and Dario became friends, from what I thought."

I bite my lips and fall into thought. I've wondered about that memory since the other night. The two pretty women were coaching me and teaching me to protect myself. I was so tiny and excited to play with them, but we weren't playing. My little mind didn't comprehend what I was being taught.

My phone rings, pulling me from my thoughts. I pull it from my pocket and answer when I see it's Rio. I should have known.

"Hello."

"Hey, gorgeous. How's my baby? Have you eaten?"

"*Our* baby is fine. No, I haven't had a chance to eat. Jace ordered something but I haven't had a moment to stop."

"Carleen, stop whatever you're doing and go eat. You have a long flight, and our baby needs to eat."

"Okay, fine," I pout.

"I'm going to fuck the shit out of you when you get here. You'll need the fuel," he says in a sexy, deep voice, taking the sting out of his initial demand.

I squirm in my seat. "Is that a promise?"

"They're changing the sheets and setting our room up as we speak. I can't believe you're going to be here soon."

"We still have an entire day."

"Don't remind me. You know I used to wish summer after summer that you could come here with me. This all seems so surreal. I love you."

I swipe at a tear as my emotions get the best of me. I used to miss him so much when he would go to visit his grandfather. I'd be so angry with my parents for not allowing me to go along. Now, I get they were protecting me from a world I didn't and still don't understand.

"I love you too."

"But?"

I sigh. "I'm scared. There's so much I don't understand, so many things I still need to tell you."

"Soon, baby, soon. Listen, I have some things I need to handle before your arrival. If you can't reach me, but you need something, call my brothers. I'll see you when you get here. Go eat. I love you."

"I'll see you when I get there. Love you too."

I hang up and sit thinking for a second. I wonder what he may know or remember about my auntie. We never talk much about before Ava left, at least not about things that involved her.

"You okay?" Toni asks, reminding me she's still here.

"Yeah, I need to eat, then I can get back to this."

"Good, I'm starving. You can cook for us all. None of that Italian shit either. I want some rice and peas. You have time to season some chicken or oxtails?"

"Girl, get out." I laugh, knowing I'm going to make her request.

My phone rings again. I look at the name and frown.

"Oh, who's that? Your face looks like you smell shit," Toni asks.

"Lou," I reply as I send the call to voice mail. He's been calling a lot since the morning after the attack. He can go fly a kite for all I care.

Dario

I hang up with Carleen and dial Gio. I need him to make some things happen for me. I have a small window to do it all in but I need it to happen.

"Hello," he answers.

"What you have for me?"

"An address. I can get it to Apollo within the hour."

"No, I need you to clear me a path. I'll be in and out. This is a problem I want to handle on my own and I need to see someone. That's my woman and child. I'm not going to feel right if I don't do this."

There's silence on the other end for a few beats. I check the phone to make sure we're still connected. When I place the phone back to my ear, Gio grunts.

"I'll have a jet there, fueled and ready to go within the hour. When you land, I can hold open a ten-hour window. Get whatever you need done in that gap. It's all the path I can give."

"It's all I need."

"Some salty situation, that's what this all is. I'll send the package to you. Check the warehouse."

I understand right away, he's talking about the warehouse we keep for curing meat. That's going to place me in the center of the airport and this other thing I need to do.

"Thanks, Gio."

"You're welcome. Have a safe flight."

The line goes dead, and I make one more call before I head down for the car to leave. This will be a long seven and half hours by private jet. Long enough for me to allow my demons to surface.

CHAPTER THIRTY-EIGHT

The Butcher

Dario

"Did you get the box from the safe?"

"Yes," Apollo says from the driver's seat.

When the plane landed on the tarmac, he was waiting for me in a black Jaguar. I climbed in and gave him instructions for our first stop. I'm glad to see him, because I know in my bones, if he weren't driving, I'd be on my way to Carleen.

I need to make these visits and head back to my plane to get back to Italy before the feds are tipped off that I've reentered the country. I focus on my sole purpose for this trip. The security of my family.

"Wait out here for me," I say as I look out the windshield at the mansion we're pulling up to.

I know this home well. However, I never thought I'd be coming here for this. Not in this lifetime. I step from the car and fix my suit jacket before tugging at my cuffs.

Reaching into the back of the car, I pull out the gift I asked Apollo to get for me. Inhaling a deep breath, I turn for the front door. I ring the bell and wait.

A few calls and I was told both Mitchells would be home tonight. However, it's Patricia Mitchell who answers the door. She gives me a huge smile and tugs me into a hug. I return the embrace with my free arm.

"Dario, it's so good to see your face. It feels like forever," she sings.

"Likewise, Doc. How you doing?"

"I'm well. Come on in." She waves me into the house. "I thought you were in Italy."

"I was. I'm returning tonight. I just have a little business to handle."

"Does Carleen know you're here?"

"No, ma'am, my business is with your husband. I don't want Carleen to know I'm here."

"Oh, I understand." She bites her lip and wrings her hands. I hand over the gift bag. "Oh, thank you. Good luck, Dario."

She leads me to the great room, then turns to leave me with her husband. Dr. Mitchell is seated in his recliner with a book in his hands. When he looks up from the book, he frowns at me.

"Good evening, sir."

"Humph."

"May I have a seat?" I ask before moving any farther.

He grunts and nods his head toward the couch. I move to the sofa, open my jacket, and take a seat. I sit staring into my palm, rubbing my thumb into it.

"I can remember the day I knew I was in love with your daughter. I wasn't more than eight. We were on the playground, and she tripped over her feet and skinned her knees.

"It was that day that I knew I'd do anything to protect her. My love for her has only grown. I have desired to be her husband for years. To provide for her, to cherish her, to be her best friend and comfort. Carleen is an amazing woman and I love her with everything I am.

"I just found out we're expecting our first child together and I feel I may have done this way out of order, but I hadn't planned to get involved like this at this time. What's done is done and I couldn't be happier." I pause to take a breath and look up into his intense eyes.

I continue with conviction as I look into the face of the man who blessed this world with the woman I love more than anything. "Well, actually, I could. It would make me the happiest man in the world to marry Carleen before my son or daughter is born. I've come to ask for your blessing," I finish.

"Get out," he shouts at me and stands, his body trembling with his anger.

I sit stunned. This is not the reaction I thought I'd get. I scramble, trying to figure out where I went wrong.

"Percy, stop it. The boy is coming to you out of respect."

"Respect? She's my only daughter. He wants to rush her into a marriage after knocking her up. Give me a break. I will not be robbed by his family again. Not of my daughter's wedding and not of my daughter. No. Get out."

"Don't move, Dario. You sit right there," Dr. Mitchell says, she turns her glare on her husband. "You can hate my family and me for what happened, but I won't allow you to take this from Carleen. He didn't have to come here for this. God knows that girl loves him enough to marry him without our blessing."

"And there is the problem. I wasn't raised like this, Pat. How can you turn a blind eye to all of this?"

"The same way you turned a blind eye when his grandfather helped you close on that property they weren't trying to allow our Black asses next to. All-cash offer or not."

Her husband scoffs. I wipe my hands on my thighs, still not entirely sure what's going on here. To be honest, I'm at a loss for what to do next.

"If you have never benefited from our connection to his family, go on, tell him no and break our daughter's heart, but as you think of all the times we've received donations, invitations, and favors because of the Di Lorenzo name you think about Carleen and that baby she's carrying. His baby.

"We are well beyond acting Indignant about who they are. If you have a problem with his family, you go ahead and take issue with mine. Kington runs things and has since you met me. Don't try to turn a blind eye to that and condemn this child." She points at me as I sit with my mouth open.

Not that I didn't know about the Thompsons. I'm just shocked to see her go to bat for me like this. This is a couple I've never seen disagree. I've admired their love growing up.

Percy shakes his head and sits back down. "She's my only daughter. You can't ask me to give up walking her down the aisle. I have an account I've been putting money into since she was born, just for this day. I've lost enough. Don't ask me for this."

Dr. Mitchell comes to sit beside me and takes my hands. "Maybe we can compromise. Dario, if my husband gives you his blessing, can you promise us we'll get to throw her a proper wedding? Her uncles will want to be there. I understand you want to be married before the baby comes, but this is important to the men in my family."

I nod. "She will be in Italy with me, I want her and the baby with me, but a wedding isn't out of the question when we return. We can have a small ceremony before the baby comes. My brothers and father won't be there either, if that's any consolation."

Dr. Percy nods. "I may not be into all of this gangster shit, but if anything happens to my daughter. I will make sure you are the next one my brothers-in-law make disappear."

I smile. I've heard the rumors about the Thompsons and how they make entire families disappear. I get the reference, but I'm not scared. I'd welcome death if anything ever happened to Carleen.

"Thank you. And for what it's worth. I'm a chef. I run a restaurant. That is what the world will know me for, but if anyone ever and I do mean ever, threatens my wife or child, I will show them a true Di Lorenzo. Your daughter is always safe with me."

"Humph."

***

Like I said, I'm a Di Lorenzo when it comes to my woman and child's well-being. What happened the other night has awakened Rio the Butcher. I won't rest if I don't do this.

I unfasten my jacket and remove it as I make my way to the car. Tossing the jacket over my arm, I flick out my wrist to check the time. I still have four hours until I need to be back on that plane.

"Very good," I say to myself as I climb into the Jag.

Apollo revs the engine, then tears out of the Mitchells' courtyard. He and I understand the faster I get to my next destination, the longer I have to create suffering. My mood turns as black as the night as we get closer to the warehouse.

"Your bag is in the trunk. I sharpened them for you," Apollo says as he parks in front of the warehouse.

"Thanks." I look at my watch. "If I'm not out in two hours, come stop me."

"You got it, boss."

I step out of the car and grab the bag from the trunk. It's been so long since I've used this bag. However, I'm no stranger to its weight or the objects in it.

I walk into the warehouse and a deep growl rises in the back of my throat as I think of Carleen's scream over the phone. I stop in front of the sniveling piece of shit in front of me and drop my bag to the ground.

"Vito, how you doing?" I say casually.

He whimpers through the tape over his mouth. "I have no idea why you wanted my attention, but you've got it."

I crouch and unzip my bag to pull out the twin, ornate axes inside. They're heavy in my palms, but old acquaintances. I stand and turn to face Vito.

While sharpening the blades against each other for good measure, I say, "You know, Jace gave these to me when I was about nine. It was a birthday gift. He gave my twin a blade with matching engravings. It took years for me to grow into these though," I say and rotate the axes in my hands effortlessly.

I toss one in the air and catch the handle, then point the blade at Vito. Tears fill his eyes. He jerks against the hook and chains he's hanging from, his arms and legs spread out. He's at the perfect height to be slaughtered.

"You fucked up. That's my fiancée you sent those fucks after. I listened to the mother of my child scream as they busted into my place. Now, you're going to scream for me as I butcher you."

I move in and tear the tape from his mouth.

"Dario, it wasn't me. I swear, I don't know what you're talking about. I don't even know how I ended up here. Gio asked me to meet with Dante. I thought they wanted to renegotiate terms or something. Business has been up. I got there and some guys ambushed me. Please don't do this," he cries.

"Why do I not care about a single lie coming out of your filthy mouth?" I snort, looking down my arm at my blade.

I drop both arms to my sides and rock back on my heels as I glare in his eyes. This motherfucker farts, before shitting himself. I pull a face, looking at him in disgust.

"I'm a made man," he sobs. "You can't do this. My father is going to have your head. Your whole family will have to answer for this."

"Say something I actually care about if you must speak."

"I swear, man. I wasn't going to give you guys up to the feds. I never mentioned your family. I swear," he sobs.

I furrow my brows. Rage fills me. If it weren't for the feds, I'd be back home by now, and Carleen wouldn't have been alone to begin with.

"Wrong shit to say," I growl and swing at the joint of his right shoulder, severing the arm from his torso.

His howls are like music to my ears. I hum to myself as I cut into his left hip next. He's only held up by his left arm and right leg now. His screams get louder.

"Shut the fuck up," I bellow, spit flying from my mouth. My chest heaves as I rotate my wrists with the axes in my hold.

I drop them and go for one of my knives to cut his tongue out of his head. Fucking rat. I pry his mouth open with a mouth gag and grab his tongue with pliers. I chop his tongue out with one swift slice.

"My knife skills are still award winning. Don't you think?" I slap his cheek as he gargles on his own blood. "That will teach you to keep your fucking mouth shut."

An hour later, I'm covered in blood as I whistle and grind this cocksucker up in the meat grinder. I let the ground meat fill sausage casings to send to his family.

Footsteps grab my attention, I look up to find a woman walking toward me in high heels, her hips swaying. She's on the tall side. Her dark hair is pulled into a messy bun on top of her head and her green eyes stand out in her pretty mocha-colored face. Her full lips turn up into a smile.

I pull my gun and point it at her. "Who the fuck are you?"

She holds one hand up, the other weighted down with a duffel bag. "Relax, the collector sent me. This is for you," she says and tosses the bag down.

"I'll take your tools to have them cleaned."

I put my gun away and nod over to my bag with the axes and other tools. "Thanks."

"I'll take the clothes too." Her eyes roll over me. She's pretty but not my type. Which reminds me, I need to get going. I want to reach the other side before Carleen.

I grab up the bag she tossed my way and find clothes inside. "Give me a sec," I say and turn to head into the private office.

"Take your time," she calls to my back.

CHAPTER THIRTY-NINE

Flight Company

Carleen

Jace opens the back door of the SUV to let me out onto the tarmac. I step out and look at the private plane that's going to take me to my man.

I cover my belly with my palms. I can't believe I'm getting ready to board this plane. This seems so surreal. I reach to tug Jace into a hug.

"Thanks. I mean it."

He releases me and looks down at my face. I love the smile he gives me. It's open but hides a little secret as if he knows something I don't, and it amuses him.

"No problem. Be safe. I can't wait to meet my niece or nephew."

I smile. "I can't wait to introduce them to you."

He kisses my cheek. I turn to Gio and smile. He pulls me into a hug, his scent surrounding me. Wow, these men smell nice.

Gio rubs my back. "I'm proud of you. A woman is never beneath her man, but the anchor at his side. You're ready for who my brother has to be. I'll bring you both back when it's time."

I step out of his embrace and knit my brows. He gives me a wink and kisses both my cheeks. Placing a hand on my bump he leans into my ear.

"Gwen would be proud."

I give him a teary smile and follow Jace to the plane, where he hands over my bags to the waiting attendant. I climb the stairs and step into the aircraft. To my surprise, Uncle Lucas is already on board.

"Ah, Carleen," he croons as he stands.

This man has been in Dario's life for as long as I can remember. He's been so nice to me through the years. He treats the guys like his own sons. Even Jace.

He's just an all-around nice guy. However, there's always something so sad in his eyes. I've always wondered if it's because he doesn't have children of his own. I've never seen him with a woman either.

I move to give him a hug. "Uncle Lucas, what are you doing here?"

"I'm here to do what it's always been my job to do. Protect the Di Lorenzo heirs," he says and looks down at my belly.

"Aww, you didn't have to take this trip with me. I'm grateful for the company, but you really didn't have to."

He winks. "Trust me, I wouldn't have it any other way. Come, sit. Can they get you anything? Water, something to eat. There's some really fresh fruit."

"Water is fine," I reply as I sit in the seat across from him.

I'm brought a water and a plate of fresh fruit. As I settle in, I think over his words.

I'm here to do what it's always been my job to do. Protect the Di Lorenzo heirs.

My mind goes to Auntie Gwen. Lucas was around back then. Maybe he can help me to learn more about my aunt and the mystery woman from my memory. Too nervous to come right out and ask, I start on the fruit. It's so good and hits the spot. I didn't eat much this morning. I was so afraid I'd forgotten something. I don't know how long I'll be away. I didn't want to leave anything important behind.

"Pregnancy agrees with you," Uncle Lucas says. "Dario will be in for a treat when he sees you."

I duck my head and smile. "I can't wait to see him. It feels like it's been forever."

"Love can do that to you. Moments turn into little eternities when you're apart."

I tilt my head and study him closely. His words come out with a knowing sound, mixed with a bit of pain. Uncle Lucas is a very handsome man, his jet-black hair stands out against his tanned skin and hazel eyes, eyes that are arresting. His Italian features are strong and charming, giving his face a familiar but comforting feel.

His presence puts me at ease. We fall silent as we take off. I had brought along my backpack with my journals, planning to write some. I have a few recipes in mind. Dario and Apollo made me promise not to work on the staff scheduling. Although that had been my original plan.

Uncle Lucas looks at my recipe journal as I take it out and smiles. "I remember the first notebook I gave Dario for his recipes. He filled it up in one summer with Giuseppe." He pats his stomach. "I was stuffed for months when he returned and wanted to make every single one. Good thing we Italians love to eat."

I take this as my lead into my questions, hoping he will stay open with me. I want to know who the other woman was. In my gut it seems important, for some reason.

"You have known the Di Lorenzos for a long time, right?"

"Yes. However, I was a friend of the Esposito family first. Frances and I grew up together. We were best friends."

"Were?"

"We are still friends, but years change people. Decisions, love, and loyalty get in the way of what was once simple."

The sadness I always see in his eyes, deepens. I'm more curious now as to what has placed it there. I've rarely seen the two men apart. I was sure they were in business together. I shake those thoughts away and push forward.

"Do you remember my auntie Gwen?"

A fond smile comes to his lips. "Yes, Gwendolyn was an amazing woman. Brilliant in fact. She and Ava were like sisters. Ava and her soldiers waged the wars, while Gwen handled the mental strategies to win.

"Back then, no one wanted to give women the kind of respect those women deserved. And Black women, forget about it. I was in awe of the three of them—"

He cuts off as if he has said too much and just realized it. His eyes come back into focus as if he were living in the past for a moment.

"I remember Ava, Auntie Gwen and another African American woman. What was her name?" I snap my fingers as if trying to remember, hoping he will fill in this missing piece for me.

If at all possible, his eyes grow sadder. He looks down at the table and runs his hands across the top. My heart aches from the change in his demeanor.

"Beth, we called her Beth." He balls his hands on the table. When he looks at me, his eyes are suspiciously moist.

"Oh, yeah, Beth. Now I remember."

"She was very fond of you, as was Ava. Gwen would smile proudly as they fawned over you. You all were their future. The rest of us became pawns," he says and looks away.

I reach over and cover one of his hands. I know I've stumbled upon something heavy here, so I don't push. He clears his throat and looks back at me.

"All it takes is one drop of other blood and you are nothing more than a friend who earns, consults, or protects. Never can you be one of them, no matter how much they love you," he chokes out.

"Ava wasn't willing to accept that. She couldn't. If she did, it meant the end of all she fought for, all of those she loved most were from other cultures. The Dane, her two Black best friends. The deck was stacked against her."

"How so? What do you mean?"

"Can I be frank with you? This never leaves this plane. I've never told a soul."

"My lips are sealed."

"She was a woman in a man's world. Donnas weren't nonexistent, but they had to be more ruthless. Ava was ruthless, all right, and a mastermind. I respected her for it. I became a more calculated, ruthless man myself in her presence.

"However, Ava was a free spirit as well. She loved who she loved. I was so captivated by her, from the first time we met. Others were put off by her choices, but I was intrigued. I wanted to understand.

"She brought me into her world, and I learned so much. Emil, Beth…we all served a need for her, something the other couldn't. We were her compass, we grounded her in a life that was all-consuming. If the Five Families would have found out about us, it all would have fallen apart.

"We already had secrets to uphold. Don Giuseppe was growing ill, and he wasn't ready for who Ava really was. He would have killed us for the web of confusion we created. Especially me.

"In the end, we lost our bond but gained something else. And then, just like that, it was all gone. Gwen warned us," he says brokenly.

My mind races as I read between the lines. I believe this man has just told me he was in a relationship with not just Ava but Beth and this man, Emil. However, I don't remember a man. Only the three women.

And that would mean, dear old Uncle Lucas was fucking his best friend's wife. I'm blown away. My brain hurts and seeing this sweet man on the verge of tears makes me keep my mouth shut.

What the hell is going on here?

CHAPTER FORTY

Beautiful Love

Carleen

I have butterflies in my stomach as we pull up to the huge house. It's unbelievably gorgeous. The backdrop, the design of the house itself. I feel like I'm in a movie.

On the drive here, my breath was taken away, but this house. My God, it's stunning. I envy the summers Dario got to spend here.

"Welcome to Cosa Di Lorenzo," Uncle Lucas says. "Go on in. I'm sure Dario is waiting. I'll get your things inside."

I wipe my sweaty palms on my dress. I wish I had time to freshen up before seeing Dario. I shake the thought off, hoping he'll come freshen up with me, I hurry to the front door.

Pushing open the heavy doors with the wrought iron inlay glass, I step inside. The foyer opens to a massive staircase. I look up to the top right as Dario comes into view with his head bent over his phone and one hand in his slacks pocket.

My lips part and I take in a deep breath. He looks gorgeous. He lifts his head and his face transforms as he gives me a breathtaking smile. He smiles so wide; his ears lift with it.

The dark-blue suit, crisp white shirt, fitted vest under his suit jacket, and the way his hair is blown away from his face, everything about him has me weak in the knees.

He takes me in for a beat. When his gaze drops to my stomach, he's in motion. He jogs down the stairs smoothly, while putting his phone in his pocket.

I take a few steps to meet him as I snap out of it. Dario palms my face and devours my lips. My entire being relaxes. He smiles into the kiss as he deepens it.

"You're here," he says against my mouth.

I run my fingers through the hairs at his nape. He brushes his thumb over my lips. I'm completely lost in his eyes. They are so bright as he stares at me.

He reaches for my hand and gently tugs me over to a decorative mirror on the wall as he fingers the bracelet he gave me. Stepping behind me, he palms my stomach as he looks at our reflection.

"It's real. My baby is in here. I've dreamed of this." He pinches my chin between his fingertips to lift my face.

He gives me the sweetest forehead kiss. As he stares into my eyes, he skims the back of his finger over my jaw, down my neck, down between my breasts and over my mound until he reaches my nipple, where he brushes his thumb back and forth.

He then palms my stomach once again with his other hand and places a soft kiss to my lips. "You two mean everything to me. I love you."

I fight back my tears. Hearing those words over the phone, was so much different from him looking into my eyes while he says them.

"I love you too."

He kisses me breathless. I turn in his embrace and wrap my arms around his neck. He holds me tightly, as if I'll disappear. I know the feeling. I tighten my hold on him, pushing a hand into his hair to hold him close as he consumes my mouth.

"Come, let me get you upstairs before Nonno finds us fucking in his foyer. I need you."

I bob my head in agreement. I can't find any words or proper thoughts after that kiss.

Dario

I can't believe she's here. Carleen is so beautiful. The purple dress she has on gives her a sexy but innocent look. I can't for the life of me reconcile this woman with the killer Jace and Gio described.

She'll never have to experience such things again. I swear, I'll protect her and this baby with my life. I've never desired anyone the way I desire to be inside her right now.

"I'd planned to feed you first. If you're hungry we can have dinner now," I say, remembering myself.

"Food can wait. I ate on the flight. I'm starving for you," she replies as we reach our room.

I open the door and let her through first. I slip inside right behind her, before someone can come looking for me. Closing the door, I pull out my phone and start to play the song that comes to mind as I look at her.

Michele Morrone's "Beautiful" fills the air. I move to toss my phone on the nightstand and shrug out of my suit jacket. Carleen sits on the bed and starts to take off her shoes.

"No, allow me," I say and kneel before her.

I unfasten the cute little flats and place them down on the floor. Placing my hands on her calves, I slide my hands up her legs, pushing her dress up as I go.

"You're so beautiful. You're glowing. My baby is growing inside you. I'm in complete awe of you."

There's one thing I understand about women. There's good pussy and then there's good sex. Good pussy doesn't mean the sex will be good. Carleen has both. I crave sex with her like my next breath.

Her pussy is tight, wet, warm, and she fucks with me, matching me passion for passion. The thought of it has my lips on her inner thighs, wanting to arouse her so I can slide inside and take us both to that place that makes me see stars.

"Rio," she pants as I nuzzle her folds over her panties.

I bite the fabric, pulling it away from her slick center. I release her panties from my teeth and inhale her deeply. She smells like heaven even after a seven-and-a-half-hour flight.

I hook my fingers in her underwear and peel them down her long legs. My eyes go to her belly. It's evidence of our love. It turns me on so much, I'm ready to bust through my pants.

"You look amazing carrying my child."

She moans in answer as I place my palm on her stomach and dive in to eat her sweet pussy. I groan. Oh God, how can she taste better than the last time I went down on her?

She lifts her legs and pulls them back into her chest. I pin her thighs in place and dive deeper. Soon her voice is louder than the music.

I smile and push in two fingers to beckon her climax. Her thighs begin to shake.

"Did you miss me?"

"Fuck yes, Rio, please. I need you."

I back off and quickly come out of my clothes. She sits up and tugs off her dress. When her breasts come into view in her bra, my mouth waters. They've gotten bigger. I didn't think they could get more perfect.

She scoots back to the edge of the bed, sitting with her hands on her stomach as she looks up at me. I palm her throat and tilt her head back. Bending, I give her a searing kiss.

A groan rips from my lips as she palms me and starts to stroke my length. I release her and stand straight.

"On your knees, in the center of the bed, now," I command.

I climb on the bed with her and sit on my butt on my heels. I guide her to turn her back to face me. Backing her up until she's sitting on my thighs. I ease my length into her from behind.

"Oh, yes," she pants as she starts to ride me, bouncing on my length.

I hold on to her hips as she moves up and down. I can't help but thrust up into her, throwing her off pace. She falls forward on all fours. I place my hand in the center of her back and hold her in place as I start to drill into her.

"Fuck," I hiss. "This pussy is better than I remember. My beautiful girl. You kept this shit tight for me. I want to come deep inside you. Argh. That's it, keep coming on me."

"Rio, please. Harder. I can take it."

I growl and reach for her shoulders before I pound her ass into the mattress. I don't know how long we're going at it before we're both spent and all she can do is shake and quiver in my arms. I fuck her tight pussy until it dries up and my cum is the only lube she has as she tries to keep humping my semihard cock.

"I think that's enough for now," I pant and chuckle, then kiss her sweaty forehead. I'm on my back now, with her on top, pressed tightly to my chest.

She moves to my side and snuggles in close. Tossing her leg over my thigh, she places her palm in the center of my Adonis belt. Turning her face up to me she smiles.

"I love you," she purrs and kisses my jaw. "God, it feels good to say that in person."

"It feels good to hear it. I love you too."

"I always wanted to ask you something."

"Then ask."

"Why'd you get butterflies?" she asks and brushes at the swarm I have tatted across my stomach, leading toward my cock.

"Do you remember when I got them?"

She bites her lip and looks up at the ceiling. "Around the time I told you that I was thinking about handing over my *V*-card."

I snort. "Exactly. I don't know. In my head it made sense at the time. You loved butterflies and when we were little you would trip over your feet to chase after them whenever you saw one."

She sits up and looks down at me as she laughs. "Boy, tell me you didn't get them tattooed there so I'd trip onto your dick."

I gave her a sly smile. "I hoped you'd chase them down."

She laughs harder and I join in. Subconsciously, I really did hope she'd catch the hint back then. Dante teased me about the butterflies for weeks when I first got them done.

"Let's shower," I say as I sit up and wrap my arm around her head in a headlock to tug her in for a kiss. "We have a lot to talk about."

CHAPTER FORTY-ONE

Walk on the Beach

Carleen

As I tug my cape closed tighter, I'm glad we chanced the brisk wind to take this walk on the beach. The night sky is magical. Even with my ponytail whipping in my face, I can't help smiling and taking in this gorgeous place.

"So we're in Sicily, right?"

"Yes, I'll take you to Naples this week. We can take a ferry or fly over. We have family there. Nonno had two younger brothers who have a bunch of children there. His sister lives there as well."

"Had?"

"I believe they were killed. It's something he doesn't like to talk about, but I think it's one of the reasons he's pushed us to be so close."

"Oh, that's kind of sad."

"I still can't believe Gwen was your aunt. When she took off with Ma. I felt like I lost two mothers."

"Do you remember Beth?"

"You know what's crazy? You're the one who lost their memory, but I feel like I buried those times so deep that I forgot almost everything about life before Ma disappeared."

"That makes sense. It was a traumatic time. If I hadn't had the accident, I don't know how much I would remember. All I can remember for sure was how depressed everyone was."

Dario squeezes my fingers. "I still have so many questions. Something more happened. I know it in my gut. Did your parents say anything else?"

I think of the things Uncle Lucas told me, but I hold my tongue. I can't tell Dario any of that. Not that I think any of that will help.

"No, I told you all they told me."

"The more I think about it, the more I believe Gio knows the entire truth. I was so relieved when *Nonno* told me I wouldn't become Don. All I could think about was getting home to you so we could start a life together. I never stopped to think about all *Nonno* had said."

"Gio was so cool about it. In fact, we never addressed the subject." He pauses in thought for a moment. "Damn it."

I place a hand on his chest and stop walking. Looking up into his eyes, I search his face. He looks so frustrated.

"Be patient. Your grandfather promised you the truth. For now, let's enjoy this beautiful place. I'll need your help finding a doctor for me and this little one. My Italian is rusty."

"Your Italian sucks," he teases. "*Nonno* already has a doctor coming in to check on you next week." He brushes his fingers across my cheek. "How are you feeling? You must be tired. Do you want to eat again?"

"Oh God, no." I laugh. "I'm so full. I am tired, but I'm still taking all of this in."

"Come on, let's head back. This place isn't going anywhere. It's been here since before 729 BC. It's survived pirates, famine, earthquakes, civil unrest, volcanoes, and epidemics, you name it. This city will survive one night of rest."

I smile up at him and lift on my toes to kiss him. When I pull away, he inhales deeply and presses his lips to my forehead. We stand like this for a few beats before he pulls away and looks down to search my face.

"What?" I ask as a look crosses his handsome features.

He turns me in his arms and points up to the sky. I follow his long arm and gasp as tears spring from my eyes. I've cried more in the last few months than I ever have in my life.

Looking up, the words *Will You Marry Me?* are scrolled against the night sky like a Bat-Signal, lit brightly for all to see. I turn to face Dario and he's on one knee.

"I asked you to have our playground wedding after we watched Pebbles and Bamm-Bamm get married. You had this look on your face. I'll never forget it. It was almost as if you saw yourself as Pebbles.

"I wanted to be Bamm-Bamm with all my heart. Ma took us to the toy store later that day and one of the gumball machines had a ring. Dante and I used up all our quarters to get that ring out.

"I proposed the next time I saw you. I never imagined I'd grow up and have a chance to do it again. You have been my best friend all my life. The first person I think of when I wake, the last person on my mind when I go to sleep. You now know all my secrets."

He places a hand on my stomach. "You're carrying my child and you hold all my peace. I granted you your wish, now I want to ask you to grant me mine. Will you marry me, Carleen? Make our family complete and become my wife."

"Yes," I breathe through my tears, not needing to think twice.

He places the gorgeous ring on my finger and it's like my entire world settles into place. With both my hands grasped in his, he stands and pulls me into a kiss I'll never forget.

Slowly, my mind unfogs to reveal the memory of the day we watched that cartoon. I marvel at how this is yet another memory I hadn't known I'd forgotten. I can't help but wonder what else I don't remember.

Dario

She said yes. I can't even begin to name the feelings I have. I had to pull that proposal together in a matter of days and I still wasn't sure it would go without a hitch.

Nonno and Uncle Lucas were a big help. Should I feel guilty that I'm happier to have my uncle here rather than my father? It doesn't seem like it.

Uncle Lucas has been there for us all our lives. When I fell off my bike and broke my arm, he was there. When I got my braces and was pissed off and embarrassed, he was there. When I was confused about my physical reaction to Car and I didn't know how to hide or stop it, he was there.

I walk the halls as those thoughts run through my head. Carleen is fast asleep. I had to get out of bed to keep myself from touching her and disturbing her rest. I can't wait to feel the baby move, although Car told me it will take a few more weeks before that happens.

"Dario," Uncle Lucas calls, drawing my attention. I look into the study he's seated in. He waves me into the room.

"Hey, Uncle Lucas. How you doing?"

"I'm fine, my boy. Excited for you and Carleen. A baby and a wedding. Ava would be so proud."

"Yeah, I wish she were here."

"She's watching over you. I'm sure she's happy you're getting the one thing she couldn't have."

"Oh yeah, what's that?"

He takes a sip of his drink as I take the seat across from him. I sit back and spread my arms across the back of the sofa. He looks down into his drink as if his next words are in the tumbler.

"Frances didn't even want to meet your mother. She was supposed to arrive in the States for the summer. It was their first meeting. Nothing was settled as far as their marriage, but there was talk of the union.

"Frances sent me to pick her up from the airport. I was to act as him and spend time with her so he could be off with the girl he'd fallen for. He was my best friend. I was doing him a favor. "It wasn't the first time we'd disobeyed our parents together. It was only to be for the summer."

"Uncle Lucas," I hiss out.

"Hear me out. Giuseppe said you wanted the truth. The truth only I can give."

I narrow my eyes and nod for him to continue.

"She was the most beautiful woman I'd ever seen. Tall, statuesque, she carried herself with such authority. I'd follow that woman to the ends of the earth.

"I was drawn right into her life. This wasn't her first time in the States. She already had friends. Friends and lovers. I...I..." He shakes his head. "At first, I didn't understand. Beth was gorgeous, she and Ava were like two goddesses. I was young, of course, I had no problem joining them in their bed.

"Emil was when I took a step back. I was so jealous of him. The quiet strength he gave to Ava was something I didn't comprehend.

"It took me a few summers before I realized she needed all of us. The four of us became one and Ava rose to power with all of our strength. It was who she was meant to be.

"But our love was something else. She and I had a different kind of bond. Frances had all but forgotten about her. He was ignoring the fact that his father was becoming impatient and more insistent that he secure a marriage with Ava."

I hold up a hand. "What the fuck are you telling me?"

"It's called a quad in the polyamory world. I was in a relationship with Ava, Beth, and Emil. We were best friends and lovers. We were also Ava's circle. Her counsel.

"However, there was something we all wanted. Beth and Ava yearned for children. We just couldn't agree on how to do that as a quad. We were always free to see others outside of our circle."

"Un-fucking-believable. I don't think this is the truth I was looking for. I want to know what happened to my ma, not who she was fucking before she married my father."

"You can't have one without the other. Listen to me, son. It will all make sense if you listen."

"Beth found Carl first. She was the first to leave the quad. Things were never the same after that. Your mother and I spent more time together and became closer. Emil met someone and started to spend less time with the two of us. However, he and Ava remained very close. Then Gio was conceived. We didn't mean for it to happen. Ava was already supposed to marry Frances.

"She knew I wasn't him. She told me after finding out about Gio that she always knew."

"What the fuck? You're Gio's father?"

"Yes, a fact that put all our lives in danger. Your grandfather wasn't the man he is today. He would have killed me and Frances for what we did. Frances was scared out of his mind. He had a baby on the way with his girl and then there was Gio.

"Ava said everything would be fine as long as no one ever found out about the lie and Frances's other family. I was ready to go to war for her and my boy, but she made me understand so much more was at stake. She was the Donna. She had responsibilities and her father was ill.

"We had to love each other in silence, to save my life and Frances's. We never spoke of who Gio's father was. Everything was fine until Ava became pregnant again with you and Dante.

"Emil was killed, and we knew all our secrets were hanging in the balance. We just didn't know which was revealed. At least, not until Riccardo grew a hard-on for Gio and Jace."

"Stop," I bellow. "Stop."

My chest heaves as I realize this man is telling me he's my father. I look into his eyes and it all makes sense. His hazel eyes are just like ours. His jet-black hair is identical to Gio's. Dante and I could look just like this man when we turn his age.

If not for being told all my life he was only a friend of the family, I would have seen it sooner. Frances Esposito has blue eyes and his looks fall short of the handsome men my brothers and I are, but this man here fits the Rome Adonis looks we were born into.

"My middle name, Luca. It's short for Lucas. What in the entire fuck?"

"My father, Michelangelo Luca Dante Di Rienzo is who we named you boys after." He makes the sign of the cross. "May his soul rest in peace. You boys look just like him. Your mother and I never wanted to hurt you boys. It's just the opposite. All that has been done was to protect all three of you.

"I once trusted Frances with my life. Now, his main concern is his own boys. I can't sit back and watch him protect his world at the cost of mine. That time has come to an end."

"Is this why my mother never took his name?"

"They were never officially married. I was already her husband. The papers were never signed after the ceremony. Gwen handled all the logistics."

I stand and start to pace the room. My head feels like it's about to explode. There are so many pieces falling into place. I stop and turn to...my father?

"You guys, your poly thing. That's why Riccardo has it in for Gio."

"Riccardo has always had it in for our family. Gio was only an opportunity. His plan was to see you into the Don promotion, so he could murder you and move into the spot. He doesn't see us coming and if he finds out about Carleen and the baby, we're going to have to kill him."

"I'll kill him now," I seethe.

"In due time, my son. In due time. Everything has its purpose."

CHAPTER FORTY-TWO

Stranger Things

Carleen

It's only been a week since my arrival. I've enjoyed the tours of Italy Dario has taken me on. We went to visit his family in Naples and we went to Venice, Milan, and Rome sightseeing.

However, Dario has been a bit distant or detached. I try not to talk about our family drama because that seems to upset him. I'm not sure what happened between his proposal and the next morning, but things aren't the same.

Honestly, I'm starting to feel like a prisoner here. Dario had to take care of some business with uncle Lucas and I was told I had to stay here on the property. There is only so much I can find to do at almost seventeen weeks.

"*La signora* Carleen, I have a package for you," Isabella, the housekeeper, says as she enters the sitting room I'm in.

"Oh, thank you."

She brings the box over and sets it in my lap. I look the box over and there's no card or note. The white box is unmarked as well. I shrug my shoulders and remove the lid. A blue velvet box rests inside.

I get excited, thinking it's another gift from Dario. For all his being distracted, he's still been showering me with gifts. Opening the velvet jewelry box, I find a diamond necklace with a gorgeous blue sapphire pendant hanging from it.

I pick up the necklace and it's like I'm thrown back in time.

The pretty lady picks me up and places me on her lap. I smile up at her as she smiles at me. I reach out for the pretty necklace around her neck.

"You like that?" she cooed and brushed a hand over my hair.

I gave her a smile. I liked her voice and smile. As I sat looking up at her, the two other babies with the same face came over to stand by her leg.

The one who always plays with me reaches his arms up. Pretty Lady picked him up and sat him on the leg across from me. He leaned in and gave me a hug. I returned it until the pretty lady spoke again.

"Ah, I think Dario has a thing for you, Carleen. Maybe one day when he asks you to marry him, I'll give you this necklace as a gift. Would you like that?"

I have no idea what she's talking about, but I watch her lips move anyway and laugh as I bounce on her lap.

The other baby placed his hand on my cheek. I turned to look at him and pointed to his face where he touched mine.

"Cheek," I said.

"Good girl, yes, that's his cheek."

I squeal and clap my hands. I point to his mouth and look up at the lady. "Lips," I said.

"Yay, you're so smart."

I stiffened with excitement, locking my body as I clapped my hands. The other babies clapped with me. The one on her other leg leaned in and cupped my face with his hands, placing his face to mine and blowing his breath in my face.

I wrapped my arms around him and gave him a hug. "Friend," I squealed.

I come back to the present, shaking my head clear. Placing the necklace back in the box, I turn it over and read the engraving on the back.

Always meant to be.

Tears fill my eyes. I clench the necklace to my chest. My heart starts to race. Could it be…is Ava still alive? Oh my God.

"There you are," Nonno says as he enters the room. "I see you received the package. It will look lovely on you."

"Oh, thank you. I…I. Thank you."

I deflate with disappointment. I guess I'm jumping to conclusions. Maybe Ava told Nonno about her promise to give this necklace to me before…

"No need to thank me. *Cara*, I have a request. I've heard so much about your cooking, but I've never been able to get to the restaurant when I come to America. You must cook for me," he says.

"Oh, no. I couldn't," I say shyly.

"You would deny an old man this request?"

I twist my lips and side-eye him. "What old man?"

He gives me a deep chuckle and one of those Di Lorenzo smiles. I squirm in my seat. Nonno has always been so kind to me. I wouldn't want to embarrass myself by making him a subpar meal.

"Why this"—he waves a hand in the air—"hesitation? You are head chef with Dario, no? This means you are excellent in the kitchen. A master, yes?"

I snort. "I'm no master, not yet. I still have so much to learn."

"I will be the judge of this. Come, you will love the kitchen here. It's where I started Dario and where I will teach that little one." He points to my stomach, bringing a smile to my face.

"Okay," I say and exhale.

***

"This is *magnifico*. You cook as if you have Italian in your blood," Nonno says as he devours the fresh bread and ravioli I've made for him.

I nervously place a plate of steak pizzaiola in front of him. He cleans the sauce from the plate of ravioli and pushes it out of the way to pull the steak dish closer.

I stand chewing on the inside of my mouth as he takes his first bite. He groans and rolls his eyes into the back of his head. Waving his fork at me to take a seat beside him, he swallows and bobs his head.

He wipes his mouth and uses his tongue to clean his teeth as I watch with bated breath. "You have excellent skills. This is delicious. Tell me what makes you think you are not a master chef."

I sit and think this over. I've been asked this before, but for the first time, I believe I have an answer. The words start to flow before I can process them.

"I started this as a hobby. I didn't expect for it to gain momentum the way it has. My head hasn't had time to process I'm not going to be a surgeon. The one thing I had mastered.

"Day in and day out, I'm in a kitchen with Dario. He's put the time in. He has put in the hours to gain mastery. He does it effortlessly. I guess I didn't realize, but so do I. I was scared to admit I belong."

"But you do," Nonno says fiercely.

"That she does." I turn to find Dario watching us.

Nonno chuckles. "If you're not careful, she will take your place. Carleen, I've eaten from many great chefs. This meal has rivaled them all. I don't compliment where it's not deserved."

Dario comes over and places his hands on my shoulders, then kisses the top of my head. He gives a gentle squeeze.

"Maybe now you will hear since it's not coming from me," he murmurs.

I swipe at my tears and nod. Yeah, I finally get it. I earned my spot. I'm as good a chef as I am a surgeon, if not better. It sinks in and the fear of failure falls away.

CHAPTER FORTY-THREE

Confession of a Son

Dario

I walk into find Carleen staring in the mirror. She's in her panties and bra, causing me to go hard immediately. I can't wait to find out what we're having. I hope it's a boy.

Seeing her with Nonno earlier reminded me of when I came here, and he'd take me under his wing to teach me how to cook. My chest filled with so much pride. I know my son would learn a lot from summers here.

Although, I'd be just as happy with a little princess. I'd spoil her the same way we spoil Bella. All the little dates and shopping trips. I'd go all out.

"You look gorgeous," I murmur into Carleen's neck as I wrap my arms around her.

"It seems like I'm growing so fast now that you know." She laughs.

"He knows I'm waiting for him. Papa wants to teach him how to play catch and how not to piss his mama off." I chuckle as I grin at her through the mirror.

"First, you should learn how not to piss his mama off," she teases with a little smirk on her lips.

I start to sway with her in my arms. "You act as if I haven't mastered that."

"I plead the fifth."

"Whatever." I kiss the top of her head. The necklace around her neck catches my attention. "Where'd this come from?"

"It was delivered this afternoon. A gift from Nonno. I thought it was a gift from you, at first."

I narrow my eyes. It looks so familiar. I shake the thought off and take a step back.

"Nonno was able to get us a marriage license. We can marry this weekend. You will be Mrs. Di Lorenzo before Baby Di Lorenzo gets here."

She spins to look up at me. I love the smile on her face. We'll have our small ceremony and when we return home, she can have the wedding of her dreams.

"Have I told you how much I love you?"

"I know I haven't told you enough. Come, get dressed. We can go for a walk. Maybe we should go to *Amore Domestico,* I've been meaning to take you there since you arrived."

She wraps her arms around my neck. "Did you know I thought you were coming here to take over that place? I thought that's what your grandfather wanted from you."

I laugh and kiss the tip of her nose. "Only to find out I came here to be a crime boss."

"The only crime you've committed has been stealing my heart and being too sexy for your own good."

I capture her lips for a kiss. "If only that were true."

"In my eyes it is. That's the only truth I need to know."

Carleen

I feel the moment the atmosphere changes. Dario's body stiffens and his jaw turns hard. I shiver as a chill runs through me. I don't know what just happened but he's not here with me, even though he's standing right in front of me.

His eyes go distant for a moment, and he looks away from me. I duck my head to catch his gaze.

"Baby, this is me. What's been going on with you? Talk to me."

He takes a deep breath and releases it slowly. I palm his cheek and he turns his gaze on me.

"Have you ever picked up on how much we look like Uncle Lucas? An uncle that's not even supposed to be family."

I knit my brows and jerk my head back. As I look into his eyes, the sad eyes of the older man come to me. I part my lips as I see the resemblance.

"Is he really an uncle or something?"

"No, he's my father. Our father," he seethes.

"*Ohhhh,*" I draw out. So I guess my assumption on the plane was right.

I take his hand and lead him over to the bed. He sits and draws me onto his lap. I press my nose into his cheek.

"How do you feel about that?"

"I don't know. I really don't know. He's been there all my life. He's been more like a father than Frances ever has. I mean, Frances treated us well enough, but Lucas talked to us, he supported everything we did, so can I be mad at him? He's been there all our lives and to listen to him tell it, he was protecting us the whole time. I don't know how to feel."

I start to rub his back. My heart is breaking for him. I can see how much this is hurting him.

"Babe, I still don't understand everything going on around us. It's like one bomb after another has been dropped on us. How about we take it one day at a time? As long as we have each other, we can face anything."

He turns to face me and palms the side of my face. His jaw working, he just breathes me in. We remain this way until he kicks off his shoes and settles back on the bed, taking me with him.

"In this room, in each other's arms, we are safe. Nothing out there can change that," I whisper.

"I'm so glad you're here."

CHAPTER FORTY-FOUR

The Dream

Carleen

I've been here for three months. I think I'm going stir crazy. Dario hardly ever allows me out of his sight, let alone this house. I'm seven months pregnant. I want to nest. I want to buy baby clothes and toys and set up a nursery.

Toni has sent me pictures of my place. It's stunning. Everything I wanted and more. I can't thank Gio enough for making sure the place got done. I have my eye on the room I plan to make the baby's.

"Car, baby, come on," Dario groans. I've doubled back three times to pee, and these overalls aren't helping at all.

I look in the mirror as I wash my hands. My face is so pregnant. I reach to smooth a hand over my pigtails.

"You look adorable. Now bring your cute ass on," Dario says from the bathroom doorway.

I turn to him and pout. "Where are you taking me? I don't want to walk the beach again. Can we go into town or something?"

A cloud comes over his face. "No, you're safer here."

"Rio," I whine. "Please."

"No, my wife and child are not going to be in harm's way. I have to keep a low profile while we're here. I can't flatten an entire town if something happens to you and that's exactly what would happen.

"For now, we stay on the property where you're safe. Baby, come on. I promise you're going to like this."

I fold my arms under my chest. "Okay, fine, but let me pee one more time."

"And how exactly were we supposed to go more than a mile away, Pissy Patty?"

I snort. "You try carrying this little guy around with him sitting on your blander and then have jokes."

"If I could do this for you, you know I would."

I smile. I know he would. I've seen his face when my feet are swollen or my back hurts. He hates it and pampers me until I can get comfortable. I love him even more for it. He's made this pregnancy so much better.

I know he's going to be an amazing father. His forgiveness toward his own father proves that. Lucas and Dario seem to have become closer in the last three months. Although Dario is concerned with how Dante will take the news once he finds out. Apparently, they have to keep it from him a bit longer.

"Car?"

"Um?" I reply as I finish up and pull my overalls back up.

"Where'd this basket come from?"

I wash my hands and waddle back out into the bedroom. Sitting on the bed is a huge basket with baby things inside. A teddy bear, onesies, and other items for a baby boy.

"I don't know where that came from. It wasn't there when I went in the bathroom. Are you sure it's not from *Nonno* or Lucas?"

"I've been with them both all day. It appeared just now. I didn't hear anyone come in. I came out and it was here."

"Babe, I don't know, but it's so nice. It's sweet of whoever sent it."

"But where did it come from?" he bites out through his teeth and goes to turn to storm from the room.

I throw my arms around his waist. My husband can be such a hothead. If I let this get out of hand, he will stew about this all day.

I want my darn date. I'm not spending another day locked in this house doing nothing. I'm so tired of online shopping. I know the delivery guys have had enough of me.

"Rio, baby, it's a gift. Anyone from the staff could have brought it in. Aren't you supposed to be taking me on a date? I want to spend time with my husband. Don't make me beg," I pout.

He looks up at the ceiling and blows out a breath. I can see on his face the war happening in his mind. I lift on my toes and peck his lips.

"Please."

He looks down at me and runs his hands down my pigtails. "Only because you're too cute for me to resist, but don't open that thing until I find out where it came from."

"Babe, the bear is not going to jump out and attack me."

"I've seen worse. Don't touch it."

I groan but give in. I'm sure it's a gift from *Nonno* or maybe Gio and Jace sent it. I'm not worried.

"Baby, I've been so focused on my father, you and the baby. I still haven't gotten the answers I came here for."

I look into his eyes and search his face. There is pain clearly there.

"Listen, babe, as much as you and I both wish Ava and Auntie Gwen would jump out of one of the closets to be here with us now. That's not going to happen.

"Whatever you find out, it's not going to change that and we can't get our hopes up over gifts that appear in the middle of the afternoon," I say softly.

"That's just it, Car. I don't know about your aunt, but I don't think my mother is gone. *Nonno* and Gio are still holding a trump card and I have this feeling it's going to pack a hell of a punch.

"Learning the man I thought was my father all my life isn't will pale in comparison. I can almost promise you that," he says.

"And I'll be here for you, whatever the outcome. For now, let's go have our date. Today we live the dream."

Dario

My father's words have stuck with me since the night he said them. Carleen and the baby could be in danger if news gets back to America. Riccardo stopped calling for weeks after I arrived in Italy. Suddenly, he's back to calling nonstop.

I swear, I'm going to be the one to bury him. He's working my last nerve. I still owe him for his words to my wife. Who talks to a child that way?

I seethe every time I think about it. However, I force all of this to the back of my mind as I lead Carleen into the backyard where our date will be tonight. I know she needs this.

I have been high handed about her safety. However, knowing she's here safe helps me to think more clearly. Nonno says the other families back in the States have been acting strange.

That doesn't make me want to head back anytime soon. The instability is something I want to avoid until Gio does whatever he has planned.

Even when Gio gives the all clear. I have to think about my little family. What if Vito wasn't the only one who decided to be bold enough to come for me and mine? I don't want to take that risk.

"*Rio*," Carleen growls at me.

I focus on her and smile. I give her a wink. This is what happens when you marry your best friend. They know you too well for you to hide when your mind is elsewhere, but I wouldn't have it any other way. I've enjoyed being married the last few months.

"Come on," I say and tug her through the bushes that lead to the private area I had set up for us.

"Oh my God," she gasps. "Yes," she cheers as she spins in a circle. "A popcorn machine, candy, slushes. Babe, this is so cool. I love it."

I smile wide at her happiness. She mentioned wanting to go to the movies. I had the garden area turned into a private viewing area. Our own outdoor movie theater.

I move to the soft pallet-like seating. I hold a hand out to help Carleen sit. She's still smiling from ear to ear, looking around like a kid in a candy store.

"Seriously, babe, when you do all the romantic stuff, you nail it. Like over the top, nail it. I'd be so jealous of your wife if she weren't me."

I sit behind her and tug her into my chest, banding an arm across her chest. Kissing the side of her face, I move to talk into her ear.

"That would never happen. I wouldn't be married if I couldn't have you."

She looks over her shoulder at me. "Really, you never planned to marry?"

"Nope."

"I thought I could try, now I know I would have been miserable. It was you or nothing. I was kidding myself otherwise."

I scoff. "I would have lit his ass on fire eventually. Anyway, new subject. What do you want first? There are honey barbeque chicken skewers, popcorn, jelly beans, roasted nuts."

"I'll have a slushy and two skewers with a side of popcorn and jelly beans."

"I still think that shit is disgusting. Jelly beans in all that butter with popcorn. Yuck."

"The joys of carrying your child. Come on, let's get to this movie, buddy."

I kiss her lips and stand to get her goodies. Filling a box with popcorn and shaking my head as I pour in jelly beans. I toss two hot skewers on a plate and walk them over to her before I go back for slushies for us both.

"What are we watching?" she asks as I take my seat behind her again.

I grin. Now we can't have a movie night and not watch her favorite movie. *Purple Rain* is always the choice when she wants a movie night. She starts to laugh.

"Good choice, but we make it through this time. I'm not giving up my drawers in the middle, big man."

I laugh and snatch a piece of chicken from her skewer. I pop it into my mouth and chew. She glares at me. I peck her lips.

"Let's see you keep your hands off all this for two hours."

She snorts. "I can hold out for an hour and *fifty-one* minutes," she says pointedly.

I wink. "Challenge accepted."

***

We make it through her finishing her food and about thirty minutes of the movie before she has her hands down my pants and I'm tearing her overalls off.

My wife is the sexiest woman alive. I've enjoyed having to maneuver around her growing belly. The positions we resorted to have become some of my favorite.

Like now, I have her leg in the air as I drive into her from behind. Her back to my front as I palm one of her tits. I look down at her ass bouncing back on me and bite my lip.

"Yeah, baby, just like that," I breathe.

She moans and throws her head back. I capture her lips and breathe her in. She feels so good around me.

Placing my forehead to hers, I absorb her energy and give her mine. I can feel our souls connect. She cries out as I hit her spot and reach to press my hand against her sex, massaging with each thrust.

She gushes all over me and I swear my heart skips a beat as she squeezes me. As if this were the first time making love to her, it hits me.

I've loved this woman all my life. She has been my soul desire from the beginning. My best friend, my companion, the source of all my happiness.

I no longer regret reading her journal. It was only a mirror of my thoughts that I needed a look into. I come deep inside her as we seem to take each other's breath, like an exchange of mind, body, and soul.

"I love you," I groan and kiss her nose.

CHAPTER FORTY-FIVE

My World

Carleen

My back has been killing me all day. I can't find a comfortable spot. It's a week before my due date, but I think this little guy is pushing for his arrival.

"*Mi scusi, signora, tutto bene?*" Isabella asks as she passes by me pacing at the top of the stairs. I'm waiting on Dario, Nonno, and Lucas to return from their outing. I opted to stay behind to take a nap.

They were only going for a walk on the property. They should be back any minute. A sharp pain runs through my back. I yelp, reaching for the banister. I drop my head between my shoulders and rock my hips back and forth, trying to breathe.

"Oh God," whooshes from my lips.

"*Signora*, should I call for *Signore* Di Lorenzo?"

My water breaks before she can finish her words. "Yes," I exhale.

The front door opens and Dario is the first to appear. I groan loudly and he looks up the stairs. He's in motion before I can say a word.

"*Signore, le si sono rotte le acque. Il bambino sta arrivando,*" Isabella says as she takes my hand and leads me toward our room.

"I've got her. *Nonno,* please call the doctor," he says as he scoops me up into his arms.

I cling to his neck as another contraction hits. I bury my face in his neck and hiss through my teeth. The pain is blinding.

"I'm here, baby. I've got you. We're going to do this together. I won't leave you."

I tighten my hold, remembering when I was a little girl and he held my hand on the playground. I know I can do this with him by my side.

"I'm going to be a mother," I whimper.

He kisses the side of my face. "The most beautiful mother in the world. We're so lucky to have you. I can't wait to do it again."

"Can I get this one out first?" I groan as small pains ripple through my back.

Dario chuckles. "Too soon?"

"You think?" I cry out as a bigger pain sets in. "Oh, babe, he's not waiting. I feel him crowning."

He places me gently on the bed. I hold my stomach and sit with my back to the headboard. Dario tries to place a few pillows behind me.

This is really happening. Our son is really coming. Holy shit.

Everything happens in a blur after that realization comes. Soon my son is lying in my arms, and I couldn't be happier. However, if I thought my husband was over the top in being my protector, our Matteo has taken him to all-new levels in a matter of moments.

Dario

Looking down at my wife and son, I'm looking at my entire world. I'm so proud of them both. I run the backs of my fingers over Matteo's thick black curls. He's a handsome kid.

"Call Salvatore, I need him here. Double security. No one comes on the property without signing in and out."

"Is that necessary?" Carleen says, looking up at me worriedly.

I bend and kiss her lips, then my son's forehead. "We won't find out. I'm not taking any risks."

CHAPTER FORTY-SIX

Retaliation

Frances

I walk into Sylvia's home to the sound of wailing. I rub at my temples, knowing I'm about to be pissed off. As soon as I see my father in the living room, holding Sylvia's sister, my blood pressure goes through the roof.

"What's going on?" I ask Sylvia as she rushes into my arms.

"It's Mikey. Someone sent Theresa a picture of his bloody body. Who would do something like this?"

"And we still haven't heard from Franky," Theresa sobs.

My father looks over her head at me. I want to pick something up and throw it. Mikey is Sylvia's nephew. Peter's older brother. This is the last thing I need. I work my jaw as I glare at my father.

"Can we talk outside?" I seethe.

He nods and stands. This will be another situation that will cost me one way or another. I hate this shit. I swear to God, I wish

I had gone to pick Ava up from the airport myself. Sending Luca in my place is my biggest regret in life.

It's like this whole thing has made my father worse in his quest to reestablish his family's name. I'm paying for my father's father's sins as well as mine.

I step into the backyard and close the door behind us. When I spin on my father to give him a piece of my mind, he's already in my face.

"I want them all dead. I don't give a shit who you think is a friend or how you feel about any of them. Dario, Dante, Gio especially and if I have to kill him too, Lucas can be the first."

"Are you forgetting something?" I hiss.

"Ah, who gives a shit?"

"You should. You know good and damn well there were several reasons Giuseppe didn't have Lucas murdered in the street. I wouldn't touch his grandsons and I damn sure wouldn't touch Lucas. You're lucky to be alive after your stunt with Ava."

"Luck has nothing to do with it. No one can prove I did a thing to her. I was so far removed from that hit, you would have had to be in the room when I set it in motion to prove I was involved," he snarls.

"Do whatever you want but keep my sons out of it. And so help me God, if I don't find Franky or Theresa loses another son because of you, I'm going to lead Gio right to your door."

He moves to get closer. So close our noses touch. "Are you threatening me?"

"I don't think I have to. Ava's boys are going to settle things with you."

He grabs the back of my neck. "Those should have been your boys. Your blood and hers. Not some—"

"Frances?"

I snatch away from my father and turn to Sylvia. Her face is covered in worry. I pull a hand down my face. I'm betting those pictures were a warning. We will never find Mikey's body. Now, I have to explain this and deal with the fallout.

"I don't care. Yes, he's at that fundraiser. Make it happen," my father snarls into the phone.

"You're making a mistake. You're not going to like the response."

"There will be no response."

"Find Franky and keep my sons out of this," I snarl.

"You can unclench your ass cheeks and dry your pussy. I went outside for this."

With that, he storms away.

"*Fuck*," I roar.

Gio

"We got the call," the asshole on the other line says.

Arty and his guys are a low-level crew. They have been running for Gustloff for the last past year. They're a loose end I need to tie off. I knew Riccardo would use them to retaliate for Frances's goomar's nephew.

I've just been waiting. Again, two birds with one stone. I'm never wasteful with my moves. You don't run the board with singular focus.

"Do the job, but make sure no one is hit. Your payment will arrive at your warehouse tonight once it's done. There's no room for error, so don't make any," I reply and hang up.

"Want me to handle this?" Jace asks.

"No, send Ming. You come with me and make sure Dante is safe. Give Mitch a heads-up that something is off so he's alert. Let it play out from there."

CHAPTER FORTY-SEVEN

Drama back Home

Carleen

It's been two weeks since our little stink was born. I love my son so much. I didn't know I could love anyone this much. This little boy has my whole heart. I love Dario even more for giving him to me.

It's only been two weeks and I'm wrapped around his tiny little finger. He's so alert for a newborn. Like now, I'm breastfeeding him and he's looking up at me as I talk to him.

"You're a smart boy, aren't you?" I run my hand through his thick locks. They're so silky. Not as dense as my natural hair, but soft and just as shiny.

He unlatches as if to answer me. However, he only breathes at me. He's been doing that a lot. As if he can't wait to talk to me. I'm amazed by him.

"Here you go," Dario says as he places a glass of water and a sandwich down on the bedside table.

Matteo woke us both and my stomach wasn't happy about it. Dario offered to go down and make me a sandwich. He leans to kiss my lips, then plants a kiss on the baby's cheek.

"Thanks."

"No problem. You need anything else?"

I shift Matteo so I can burp him. "No, I'm going to change him and try to get him back to sleep."

"I can do that. Here, let me have him."

He takes the baby and places him on his bare chest. Matteo looks so small in his arms. I'm not going to lie. Rio looks hot as he burps our son while cooing at him.

"What are you looking at like that?"

"You. Being a dad looks good on you."

"Your ass will be knocked up again you keep looking at me like that."

"Ha, you got four more long dry weeks," I tease.

"Not too dry, your mouth still works." He winks.

"I'm going to ignore that," I say through my laughter.

His phone rings on the other side of the bed. I reach over to grab it for him and hand it over. He answers and places it between his face and shoulder.

"Hello."

Dario

"Are you sitting down?"

"No." I hand the baby back to Carleen and take a seat. "What's going on?"

"Dante was shot at. He's fine, but this makes me want to come to Italy to see what's going on with management there."

"Fuck," I say and rub my palm into my eye.

I'm exhausted. I don't need this shit. Carleen already feels trapped here. I hope I don't have to lock shit down even more.

"Is there anything I can do?"

"Not right now. We can have a sit-down when I arrive. I think it's best to show a united front with these guys. I just wanted you to know. I'll see you soon."

"See you soon." I hang up and toss my phone.

"Babe, what's wrong?"

"Someone shot at Dante."

"Oh my God, is he okay?"

"Yeah, he's fine." I run a hand through my hair. My heart is racing. Dante isn't just my brother, he's my twin. I don't know what I would do if something happened to him.

Carleen moves behind me and presses against my back with Matteo in her embrace. Peace washes over me as I draw strength from the love of my wife and son. For them I can hold it together.

CHAPTER FORTY-EIGHT

Going Home

Carleen

Four weeks later...

I sit on the bed humming to myself as I pack Matteo's tiny clothes into my suitcase. I peek over at him in the middle of the pillows I've surrounded him with. He's so adorable in his sleep. He's starting to look more like his father. He has my smile though.

Lizzy thinks he's all me. Dante agrees with Dario that my son is all his father. Gio only stares with a look I've yet to place, while Jace always has this look of...longing?

It's been good to have everyone here. I've gotten to know Lizzy more and I was so happy to see Dante propose. It was so romantic, and it felt good to get back in the kitchen to cook for them. I think Nonno enjoyed himself while babysitting that night.

Dario has become lax in security with his brothers here. It's been a month of good times and laughter. It's been good to see Dario with his brothers and grandfather.

It's not lost on me that Lucas returned to the States, at least that's where I assume he went. I had thought he would stay behind to spend time with his three sons. However, once Dario warned me not to mention who Lucas truly is, I got the feeling that secret isn't fully out of the bag and won't be for a while.

All in all, I was happy to hear we're going home today. Matteo has just turned six weeks. My family can't wait to meet him. I also have a wedding my mother can't wait to plan. It's been hard trying to pack and take care of the baby. I have so much stuff I've accumulated while here.

"Hey, you need me to help out?" Lizzy asks as she pops her head into the room.

"Could you sit with him while I run down to grab a bite? He's sleeping, I don't want to wake him," I reply.

"Sure, no problem. If you want, I can watch him while you finish packing. Bella and I are all done. Dante took off to wherever Gio wanted to go."

"Thank you so much. I won't be long. He sleeps pretty well once his belly is full. I just fed him. I'll whip something up quickly. Can I make you something?"

"I'll take whatever you leave down there for me."

"Gotcha."

I stand and head out of the room as she enters and sits in the rocker Dario had brought in for me. I'm going to miss this place.

I get to the main floor and turn for the hall that leads to the kitchen. I freeze in my tracks as Nonno and Nyla step out of Nonno's study.

I'm stunned because in the last four weeks everyone has been here, I haven't seen her once. The last time I saw her was during that sensual fight slash dance between her, Jace, and Gio. When I asked Jace about her, he said she had work to do and couldn't join us.

She turns to Nonno and he pulls her into a hug. I tilt my head as I study their embrace. There's a fondness about it on both sides.

Like a father embracing his daughter. When Ny pulls away, Nonno cups her cheek and says something I can't hear. I think I see moister on her face from here.

Then Ny turns and heads out of the house without a backward glance. Nonno turns to me and gives me a strained smile. I give a small wave and turn to head to the kitchen and mind my business. However, the melancholy look on Nonno's face sticks with me. It haunts me if I'm honest. Hours later, it still plays in my mind.

Dario

"Is everything all right?" I say against Car's forehead as we sit on the plane to head home.

"I was expecting Nonno to join us. Is everything okay?"

"Yeah, he felt he needed to stay behind. I'm sure he'll come in for the wedding. Are you ready for this? Your mother sounds like she started planning without you."

"I'm excited. It looks like we'll have two weddings in one year. I'm so happy for Dante. Lizzy fits him."

"You can say that again. He looks a hell of a lot happier."

Matteo stirs in this car seat, bringing a smile to my lips. Carleen places a hand on his chest and coos at him. Once he's settled, I can't help but to pinch her chin and turn her face to mine. I kiss her passionately.

"Thank you," I say when I break the kiss.

"For?"

"Making my life complete. For the first time, I feel whole."

"Even without the answers you were looking for?"

I think back to the trip I took with my brothers. I felt like we were being watched the entire time. As we were leaving the old church, I said a prayer for the family I do have.

I think it's time I let go of the hopes of a little boy. I have grown-man responsibilities right here with me. My wife and my son are what's important.

Besides, Gio is up to something. If I focus, I might be able to see what it is before it bites me in the ass. If he doesn't take over as Don, it will fall right back into my lap.

I need to watch for his endgame, so it doesn't disrupt my little family.

"It's time I stop chasing ghosts," I say and kiss my wife.

CHAPTER FORTY-NINE

Clap Backs

Carleen

We sit in my parents' living room with all my uncles and some other family who wanted to see Matteo for the first time. The place smells good. My aunts are cooking in the kitchen and my father has the grill going outside.

I'm sitting next to Dario in the living room with my uncles and Toni. Mom walks in with a tray of drinks for everyone. I love the smile on her face. She's in love with Matteo. This is the first time he hasn't been in her arms. The spoiling has started.

"Eh, the boy cute," Uncle Kurt croons.

"You say that as if my son was going to be ugly." I pout.

"Oopies, you had a big head when you were a baby," he says.

"But half of them babies you got look like aliens," Toni says and sucks her teeth.

I can't help bursting out into laughter. Uncle Kurt's face turns salty looking, but she's not lying. His kids have some big ass heads. Especially the ones outside his marriage.

"Didn't get that from our family," Uncle Rick says. "You have to be careful who you out here mixing with. Look at Lefty, the boy never seen anything on his right side just like his ugly mama."

"Oh my God, good one, Daddy," Toni gasps.

Uncle Kurt sucks his teeth. "I told you that boy not mine, eh. I was drunk and she's been trying to pin him on me since."

"But he has the same amber-honey-colored eyes and silky black hair as you and all your brothers," Toni tosses at him.

"I hate y'all," I breathe through my laughter.

"You should hate them feet. Rio, don't allow her to carry that boy around, she'll trip and drop him…oops," Uncle Ernie throws in, shocking me.

"Someone tell Uncle E that growing his hair out and trying to look like he has a jheri curl, isn't going to get him more votes," I shoot back and fold my arms under my breasts.

"*Ohhh*, that's my girl," Toni sings and gives me five. "Besides, y'all didn't see her walk up in here. I think my boy done knocked them feet straight."

I groan and bury my face in my hands. Rio chuckles and pulls me into his arms to kiss the top of my head.

"Give me my grandson, Kurt. Carleen, come with me, we have a wedding to plan." My mother comes to the rescue.

"But I thought she already married the boy."

"She did, but they saved the wedding to have you heifers there," Mom replies.

Dario's phone starts to ring as he sits beside me. He pulls it out and answers.

"Wait, slow down, Dante. Bella was what?"

His face goes pale and then red in a matter of seconds. "I'm on my way," he says and ends the call.

"What's wrong?"

"Bella was kidnapped. I have to go. You and Matteo stay here. I'll come back for you myself."

"Okay," I nod as he kisses my forehead.

Dario

I'm fuming as I ride the elevator up to Dante's office with Apollo and Salvatore. I can't believe this is happening. My twin sounded like he was losing his mind. I know how much Bella means to him. I'm not her father and I feel like setting some shit on fire.

The elevator dings and we step off, headed straight for the conference room Gio texted for me to head to. We're going to homeschool our children or have a guard sit in the back of their classrooms. As I think about it, maybe I should assign Carleen a personal guard.

She's not going to go for that. Fuck, I'll try anyway.

I storm into the conference room and scan it for Dante. When I lock eyes with him, I give him a nod to let him know I'm here for him. Whatever he needs, I've got him and Bella. My niece will be returned safely.

"What do you need?" I ask as calmly as I can.

"He's giving me two hours to get there. I need all of the men we have and someplace to bury the pieces of this fuck after I'm done with him."

"Let's go. I have all of that covered," I reply with an ease I don't feel.

"We can help," Elijah says as he and the woman next to him step up. I narrow my eyes at the woman. Something about her nags at the back of my mind. I don't have time to put my finger on it.

"I'm coming with you," Lizzy says, breaking into my train of thought. I lose the thread I'm about to pull and focus on the task at hand.

"No, you're not," Dante barks, completely killing my train of thought. I shake it off and tune into the conversation.

"Dante, don't," Gio says firmly. "Let her come. We may need her skills."

I watch my brother seethe as if wanting to argue. We don't have time for this. From what I hear, Lizzy can handle her own.

It's the only reason I allowed Carleen out of the house with her back in Italy. Gio told me my wife would be more than safe with her. Jace confirmed that she's more lethal than Carleen has shown herself to be.

Knowing how much Carleen wanted to go out, I agreed. I get the feeling Gio is advising Dante correctly in the case, as Dante exhales. I know we are all on the same page.

"Fine, but not alone," Dante says.

"I'll call the girls," Lizzy says.

Gio grunts and nods. This catches my attention. *The girls? What girls?*

***

I'm happy my brother has his daughter back, safe and sound. Although, I think I can speak for us all. While it was amazing to see Lizzy in action, we all wanted to be the one to put a bullet in that asshole.

Which leads me to my other burning thoughts. I've sat in my living room all night thinking this over until my curiosity needed to be quenched.

Gio is more than thorough. I can't for the life of me see him allowing that Peter guy through as an intern. Not the all-seeing Gio and what Gio doesn't see Jace does.

I'm starting to feel like I'm being played. Some shit just ain't adding up. I know I said I was done chasing ghosts, but Gio and that crystal ball of his are very much alive and I want to know what he sees that made him give that motherfucker a pass that could have gotten Bella hurt.

I step into his penthouse, off the elevator. No, I'm not invited and at this point, I don't care. I'm still a boss in this family and Gio has some answering to do as one of my captains.

Music and moans fill the air as I move through the apartment. I follow the sounds, stopping short as my brother comes into view. I'm so stunned, I stand staring with my mouth open. In my shock, I don't register the gun Jace has pulled on me.

"Jesus, Dario, I almost blew your head off," Jace breathes.

Nyla jerks away from the passionate kiss she's locked in with Gio and covers her naked breasts Jace had been sucking and kneading. I don't know what to think or say.

"You need something?" Gio asks as he cuts off the music and crosses his arms over his bare chest.

"We need to talk," I reply.

He leans over to grab a dress shirt from the accent chair and covers Ny with it. She climbs from Jace's lap and turns to look up at Gio. He palms her neck and tugs her into a kiss.

Jace stands with a clear hard-on in his pants and shields Ny with his body as he pushes her gently forward and guides her from the room.

I pull a hand down my face. My brother is a lot more complicated than I thought. I stare after Jace and Nyla wondering what the fuck I just walked in on.

"Do we have a problem?" Gio asks, pulling my attention.

I shake my head clear. "What's that about?" I nod toward the direction Jace and Nyla went in.

"Nothing you need to be concerned with and I'm sure that's not what you came here for."

"You want to explain to me how Peter Hall ended up working for Dante in the first place? And Lizzy shocked the fuck out of me. Nyla is a sniper for fuck's sake. You had her and some other board around Carleen while I was gone, and I know it wasn't for Car to have new friends. What are you up to, Gio?"

"*Stugots.*"

"Bullshit. I don't believe for a second you don't have anything to do with all this. You know something."

"It's better you walk out that door and act like you know nothing. I'm not ready for this conversation and neither are you," he barks.

"Mama, she's still alive, isn't she? You've known where she is all this time."

He closes the gap between us and gets in my face. His chest heaves as he cracks his knuckles at his sides. I hold my head high and glare back at him.

"Always with the questions. I told you it's not time. I'm aware of everything. What belongs to me is never in danger. I'm controlling everything and in the right timing, everyone will be where I need them and then, you will have answers."

"Were the feds ever on my ass or was that more of your manipulative bullshit?"

"The feds were looking for the wrong twin and had your name in their mouth. You're higher on the totem pole. You were going to take the fall for Dante. All his illegal shit was about to land in your lap and he would have walked away clean. I had a choice to make, and I chose to make sure both my brothers remained free."

"I knew it. You ended all his side business. At first, I didn't catch on, but it all fit together as I sat and thought about it tonight."

"I removed any living ties that could land him or you in a cell. I told you, I'm in control here. When Toni came to me for a favor about a year ago, I told her she could have whatever she wanted if she kept an eye on anything coming our way.

"She and Talon ran into this shit around the same time. Toni was able to slow it down until I cleaned things up. Now say thank you and get the fuck out."

I ran a hand through my hair. I know Dante had ties to drug dealings as an endgame for more legit shit, but I always thought we had enough distance from it. If the feds had a RICO case against me for the shit he's tied to, I was going down in flames.

We're identical. I could be fingered for any of his crimes with no one being the wiser if prints aren't involved. Our personalities are what sets us apart.

"Thanks, but Gio, she's my ma too. I deserve to know."

He grabs the back of my neck. "What you deserve to know is that everything, and I mean *everything*, I do is to protect my family. It won't be much longer. I'm making things right, trust me." He tugs my head down to kiss my forehead and squeezes the back of my neck.

I nod and pull away. His words begin to sink in. However, I know he's not going to give me any more than that.

I drive home in a daze. When I walk into my bedroom, my mind and body are heavy. I strip down and climb into bed with my wife and son. I'm not surprised to find Matteo wrapped tightly in Carleen's arms. The kidnapping spooked her.

"Is everything okay?" She says sleepily as I wrap my arm around her and Matteo.

I release a long, heavy breath. "It will be."

CHAPTER FIFTY

Hidden in Plain Sight

Carleen

Six months later...

"Who's Mommy's precious little boy? Who's my little stinka?" I coo at Matteo, causing him to squeal and giggle with his handsome self.

I love my son. He brings a smile to my face every day. However, it's been an adjustment to be planning a wedding, running a restaurant, and being a mommy.

Rio has insisted on taking charge of the restaurant for now, while I take care of our eight-month-old. Mommy has totally taken over planning the wedding, which has given me more time to spend with Matteo and my new friends.

Like today, I'm hanging out with Lizzy as she does some wedding stuff of her own and finalizes Bella's birthday party tomorrow.

"Auntie Car, can Matteo have ice cream with me and Mr. E?"

"No, baby, he's not old enough for ice cream," I say.

As a matter of fact, I don't plan to introduce my son to sweets until he's at least three, if ever. Something my mother is dead set against. I know that woman is going to shove a popsicle or something in his mouth as soon as I turn my back.

"Oh, okay, I'll eat enough for the both of us. I'll even have sprinkles and caramel in tribute," she says.

I look at Bella and stare. What does this little girl know about *in tribute*? I swear, the things that come out of her mouth. I start to chuckle to myself.

"Is my sister here?" Ny asks as she enters the living room we're sitting in.

"Yeah, she said she was going up to the attic for some photos. She's trying to find one to put in a locket to pin inside her wedding gown."

"Hey, sweetheart," Elijah croons as he enters the room with a tray of iced tea.

"Hey, Dad."

"Are you here for my birthday? We're going to have cake and ice cream," Bella says to Ny with a beaming smile on her face.

Ny goes over to tickle her. "Oh yeah, it's your birthday? I might have heard something about that, but aren't you supposed to wait for all your guests before you cut the cake?"

Bella cups her hand to whisper. "Mr. E is sneaking me a bowl of ice cream before Daddy gets here. It's our secret."

"Well, in that case, how about I join you? Ice cream is always better with friends."

"Yes, please, I'd like that, Auntie Ny. I can call you Auntie Ny, now, right?" Bella says with hopeful eyes.

Ny kisses her cheek. "You sure can, little buddy. Come on, let's go get our ice cream before Dad eats it all."

"Mr. E wouldn't do that," Bella giggles.

"Oh, honey, yes he would. And we would have to go to the store for more, with his wallet of course."

They walk off into the kitchen as they continue their banter. I smile as I listen to Bella try to be so grown up. I look at Matteo and wonder how he would get along with a little sister. He's such a sweet child and adores Bella already.

I flinch as he pops me in the mouth with one of his heavy hands and grasps a hold of my lip. I have to pry his little chubby hand off.

"Hey, little guy, I need those," Rio croons as he enters the room and plucks the baby from my arms. "Hands off my woman."

He buries his face in Matteo's chubby neck and blows raspberries, causing him to squeal. I laugh and the two turn their hazel eyes on me. I'm in for so much trouble when this little boy gets older.

"Hey, what are you doing here?"

"Can't a man spend some time with his family?"

"Not when he's supposed to be at work. Who's taking care of the restaurant?"

"Apollo has everything under control." He moves in to dip his head in for a kiss. "When Dante called to ask if I was coming, I remembered what day it was. So I took the night off."

"I told you this morning. Are you admitting you don't listen to your wife?" I laugh.

"I've been under a lot of stress. I sort of heard you, but who was going to make sure I was on the way if not for my twin? I mean, what kind of family are you people? Getting together while I'm hard at work."

I snort. "You'll get over it." Bella comes running with her bowl of ice cream in hand. Nyla isn't far behind her.

"Uncle Dario," Bella sings. "We have ice cream, and they have bowls, so you don't have to eat it off Auntie Car's leg."

Dario starts to choke. I hiss at him, "I told you I heard something."

Bella wanted to sleep over at my place after we settled in. Dario let go of his apartment once we returned and walked through my finished brownstone. It's the perfect home for our family.

Dario swore he put Bella to bed before he made a dessert out of me. Oh God, I hope him eating ice cream off my leg was all she saw.

"Bella…" Dario turns to me with red cheeks. "Fuck, I don't even know what to say," he whispers to me.

I burst into laughter. I don't know either. She's curious, just like her uncle. However, we will not be doing anything sexual in our house in any room other than our bedroom when she's over. I warned him in the first place.

The laughter continues as the other Di Lorenzo brothers arrive. Elijah offers them all drinks and they head out back to share cigars. I breathe in the moment.

This is life.

Lizzy

"Hey, Ny," I sing as I enter the living room where I left Carleen, the baby, and Bella.

I didn't mean to take so long looking for the box of pictures. I knew just the box I was looking for, but I had to dig under a ton of stuff before I got my hands on it.

"What's up, sis? Whatcha got there?"

"Aunt Denise brought me this locket as a wedding gift. I want to put a picture of Mommy and Daddy in it to pin into my gown. Something old and something new, you know? So I feel like they're there with me."

I take a seat by Ny's feet and take the lid off the box. She runs a hand over my hair, then gives me a hug and a tight squeeze. I need the hug more than she could ever know.

"I've never seen this box before," Ny says.

"I found it years ago. I had a school project and went through the thing Dad put in the chests for us."

Ny reaches in the box and picks up several of the pictures off the top. The picture that's revealed as she does, grabs my attention. I push my glasses up my nose, then pick up the picture. The man in the picture looks just like Jace. I mean, he could be his twin. On either side of him are three women. The one on the left looks like a younger version of Aunt Denise. On his right is a woman who looks like she could be a younger version of Ny or me. Beside her is…I gasp.

It's the pretty lady. Her hair is dark the way I remember it from when I was little, but the hazel eyes stand out. This is the same woman from Italy. The one I asked Aunt Denise about.

She told me she would dig into who she is, but from the picture in my hand, she knows exactly who I was talking about. They are all here, smiling at each other.

"What's that?" Ny asks.

"Nothing, you find anything good?" I say as I quickly tuck the picture under my leg.

I don't know what makes me lie. I get the same feeling I got when in Italy, and I remembered to mention the woman to Dante. It's as if I need to keep this to myself. I only mentioned it to Aunt Denise because I wanted to use her skills to find something out.

I guess it's time I start doing some digging of my own. As a matter of fact, I want answers from the person I trust. I get up and go to call Aunt Denise.

I head out to the front of the house, swiftly tucking the picture into my pocket. When I step out of the front door, I find a nervous-looking Aunt Denise getting ready to ring the bell.

"Hey, I was just coming to call you."

"Oh yeah, honey, what's up?"

"That's what I wanted to ask you. Did you find anything on that woman I asked you about?"

"No, I tried. I got nothing."

I pull the picture out. "Maybe this will help. She's the only white lady in the picture with you and my mom."

It looks like all the blood drains from her face. "Shit," she mutters.

"Has Dante or Dario seen this?"

"No, why would…" I freeze. My brain starts to work overtime. I feel like I'm in a game, putting all the pieces together as I move through my memories.

The hazel eyes I looked up into as I sat in that safe room. The hazel eyes I look up into at night as my fiancé makes love to me. The same gazes that twinkles at me as the owner gives me brotherly hugs.

The redhead with the same eyes. *I just wanted to see. Everyone is so grown up now. I only wanted to see… I wanted her to take the job with Gio, she was the one Denise assigned.*

"That fucking Gio," I snarl. "How long has he known Ny? You never planned to assign Nyla to Dante. You're in on this."

"No, I didn't assign her, I told your father what Gio told me to say, but he came to me for you. Ny didn't know until after. She was so angry with me. Listen, Lizzy. Gio is so close to getting everyone what they want. I need him to finish this," she says with her voice filled with emotion.

"But this means—"

"Mommy, Daddy said it's time to eat," Bella says as she peeks out of the front door.

"Okay, baby. Tell him I'm coming."

"Liz, please. The twins and Carleen haven't recognized me yet. Everyone was too frantic to find Bella that day at the office. I was so worried they'd remember me then.

"Dario looked at me for a minute as if he made the connection. I was sick to my stomach. I probably shouldn't be here. It's too risky."

"Then why are you here? Why are you about to hurt the man I love?"

"Elijah, he wanted me to come. We have something we want to talk to you girls about."

"Wait, hold on. The twins and Carleen? What aren't you telling me? You knew their mom, that much I get." I pause to think.

"Gio will explain it all. Just be patient a little longer."

"I love you like my own mom, but I know how Gio can manipulate something to bend to his will. If your presence will hurt Dante, whatever you and Dad have to talk to us about can wait. Don't enter this house."

"Ny's talking about leaving again. We wanted to get this out of the way before she's gone."

I narrow my eyes. I'm a bit hurt. Not for me, but for Dante. I haven't wrapped my head around what this all means to me. Deep down, I know Nyla isn't innocent in all this.

"I promised Beth I'd always protect you and your sister. That's what I'm doing, Liz. I promise I am," she sobs when I stay silent a beat too long.

"Not at the cost of my family. Dante has been hurt enough. Don't you think the situation with his father was enough? I cried to you about it. You held me and promised things would work out."

"And they will."

"Well, today won't be the day he's hurt again."

She nods and turns to leave. I close my eyes and pray this all doesn't come down on our heads, whatever it is. My head starts to hurt.

"What's going on? What are you up to this time, Gio?" I whisper.

CHAPTER FIFTY-ONE

Princess in Skates

Carleen

This birthday party is adorable. Lizzy outdid herself. You can see the love that was put into this party.

"I'll take him off your hands for a bit," Lucas says as he takes Matteo from my arms.

"Thanks. I need to head to the restroom," I say to Denise and Elijah.

I still can't place where I know this woman from. She seems so cautious around me. Almost nervous. I brush the thought off and stand to head to the bathroom.

I look around for Dario. He was on his way to get us both skates the last time I saw him. Elijah offered to sit with the baby while we take a couple of turns around the rink. At eight months old, Matteo is a great baby. He takes to most people with little fuss.

Not seeing Dario, I shrug and head to the bathroom. I take my time doing my business before I wash my hands and fix my hair in the mirror. As I go to walk out of the bathroom, my phone buzzes. I pull it from my pocket and look down to see a text from none other than Lou. I suck my teeth. He's been texting a lot lately.

Talk about not letting go.

Lou: *We need to talk.*

Me: *No, we don't.*

Lou: *It's about your husband and his brothers. You want to hear me out.*

I freeze with my hand on the door. I haven't spoken to Lou since before my trip to Italy. How does he know I'm married? I narrow my eyes at the text.

Me: *What do you know about my husband?*

Lou: *A lot. Trust me, we should talk. I'll be out back in ten. Come and chat with me.*

I step out of the bathroom and peek in the direction of the rink where everyone is. I can see Matteo safe in Lucas's arms. Dario is headed for where I had been sitting.

Thinking quickly, I don't grab his attention. My husband will take Lou's head off first and ask questions later. Lou is well beyond receiving a pass.

Against my better judgment, I rush for the back door before I'm seen. I stand in the shadows and wait the ten minutes out as I watch Dario rush around looking for me. My heart pangs, I should say something, but he has enough on his plate. I only want to know what Lou has to say.

I look at the time and about eight minutes have gone by. I know I've made a huge mistake the moment I step outside and the door slams shut behind me.

I don't find Lou, but some guy with a gun pointed at me. I try to back up, but another guy appears to block my way. My mind races, not settling on one thought. I register one thing though. There's music playing in the distance.

It makes me think of Gio, Jace, and Ny. Strangely, my brain latches onto that thought.

"Did you hear me, bitch?" The first guy says, then slaps me across the face.

The slap is the trigger. I'm thrown back in time. I'm that small child again.

I'm crying as I stare up at the two older boys. One looks a lot like Dario and the other is a blond.

"Tears won't save your life, Car," Beth says gently.

More firmly, Auntie Gwen speaks. "Dance, baby. You have this. Dance with their asses. Lay them out, Carleen. Attack."

I come back to the present and run the back of my hand across my mouth as I taste my own blood. I look up through my lashes at the one who slapped me. Both guys are a few inches taller than me, which makes me grin.

"Let's dance, *bitch*," I seethe.

I step in and send my palm into his throat. Spinning into him like my dance partner, I face my back to his front, bring down the wrist holding the gun with one hand and reach behind him with the other hand to grasp his neck and flip him over me onto his back.

I point the gun and go to pull the trigger, but the second guy charges me. He manages to knock the gun from my hand, but I stun him as I grab his arm and spin him, using his own momentum. I have his arm pinned behind his back. I release a yell as I twist it, then kick him in his back, sending him to the ground face-first.

I'm grabbed from behind by the neck. I kick to free myself.

"You're not defeated yet, Car. Use your body. It's your weapon. No man is expecting who you are. Show them."

I snap my head back and the guy hollers. When I land on my feet, I spin and kick him in the chest. I keep attacking as he flies back. Tossing my open palms into his chest, I force him back until he stumbles onto his ass and I pounce.

While I kick his ass, the back door flies open, and Dario comes rushing out, looking like a raging bull. Music at the end of the alley grows loud. It's a reggae song I know well. Uncle Talon plays it a lot. Popcaan sings about being firm and strong.

However, I don't stop. I grab this bastard by the hair and start to bash his head against the ground as I hover over his limp body.

"Oopies, gyal. He done, done."

I freeze, knowing that voice. I look up to find Uncle Kington. His amber-colored eyes are trained on me. He gives me a nod. I release the guy and stand.

When I look around, everyone has come out of the rink, and they're all staring at me. However, the face that stands out to me is Auntie Gwen's. She has tears in her eyes as she looks back at me. It all falls into place.

I remember everything. The training, my time with her, Ava and Beth and the times when I would train with Gio and Jace because they were bigger than the twins and could fight.

Denise, as everyone calls her now, rushes over and pulls me into her arms. "I'm so proud of you," she whispers in my ear. "The one thing I needed you to remember, you forgot," she chokes. "I couldn't leave you like that. Gio promised he'd get you to remember. Honey, that was amazing. You're ready."

"Ready for what?"

"War," Gio replies.

I turn to see him staring at me proudly. When I turn to find Dario, I see Uncle Kington whispering something in his ear. Dario stands with his jaw working as he looks at the guys groaning on the ground.

Dario goes to step toward one of them as he sits up, but Uncle Kington tightens the hold he has on his shoulder. He says something else, and Dario looks to me and closes his eyes before he nods.

Uncle Kington then looks to Gio. "I'll do with these as I've done with the rest of their family."

Two of Uncle Kington's guys come and drag the three guys who attacked me to the hearse parked at the end of the alley. Uncle Kington moves to Gio.

"The deed is done, and the debt is paid. My brother can rest in peace now. You let me know if you need anything else. My crematorium is always open to you," Uncle Kington says and shakes Gio's hand.

Just like that, he walks off smooth as fuck. Only stopping to wink at me and nod as he moves by me to the waiting hearse he arrived in.

Dario

The roar I released when I watched that guy slap Carleen still rings in my head. I was in motion for the back door before I could think. I had to watch the tape back to see what actually happened in the time it took me to get outside.

By the time I arrived, Carleen was beating the shit out of a third guy I didn't see on the cam initially. I still have a ton of questions, but the one thing I know is, Carleen was made for me.

Gio has played his hand, but it has given me all I wished for and more. I just wish my mother were here to see the rise of her son.

My phone rings and I pick it up. "Hello."

"Dario, I need you to call a sit-down." I don't know what to call this man. He's not my father. "Please, I can't lose another son. You, Gio, Dante, and whatever head of the families you trust to help make this right. Can you make that happen?"

I grin. Kington told me this call would come. This is Gio's next move. Apparently, Frances's son and nephews, along with some other guys, have been going missing. His bloodline is about to be extinct. I guess funeral homes are a good business to be in. No body, no crime.

I sit back in my chair and lift my feet onto the desk, smiling broader. It's time I play my part.

"Sure, I can make that happen. Bring your sons. I think they should be there. It will show good faith. You know, I wouldn't want to find your father trying to set me and my brothers up."

"No problem. He won't be there, but I'll bring the boys. You name the time and place, and we will be there."

"I'll give you a call."

I hang up and text Gio.

Me: *Your steak is on the grill.*

Gio: *Well done.*

CHAPTER FIFTY-TWO

The Successor

Gio

"I never meant for things to get this out of hand. My father is out of control. I'm pleading with you to understand my sons and I had no part in this," Frances says. "I know Franky isn't coming home. I've accepted that. Please, I can't lose another boy."

I allow him to speak as we sit at the round table in the back room of the fish plant that formally belonged to Gustloff. Having those bad shipments come through here served me well.

My youngest brother, Dante, is smart. I knew how he set up all the supply deals and the back doors he created if those fucks ever tried to screw him. I used that to my advantage.

Now, we have a direct line for our seafood, spirits, and dairy supplies and Dante's drug dealings were cut as if they never existed. Clean, just the way I wanted, and I didn't have to make him feel less than by making it all happen. He had a hand in ending all ties. His decisions.

Not to mention, this place is a great earner. The envelopes Dante has been kicking up from this place have lined Dario's pockets nicely. When things turn over to me, he'll still see a nice ten percent on this operation.

"They're here," Jace whispers in my ear, bringing me back to the reason we're here.

I grunt and give a slight nod as Jace fades back into the background. Then I focus on the room around me. This is what all this was for. We had a score to settle.

Once this bell has rung, the war begins. Today we press play on a song that's been paused for too many years. My dolls are ready, my doll master and curator are in place and my brothers are about to learn who the fuck we really are.

I'm no one's pussy and my mother was never anyone's bitch or whore. We are the Di Lorenzos and this is what the fuck we do.

The door bursts open and my mother, Ava Di Lorenzo walks in like the Donna she is. In all her dark-haired glory. I was getting tired of that damn red wig.

She lifts her gun and blows a hole through Jacob's head first. Then she turns her gun on Louis and blows his brains out next. The sob that comes from Frances is so satisfying. After all, he was going to allow his father to do the same to me and mine.

My mother puts her gun away with a smile on her lips. I give her a nod, before I turn my eyes on Ny. I see the tears that shine in her eyes.

It's almost over, baby.

"Hi, Frances. Good to see you," Ma says. "Tell your father if he still has a problem, he can see Don Gio. *My* son, my successor."

She goes to turn to leave, but pauses and turns back, pulling her gun again. "On second thought, Gio, have Blake send that message," she says, then puts a bullet in Frances's head.

Where it Started

Twenty- seven years ago...

Italy

"You know I can do nothing for your grandsons. They will never be made. Their mother isn't Italy. It's just the way it is," Don Ferrari says as he looks into the eyes of Riccardo Esposito.

"I know, I know. All I ask is the restoration of my right to form my own family. The Esposito name once meant something. My father's father did a lot for the Ferraris back in the day."

"If I'm not mistaken, it was a move like this that brought your family down. No?"

"My father had a right to the claims he made in New York. There were no rules in America. He was only trying to establish our family," Riccardo seethes.

"And are you not Don Di Lorenzo's consigliere? How does this fit with your loyalty to him?"

Riccardo snorts. "I've never been good enough for them. I was promised a marriage for myself, his father spit on me and married her off to someone else. My son was promised a marriage and the path to be the Don of the Di Lorenzo family. That was taken away as well. What loyalty?"

"And you believe you can get rid of the Donna and hand me control of the Di Lorenzo family and their connections *if* I allow this? You know this is a bold ask."

"I know that you owned land Don Giuseppe now calls his own. I also know you are of like mind about this Donna business.

"Yes, I will bring them to their knees and hand it all to you. With your blessing and some time, I can make it happen.

"I've already rid her of that Danish piece of shit, she no longer has her version of Luca. She and the *mulignons* are next."

"Luca?" Don Ferrari grunts and snorts a laugh. "You mean Luca Brasi? You've been in the States watching too many movies. The Di Lorenzos have always been more than what meets the eye. Don't get cocky and underestimate Don Di Lorenzo."

"It is not Giuseppe I underestimate. I see the future and the Di Lorenzo bloodline has weakened. They're done.

"The oldest likes boys. If I have it my way, the next in line will do as I say. He will take to my guidance once the mother is out of the way. Giuseppe won't see it coming. He doesn't know I know the truth."

Don Ferrari lifts a brow. "Ask yourself this. If he was your friend and your agreement didn't go as planned, why didn't *you* see it coming? Do you really know Giuseppe the way you think you do and where does your son sit with all of this?

"Frances does what I tell him to."

"Yet, he has held secrets from you?" Don Ferrari holds his hand up to halt Riccardo's next words. "Say nothing more before I change my mind. If you fail, this meeting never happened.

"So whatever you do, make sure I cannot be traced. If you succeed, I will deal with the other families. What I don't want of the Di Lorenzo legacy you will be welcome to call the property of the Esposito family. Fail, and I will wipe out the rest of the Esposito bloodline personally."

"I won't fail you. This has been a long time coming. This is my destiny."

"Yet you have faced one obstacle after another." Don Ferrari chuckles.

Riccardo's face burns with anger. Frances had truly made a fool of him, as did Don Di Lorenzo, his once childhood friend. Deep down, he knew this was payback for Frances's deception. He could kill the boy himself. He knew Giuseppe hadn't because of their friendship, but as he said, this was his destiny. A bunch of stupid children weren't going to keep him from restoring his family's name. His own father had made mistakes, costing them everything.

Instead of becoming a Don himself, Riccardo had to slither around whispering in Giuseppe's ear. Enough was enough. He would ruin them all to get what was his.

He'd waited this long. When his grandsons were ready, they would make their move.

"While there are no males suitable to run their family and to keep the integrity of the Five Families, I'll agree to this. However, as soon as Don Di Lorenzo can name a strong, suitable male successor, this is forbidden. You touch no one from their family. No one. And I suggest you figure out who all that entails."

"Thank you, Don Ferrari. I won't fail you."

Don Ferrari grunts and nods. Riccardo kisses his ring and leaves. Once Riccardo had left, the Don grunted again.

"You're not really going to allow this, are you?"

"Let him think what he must. You know what to do."

ACKNOWLEDGMENTS

I'm loving this series. It's so much fun. This one is for my mom and my auntie. I believe I embedded the spirit of the real Carleen. I've pulled from the amazing women they were to build this cast. I put so much of myself in this one as well.

I'm learning and healing every day. The awakening of Carleen felt like my own. I cried because I felt it. When she found her voice and realized she deserved her success, I had to fist-pump her.

Again, thanks for your patience with me as I heal and get on track and thanks for coming on this journey. A big thank you to all of my readers. I love you guys for all of the support. Your emails and posts mean the world. Your continued support is like gold to me. Here's to more reads and good times this year.

A huge shout-out to my husband. I know you're tired of hearing about this series. LOL. ROTF. I'm almost there, boo. It's almost time for PNR talk. Ha ha ha ha. Love you.

To God be the glory. Thank you for allowing me to do what I love and for moving me out of my own way. I thank God for this gift. With all I am, I thank you for all the amazing things I can't even see coming my way. Thank you.

Next! Gio in The Ones Left Behind. Finally.

ABOUT THE AUTHOR

Blue Saffire, award-winning, bestselling author of over thirty contemporary romance novels and novellas, writes with the intention to touch the heart and the mind. Blue hooks, weaves, and loops multiple series, keeping you engaged in her worlds. Blue writes for her own publishing company Perceptive Illusions as Blue Saffire as well as Royal Blue.

Blue and her husband live in a house filled with laughter and creativity, in Long Island, NY. Both working hard to build the Blue brand and cultivate their love for the artists. Creative is their family affair.

Blue holds an MBA in Marketing and Project Management, as well as an MED in Instructional Technology and Curriculum Design. She is also an NLP Master Practitioner.

Wait, there is more to come! You can stay updated with my latest releases, learn more about me, the author, and be a part of contests by subscribing to my newsletter at
www.BlueSaffire.com
If you enjoyed *My Best Friend's Wish*, I'd love to hear
your thoughts and please feel free to leave a review. And when you do, please let me know by emailing me TheBlueSaffire@gmail.com or leave a comment on Facebook
https://www.facebook.com/BlueSaffireDiaries or Twitter @TheBlueSaffire

Other books by Blue Saffire
Placed in Best Reading Order
Also available....
Legally Bound

Legally Bound 2: Against the Law

Legally Bound 3: His Law

Perfect for Me

Hush 1: Family Secrets

Ballers: His Game

Brothers Black 1: Wyatt the Heartbreaker

Legally Bound 4: Allegations of Love

Hush 2: Slow Burn

Legally Bound 5.0: Sam

Yours 1: Losing My Innocence

Yours 2: Experience Gained

Yours 3: Life Mastered

Ballers 2: His Final Play

Legally Bound 5.1: Tasha Illegal Dealings

Brothers Black 2: Noah

Legally Bound 5.2: Camille

Legally Bound 5.3 & 5.4 Special Edition

Where the Pieces Fall

Legally Bound 5.5: Legally Unbound

Brothers Black 4: Braxton the Charmer

My Funny Valentine

Broken Soldier

Remember Me

Brothers Black 5: Felix the Brain

A Home for Christmas

Be My Valentine

Coming Soon...
The Ones Left Behind
Lost Souls Book 4: Again
Wild Hearts

Work Husband Series
Unexcepted Lovers
My Best Friend's Wish
The Ones Left Behind...Coming soon...

Work Husband Series

Lost Souls Series

★Forever: Book 1-Brick
★Never: Book 2 -Gutter
★Always: Books 3-King
Again: Book 4-Cage
Before 4.5- Thor
Sometimes: Book 5-Jackie
Lifetime: Book 6-Grim
Still: Book 7-Kevlar
Once: Book 8-Diggs, Axle, and Sugar
Now: Book 9 -Tracks
When: Book 10-Holden

Made in the USA
Middletown, DE
01 May 2022